Runner's Honor

20 Jan 2010

Dear Jonathan,

Thank you for your help with the RH website; and for your valuable professional expertise with MIPSE. This has meant a great deal to me,

Mark

Contact the author at: mjkushner@hotmail.com

Cover Design by Christine Hobbs

Visit www.booksurge.com to order additional copies.

MARK J. KUSHNER

RUNNER'S HONOR

2007

Runner's Honor

Dedicated To Coach Kallem And The Championship Burbank Bulldogs.

AUGUST 1967

CHAPTER 1

The whop-whop-whop of the blades powering the Medevac chopper bit through the night. The waist gunner wiped the rain blurring his vision from his goggles and pointed excitedly at the smoke marking their destination in the tiny clearing. The pilot nodded calmly and turned the chopper toward the beacon as the gunner sprayed bullets in the direction of the muzzle flashes on the far side of the hot landing zone.

Kneeling behind a bullet-scarred tree, Corporal Corey O'Neal watched the chopper spiral downward. He jammed another clip into his M16 and fired at the nearly unseen enemy. The battle was an hour old and his squad had taken severe casualties. Corporal O'Neal reached down and felt the neck of his wounded point man lying at his feet to reassure himself that the Medevac's mission would not be in vain.

It was too late for the other wounded. They'd died waiting for the chopper.

Corporal O'Neal motioned the rest of his squad to concentrate their fire on the enemy as the chopper set down. "Go, go, go!" he yelled. Two of his squad lifted the wounded soldier and, navigating through the tall grass of the treeless clearing, carried him to the waiting chopper. Corey diverted his attention from the battle only long enough to confirm that the Medevac had successfully lifted its precious cargo in the direction of safety. The beat of the retreating chopper was soon lost to Corey as the crescendo of the battle increased. He cursed as a Vietcong mortar crashed through the jungle only yards from his position, surely making more wounded.

CHAPTER 2

Running was more than a sport to me. It was my means of survival, my source of sustenance. No psychoanalysis could be as healing as a mind-clearing run through the dawn of a fall day. No doctor's elixir could straighten twisted insides as well as a set of 20 quarter-miles on a blisteringly hot summer afternoon. In some ways, running made life tolerable. A day's tally of abuse could be erased by an hour's run on county roads, restoring one's psyche to face the next day.

Running is a mean taskmaster. In spite of its healing powers, it is no less conniving than a snake-oil salesman, promising so much yet sometimes delivering so little, all the while demanding a lover's devotion. If you give without resisting, it will crush you. But like a demanding lover, it may rescue you in your hour of need.

Running may have saved my life.

Coach Frank Dillon may have saved my life.

Danny O'Neal may have saved my life.

I first met Danny O'Neal on August 23, 1967. Even now, decades later, I remember that date. I wrote it in the journal that still sits on my desk, an entry that I have reread hundreds of times since.

"August 23, 1967. First day in Barrel. What a hell-hole. I wish I was dead. Met Danny O'Neal on top of a hill."

Barrel, Illinois, population 12,400, was to become my ninth hometown in the span of 12 years. For a restless 17-year-old trying to find his place in the world, the eight previous towns blurred together into a frustrating stream of strange high schools and aborted friendships. I had no greater expectations for Barrel. We were nomads of the Great Plains, pitching our tents where we speculated riches might call and tearing them down in the middle of the night when the echo of that call died away.

My father, Franklin Cane, was reason for our itinerant status. To have called him uncaring would have been unfair; to have called him responsible would have been too generous. Franklin Cane was marginally more ethical than a con artist though not nearly as clever or successful. Following each failed get-rich-quick scheme, we moved to another city, another town where opportunity knocked and the innocent were poised to be preyed on. My father was like a prostitute moving to a new city and trying to start over again as a virgin. He had great aspirations to follow the straight and narrow and make an honest living, but like an aging hooker, he succumbed to the familiarity of his old habits time and time again.

We drove into Barrel over tar-and-gravel two-lane county roads. Our overloaded station wagon, trailing a U-Haul and tilting to one side on worn shocks, carried my parents and me toward the town. The horizon danced in the shimmering waves of heat that wafted up from the road, the tar and gravel cutting swaths through soon-to-be-harvested corn and just-picked soybeans. We were in the heartland, where talk in the cafes was of corn futures and new models from John Deere, patriotism trumped the realities of poverty and ambitions were expressed in bushels per acre. To me, it was just about the end of the world, one more loop in the death spiral of my youth. The only saving grace was that Barrel High School had a cross country team so I wouldn't be running alone. I might even make some friends.

The Hawks of Barrel High School and Danny O'Neal were not unknown to me. Two high schools ago, I ran on a cross country team that squeaked its way into the state semifinals only to be edged out of a berth in the finals by the Hawks. The Hawks deserved to win and we were lucky to have made it as far as we did, but that made the loss no less painful. Danny O'Neal, the first man on the Hawks cross country team, came from being trapped deep in the pack to grab second place in a display of physical prowess that I can only describe as inspiring. God had Danny in mind when he created runners. Not one motion was wasted, not one muscle was tense, not one breath was labored. Danny's legs pumped a stride that only gave the impression of striking the ground. He didn't so much as defeat his opponents as awe them into submission.

We arrived in Barrel to a temperature of 92 degrees and a humidity of about the same. Our rented house was on the edge of town, the last development before the county roads began, far enough from the center of town not to be obvious, but close enough to have indoor plumbing. My mother, Rose, saint that she was, immediately put on an apron and began unloading the station wagon, a well practiced routine. She squinted in the afternoon sun, the creases around her eyes casting shadows on her cheeks. My father wandered off to find a paper. This was his first step in sizing up his potential marks. "I'm going to earn a living," he announced and walked toward town. Why he didn't buy a paper at the grocery store we just visited puzzled me, but it was probably part of his plan. He had to get the look and feel of the place. As Harold Hill said, you have to know the territory.

I sat in the car, sweat dripping down my face, lamenting my fate until my mother returned for her third load. "Mom, how long do you think we'll stay here?"

"Hard to say. Your father's got a line on a job at the rifle factory," she said, resting against the car as she patted sweat from her forehead with her apron. "It could be quite a while, maybe long enough to get to know our neighbors." My mother, the dreamer.

"What's the longest he's ever held a job?" I asked.

"Have some respect for your father, Michael." She did love him. I didn't know why but she did. I suppose the wives of axe murderers love their husbands too.

"I'm going to hate it here. I already do."

"It's not that bad," she tried to console me as she chose the next box to lug into the house.

"Yes, it is. In fact, it's worse. If this isn't the end of the world, you can see it from here."

"We just left the end of the world. We're on our way back." That's what I loved about my mother. No matter how bad the reality, she could put an optimistic spin on it. Careening into the depths of a bottomless pit, she'd comment on how pleasant the breeze was. She must have been a good looker when she was young. The years haven't been kind to her.

"I'm going for a run," I told her. "I'll move boxes when I get back." She returned a smiling nod and hefted the box toward the house. I rummaged through enough of the boxes to find my trunks and well worn Adidas, changed, and began my first run in Barrel.

CHAPTER 3

Augustin Barrel is another way of saying inhumanly hot and humid. The corn demands it. A 90-90 day (90 degrees, 90 percent humidity) seems like a God-given respite when the day before was 95-95. On those sorts of days you can't walk across the street without your shirt sticking to your back. Paper soaks up moisture like a sponge in a bathtub. Towels never dry. Sweat drips off the brows of even the most discrete and well-mannered of the citizenry. Fans serve only to move around the heavy air. Swamp coolers are worthless. The intensity of the sun is magnified by the waves of heat that emanate from the sticky asphalt. All manner of man and beast wait out the hours of unforgiving sunshine for the small relief that evening brings. That is, all manner of life except for runners.

There is something therapeutic about running in the unbearable heat and humidity of an August day. Perhaps it is the sense of sheer accomplishment for having been successful. Perhaps it is the sense of pride that you are one of the elite who are physically capable of even attempting such a feat. Perhaps, and most likely, it is a sign of a weak mind. A 10-mile run on a county road on the afternoon of a 90-90 day defines the state of the art of running. Like climbing a mountain, you do it because it is there.

County roads are laid out in an endless grid one mile to a side. From Barrel south to Carbondale, north to Kankakee, west to St. Louis and east to Indianapolis, there is a monotonously flat and repetitive grid of county roads enclosing field after field of corn and soybeans, dotted by an occasional town and grain silo. It is difficult to deceive yourself about how far you've run on the county roads. Each intersection you cross is another mile. All you have to do is to keep count. On a 90-90 afternoon, you're drenched in sweat before reaching even the first crossroads.

I was about five miles out from town when I came upon the only hill in the county, a preposterously out of place mound of dirt a few hundred feet high. It wasn't that hard to find. You can see it for miles in the flat expanse of the former prairie. It was as if God had dropped a giant handful of dirt out of the sky, protruding from the flatness of the prairie like a scoop of unmelted ice cream on the kitchen floor. It was perhaps the one patch of ground south of Chicago that glaciers failed to scrape flat.

As I ran toward the hill, I saw that the county road sloped upwards for half a mile to reach its summit, a challenge no serious runner could pass up. There is an inexplicable joy that comes from running up hills and mountains, cresting the summit and being rewarded with a view to the horizon. As I ran toward the base of the hill the immensity of that mound of dirt grew, which only whetted my desire to conquer it. I charged up the hill, leaning forward as the slope steepened, raising my knees and pumping my arms. Sweat began pouring off me as though I had just stepped out of the shower. The burn began in my calves as I raised myself onto my toes, and then my thighs began to burn as the road seemed to turn vertical. The crest seemingly moved farther away with each step. It was nearly impossible to suck in enough of the heavy air to keep up the pace. At last, the slope waned and I reached the top. I stopped, bent over with my hands on my knees, sweat pooling on the ground below me, trying to take in enough air to slow my heart beat.

I finally recovered enough to walk little circles on the summit. Looking back, I noticed a speck approaching on the horizon. It slithered in the heat waves lifting from the pavement as it neared, like a dancing black ghost. When the speck was about half a mile away, it revealed itself to be another runner. As the figure grew larger, I became mesmerized at the perfection of his approach. There was not a single wasted movement. The grace of his gait made me ashamed of the awkwardness of my stride. With every smooth swing of his arms, the sun reflected off something on his hand, a bright metronome announcing his approach. I could hardly detect a change in his rhythm as he began to climb up the grade at the base of the hill. If water could flow uphill, it would look like this runner. It wasn't so much that he was powering up the hill but rather that the hill was moving backwards under his feet. He was halfway up the slope when I realized I would soon be in the company of Danny O'Neal.

Danny crested the summit no more taxed than he was at the bottom. He stopped, extended his hand, his gun-gray eyes looking into mine, and said. "Hello, Michael. I'm Danny O'Neal. We ran against each other at the semi-finals last year." The experience was surreal, like having Jack Kennedy know your name at a cocktail party, a totally unexpected event. Out of the hundreds of runners in that race, somehow Danny remembered me. Maybe he remembered everybody. I shook his hand and felt the class ring that had reflected the sun a few moments before.

"You ran a heck of a race, taking second in the state finals," I said clumsily. "It must have been a good day." Danny's gaze shifted to the endless fields of corn and soybeans arrayed around the hill like a patchwork quilt, as though he was looking for something.

"All days can be better than they turn out to be," Danny said. "The Hawks made it to the finals but we got blown out. I think we took last, and worse than that, the Spartans took the team title." Danny smiled and shook his head. "The Spartans, they're assholes but they're good runners." The Spartans were the acknowledged bad boys of Illinois high school sports, always winners at someone else's expense. Danny turned to me. "You're a long way from home, aren't you?"

"I'm a long way from my last one. I guess this is home for a while."

"How long is a while?" Danny asked curiously.

"Until they catch my father."

"Oh." Danny returned his gaze to the horizon, knowing better than to ask for more details.

He was tall, not so tall that he stood out in a crowd but tall enough so that his powerful strides chewed up a lot of ground. After a few months of summer running, his sandy hair was sun-bleached to albino white, making his eyebrows nearly invisible while contrasting with his deep tan. Danny was runner thin. Nothing jiggled when his feet struck the ground. Spinster aunts would have had a hard time pinching his cheeks. If not for a football-shaped birthmark on his forearm, he would have been unblemished.

"So what do you think of Barrel?" Danny finally asked.

"Hard to say. I just got here today. Seems like a good place to run." Danny gave me a big smile and then became very serious, as if playing a role.

"No, Michael, Barrel's a pit. Always has been, always will be. But it is the heartland. We have 4th of July parades, we grow the nation's food, we birth the boys who fight our wars. We are Rockwell's inspiration. You'd think there'd be nothing wrong with that but what can I say? It's still a pit." The seriousness of his reply took me back. Before I could respond, Danny let his smile return and added, "But on the plus side, the girls screw like rabbits," and he started running down the far side of the hill. I took a soon-to-become-familiar place at his side. We traded strides mile after mile, and during our run back to Barrel we became friends. That was the beginning.

CHAPTER 4

Danny spoke no truer words. Barrel, Illinois, was the heartland. Barrel took its name from the gun barrel factory around which the town grew. Barrel first prospered by providing armaments for the Civil War. It was unclear to even the town historian why Barrel was so blessed, but then, as now, not-so-altruistic people make these decisions in murky ways for sordid reasons. It's no coincidence that the town square is named after General Holden, commandant for procurement and logistics for the Union Army during the Civil War and source of the original contract for the factory. I suppose it's also no accident that after the war that same General Holden retired to a life of leisure as a gentleman farmer on 6,400 prime acres of Illinois topsoil.

Barrel has been a cog in the military-industrial complex since long before there was such a thing. In every war since its founding, the town has provided a small portion of the machinery required to wage those conflicts. During the Civil War, its gun barrels produced the deaths of countless Southern rebels and, by virtue of their shoddy workmanship, the demise of more than a few Union soldiers. During the Spanish-American War, it was Barrel's breech-loaders that sent shells on their way across Manila Bay. In the First World War, transmissions for tanks spewed forth from the factory on Main Street. The Second World War could not have been won without the B-17 tail sections that grew out of that same factory.

The years of World War II were the apex of Barrel's existence. All times before and all times after are compared to those frightening, but exhilarating years. If the town ceased to exist the day after V-J day, not a person would have objected. There was not a more determined or patriotic town in the country during the war years. Houses were literally uprooted to reroute the train tracks by the factory, just to save the few hours it would have taken to load the B-17 tail sections on trucks and haul them to the depot. Every minute that was saved brought victory over the Nazis and Japs that much closer.

The years before the next war were difficult for Barrel, but prosperity returned when the citizens of Barrel retooled the factory to make machine guns for the Korean War. Barrel took pride in the train cars full of Browning Automatic Rifles that rolled out of the factory and wound their way a half a world away to undistinguished specks of geography like Porkchop Hill. For the war in Vietnam, Barrel leveraged those skills to produce M16 rifles.

Between wars, the factory continued to be Barrel's reason for being, even if it provided for only a meager living. If you can make transmissions for tanks, you can make them for tractors, and that's what Barrel did. If you can manufacture a rifle, it is not so hard to link together the undercarriages of Fords, and Barrel did that as well. With every new contract, the factory retooled and a street or a square was named for another silent benefactor. But the price for Barrel's tenuous security went far beyond the bestowing of the occasional honorific. Barrel paid for its war-fed good fortunes with the lives of its boys. These young patriots marched off to battle largely without question, without protest and without remorse. It was a sense of duty that permeated the very soil of the town. I can't say how this propensity for patriotism began. Perhaps it was a genetic trait passed from father to son or the result of an unknown mineral in the drinking water.

The monuments in Holden Park are testimony to the valor of Barrel's young men. In almost mocking symmetry, they circle the statue of General Holden, one monument for each war. Each spire is adorned with brass plaques etched with the names of the dead, permanent remembrances of the young men from Barrel who died in war for their country while answering the call of duty. With the start of each new war, a new monument is erected with the knowledge that the young men of Barrel will be the first to volunteer, the first to fight and the first to die. With the news of the death of each young man, the appropriate plaque is removed from the monument, its surface is etched with his name and it is replaced on the spire. It always puzzled me how the size of the monument and the number of plaques could be so precisely chosen at the outset of the war, for at the end of each war, the plaques are filled to perfection without a space unfilled or a name wedged in. I suppose practice makes perfect.

It is only now that I understand what so disturbed me during my first visit to Holden Park. It was not the eeriness of the shadows the monuments cast or the sense that hundreds of silent voices were calling out a warning to me from their unmoving positions on the plaques. What caused my heart to race and my hands to grow cold was the enormity of the monument erected for the war in Vietnam. It was covered with what seemed like endless acres of blank plaques dwarfing the growing cadre of names that were already etched on their surfaces. It was not a good omen for the young men of Barrel whose names would one day fill the blankness, and I was now one of those young men.

The pace of our run slowed as Danny and I entered Barrel, the county roads morphing into the small patchwork of asphalt streets of the town. We ran by the rifle factory, the shuttered storefronts and the sidewalk fruit stands. We passed tired houses with well-kept yards and jogged by porches of senior citizens trying to fan away the heat and humidity. We ran in silence by the funeral procession assembling around a flag-draped coffin being carried by an honor guard to a waiting hearse. Another name would soon be etched on the Vietnam monument in Holden Park.

We slowed to a halt on the infield of the Barrel High School track as the clouds that would bring that afternoon's thunderstorms began to obscure the horizon. There I met my soon-to-be teammates, the Hawks of Barrel High School. They had just finished their own runs and were lying shirtless on the infield grass while they recovered from their efforts, glistening in the sun as sweat dripped off them. They were an unlikely collection of athletes whose only common traits were their lack of hand-eye-coordination that otherwise would have allowed them to succeed in other sports, their dedication to the one sport that welcomed them and their devotion to the man who was their coach. The Hawks' hierarchy was clear in an instant. Cross country is a team sport and Danny was not only the Hawks' best runner, he was also their captain and leader.

A cross country team must have at least five members, though seven can run in a race. In a dual meet, the two teams line up at the starting line, alternating spots between the teams, 14 runners abreast. In an invitational, there might be 20 or 30 teams, 200 runners poised on the starting line. With the blast of the starting pistol, the runners leap into stride on a course that may take them through woods, on city streets or county roads, up hills, over creeks or just in circles around campus. For three miles, they jockey for position. The foolish and unprepared quickly take the lead only to fade halfway through the race. The fit and cunning keep the leaders in sight, maintaining contact as they work their way through the pack so they are positioned for a closing-mile kick into the finish.

The race finishes in a chute, a funnel-like arrangement of ropes and stakes with the finish line, only a lane wide, at its throat. The chute tapers the pack of runners into a single file by the time they cross the finish line so there is no doubt as to their finishing places. Sometimes flying elbows accompany the mad dash to the finish line, three or four runners across desperately lunging to the front to take the prized position that allows them entry into the apex of the chute first. Crossing the finish line, each runner is given a stick, usually a tongue depressor, with his finishing position on it that designates the points he earns. You add up the points of the first five runners for each team and the low score wins. It is as simple as that. It's not rocket science.

Here is where cruel mathematics separates a collection of a few talented runners from a championship team. In a dual meet, in order for your team to win the race, all you need is three good runners and at least two stragglers who can finish the course. If you take the first three and last four places, you win 29-30. If you take the first seven, you win 15-50. Here's the gotcha: Winning dual meets with only those three good runners with scores of 29-30 will probably get you to the conference or state finals. But if all you really have is three good runners, even if they take the first three spots, you're going to lose the big meets if your next two runners finish deep in the pack. Their points will simply exceed those of an opposing team that manages to finish five runners in the top 20. The only teams you need to fear in the big invitationals and state finals are those who are winning their dual meets 15-50. If they're winning dual meets 29-30, they don't have the depth needed to win the big races.

That had always been the Hawks' problem. They could win the dual meets but their lack of depth spelled doom in the big invitationals and state finals. Scouring the farms that surrounded Barrel, the Hawks could always conjure up three decent runners but they never seemed to be able to close the deal. The strong fourth and fifth runners needed to win the big meets eluded them, and whatever had passed for their fifth man last year graduated. That lack of depth cost them dearly. The Hawks last won the state championship in 1942.

As we sat in a circle on the infield grass, Danny introduced me to the members of the Hawks while fingering his oversized class ring. I could tell instantly that Danny took pride in being captain of this less-than-renowned collection of runners.

"Hawks, this is Michael Cane, runner extraordinaire, and soon to be a Hawk himself. Michael, these are the Hawks." I knew I would be welcome. I would be their fifth man. "That bag of bones over there is Shaun Ryan," Danny said pointing to the first Hawk in the circle.

Shaun gave me a smile and what seemed like a wink. "Good to have you aboard," he offered. Shaun was a good-looking kid. He had talent but needed motivation. On a good day, he could keep pace with Danny in practice but would probably never beat him in a race. Danny held the school record on the Hawks' three-mile home course in 14:22. Shaun had barely broken 14:50. He'd been second man to Danny from his first day on the team. Shaun seemed at ease with that role, important but not so important that he carried the pressure of expectation that Danny did. Shaun ran because he had little else going for him other than his good looks. He rarely opened a book other than the maintenance manual for his car and had few ambitions beyond taking his place next to his father on the assembly line at the factory. His world seemingly ended at the county line. It was difficult for him to conceive of a place called Chicago, let alone a place called Vietnam, which, ironically, he was more likely to see.

"….and his partner in crime is the notorious Billy Johnson," Danny continued as he introduced the team.

"Hey," Billy offered, with a tip of the brow salute. Billy was the religious one, a consistent third runner who followed instructions, turned in all of his assignments on time, went to church every Sunday and sang in the choir. Billy was also the first to be found drunk under the bleachers during Friday night football games or naked with a sophomore girl in the back seat of his car. He was a Dr. Jekyll and Mr. Hyde, the Eddie Haskell of Barrel. Billy was blessed with speed. He could run a half-mile in 1:55 but didn't have the endurance to be a leader at three miles. His 15:15 on the Hawks' home course was respectable, but only approaching what was needed to bolster a championship team. Billy would eventually marry a nice Baptist girl because that was what his parents wanted him to do. He would also eventually end up on the short end of more than one nasty divorce, unwanted outcomes of affairs with secretaries and delivery girls.

"…and that mountain of a man casting a shadow across the infield is the pride of the South, Amos Danforth," Danny said, hardly able to contain his admiration of his teammate.

"The South will rise again, boy. Keep your powder dry," Amos offered with a smile. Amos was an enormous barrel-chested specimen, more suited to weightlifting or wrestling than distance running. His thighs were as big around as my waist and his arms matched my legs. His muscular torso stretched the extra large Barrel High School running trunks he wore beyond the point of modesty. Amos, the fourth of an unending stream of siblings, acquired his bulk working the family farm. I had visions of Amos in harness pulling the cultivator like a comic book superhero pulling a disabled train. Amos' running style was an agonizing mixture of stomping and shuffling, which surprisingly worked well enough for him to be fourth man on the team. His bulging muscles may have been forged by lifting bales of hay and pounding in fence posts but they were adaptable enough to power his hulk across the Hawks' course in 15:30. Two of Amos' brothers were fighting in Vietnam and one had his name etched on a plaque in Holden Park. Amos was destined to be the fourth of his family to serve there.

Danny paused before making his last introduction. "...and the team wouldn't be complete without Carl Hager."

Carl, sweet Carl. Carl was too short to be a really good runner, too unkempt to be popular, and too poor to make a difference. Carl lived so far on the wrong side of the tracks that he couldn't even see the tracks. He ran with more heart and more perseverance than any runner I have ever known. Every mile run in practice was executed with the intensity of a zealot, but it never seemed to do much good. Carl was entering his senior year and he had improved by only a handful of seconds on the Hawks' home cross country course since the 16:10 he ran in his freshman year. In all that time, he had never finished in the Hawks' top five. My arrival might again deny him that honor. Carl was an observer who spoke little and for whom school was a challenge no greater than his running. In those politically incorrect times, Carl was described as being "slow." He lived with his war-widowed mother. The name of the father he wished he could remember is etched on one of the plaques in Holden Park on the monument for the Korean War. I waited for Carl's greeting but he only looked at me as though mute.

"Hey, nice to meet you all," I offered, taking my place on the grass.

"So where're you from?" Shaun asked.

"We move around a lot," I explained. "Most recently, from Marion."

"You know Cathy Monroe from Marion High?" Billy asked, suddenly perking up.

"Can't say that I do. A friend of yours?"

"Well, you can say I knew her...in the Biblical sense, that is," Billy bragged.

"Ignore him," Shaun chided. "He's a bullshitter, and not a good one at that."

"Men, men," Danny implored, "let's not give Michael the impression that we're a bunch of lowlife crawlers."

"Yeah, let him learn that on his own," Shaun said, throwing a tuft of grass at Danny.

"I really did have her," Billy defended himself. "Remember the Peoria Invitational?" That seemed to be a cue, as Shaun, Danny and Amos chimed in unison, barely able to finish the words before bursting into laughter.

"Don't invite us in unless you're going to have us in!"

It must have been an inside joke. I laughed anyway to be polite.

Carl was silent, carefully looking me over as if he was contemplating the purchase of a prized dairy cow. After squinting at me for a while he asked, "You any good?" Carl was clearly a man of few words. Billy, Shaun and Amos turned my way, anxious for an answer."

"Well, I've had a few okay races."

"14:45 at his conference finals last year," Danny cited for me. How he knew that I'll never know. The Hawks all quickly did the mental arithmetic.

"Whew, doggy!" Amos exclaimed, "looks like Shaun's going to have to run for his supper!"

We all got up, said our goodbyes and began running off in different directions to our homes. The first day of the fall semester was the next day but we would see each other for a morning run before school. "See you tonight?" Danny confirmed as we jogged off. He'd asked me to dinner at his house as a welcome to Barrel.

"See you in an hour."

CHAPTER 5

Danny's upbringing was stern but not totally without love. His parents met at a USO dance in San Diego the night before his father, Ben, shipped out to the South Pacific of World War II. Ben proposed to Danny's mother Alice that same evening. It was a crazy time. Alice had enjoyed a life of privilege in a family whose blood was blue and whose hands were uncalloused. She must have fiercely loved Ben to follow him back to Barrel after the war. Barrel was surely as foreign to her as Sherpa villages in the Himalayas. The plain manners of the people of Barrel were downright primitive compared to her exquisite ways but she accepted their welcome and eventually became one of them. Love will make you do strange and irrational things.

The love that brought Alice to Barrel faded in the years since the war but Alice's devotion to her family could not be questioned. Following in the footsteps of his father and grandfather before him, Ben had been a Marine in the war. He waded ashore on Iwo Jima, was wounded on Okinawa, and still had nightmares to remind him of his service and the atrocities he had witnessed. The names of Ben's brother and father are etched on plaques in Holden Park. Service and sacrifice were not strangers to the O'Neal household.

Patriotism and the edicts of Ben O'Neal were not questioned by the O'Neal family. Issues were black and white with no gray in between. There was little tolerance for discussion and less for debate. The fledgling antiwar movement protesting U.S. involvement in Vietnam infuriated Ben as an assault on the very core of the American spirit. As far as Ben O'Neal was concerned, there was no middle ground. If you served, you were a patriot; if you were not a patriot, you were a traitor. If you did not salute the flag, you must want to burn it. If you questioned your duty to country, you were a coward. It was as simple and unquestionable as that. Ben's stark opinions may have been difficult to accept but they made the topics of dinner table conversation easy to predict.

Danny's sister Hannah was too young to understand the oppression of Ben's uncompromising standards and Alice was too devoted to her husband to object, so Danny was more often than not the target of Ben's frustration. Danny's brother Corey accepted the seemingly unavoidable destiny set before him, not in blind agreement with his father, but with the stoicism of accepting his obligation as a citizen. Upon graduating from high school the year before, Corey enlisted in the United States Marines and was somewhere in Vietnam that very evening. Danny missed Corey desperately. Corey served as the father to Danny that Ben could never be, and the devotion Danny gave Corey was deeper than any father-son relation could ever hope to be. Danny vowed to wear Corey's high school class ring—the ring I saw earlier that first day reflecting the afternoon sun—until Corey safely returned from the war. Danny prayed every night that his brother's name would not one day be etched on a plaque in Holden Park.

The humidity of the day had barely dissipated when I climbed the steps of the front porch of the O'Neal home. My fresh shirt was already wilted and showed the sweat stains of my walk across town. A paunchy, unsmiling man answered my knock. His unwelcoming glare startled me. "We start meals on time in the O'Neal household, boy," he said through the unopened screen door, and turned away to return to the dining room table I could see beyond the living room. A wrong turn had cost me a few minutes and it seemed as though I would pay for that transgression. I thought about opening the screen door and stepping in but Alice appeared an instant later and opened the door for me.

"You must be Michael," she said, smiling while putting her arm around my shoulder to escort me inside. "Danny told us all about you. Welcome to Barrel."

The impeccably kept house was museum-like in chronicling the service of the O'Neal family to their country. An entire wall of the living room was covered with photographs of O'Neal men in uniform and official platoon pictures. The photos dated to the First World War, a grandfather or great uncle peering at us from under the helmet of the era. The most recent, most prominently displayed picture was of Corey O'Neal in full combat gear. He was framed by the jungles of Vietnam while smiling at the unacknowledged photographer. A glass-doored china hutch held more than one triangularly folded flag that once covered the coffin of an O'Neal soldier.

Ben sat irritably at the head of the table with Danny at one side and his sister Hannah at the other. Danny, uncharacteristically silent, gave me a small wave as Alice guided me to a chair by Hannah and quickly began dishing out the food. Dinner commenced without conversation, following a clearly orchestrated routine. The plates went from Alice to Ben to Danny to Hannah and back to Alice. The sounds of dishes clicking and spoons scraping the bottom of bowls seemed deafening in the absence of any spoken word. Hannah easily amused herself by tormenting her food while Danny ate staring at his plate. Ben broke the silence.

"I spoke with the Marine recruiter today," he said to no one in particular but clearly intending his comments for Danny. For a town of only 12,400 people, Barrel was surprisingly blessed with active and well-staffed Army, Navy, Marine and Air Force recruiting offices, a testimony to the town's record of service. "He'll guarantee Danny's assignment to Corey's unit if he enlists now and reports when he graduates in June." Ben looked up to his wife. "I can't think of anything more rewarding than having our sons serve side-by-side."

"Rewarding for who?" Danny asked without looking up.

"That would be nice," Alice ventured before Ben could reply, giving Danny a cease-and-desist look.

"It's an empty promise," Danny continued. "Corey will have finished his tour in Vietnam before I could get there."

"Then he'll volunteer for another tour," Ben concluded.

"So you're making decisions for Corey too?" Danny popped. This was obviously a conversation that had been held at least a few times before. I didn't quite know what to say so I said nothing. The ensuing silence hurt my ears.

"How long has Corey been in the Marines?" I finally cautiously asked.

"Just over a year," Alice answered. "He enlisted the day he graduated from high school. Corey was a runner, just like Danny."

"Only not as good," Hannah corrected.

"He would've been drafted anyway," Danny said.

"Don't belittle his service," Ben spat angrily. "At least he knows where his duty lies."

"And I don't?" Danny countered. "Maybe my duty is not to blindly enlist to fight in a trumped-up war. I'd rather take my chances with the draft." Ben's fists hit the table in an instant.

"You will not talk that way in my house," Ben commanded, his eyes unblinking. "Your brother is risking his life this very instant in the service of his country. Your uncle died fighting the Nazis in the Argonne Forest. I took two bullets serving this great country. Don't you dare belittle that. You have a duty to your country and you will fulfill it!"

"What about my duty to myself?" Danny asked. "When do I serve myself?"

"We are not going to have this conversation again!" Ben's voice rattled the china hutch. He threw his napkin onto his plate, got up from the table and disappeared into the living room.

"Danny and Daddy fight a lot," Hannah explained.

"More potatoes, Michael?" Alice offered as though nothing had happened. Danny stood up as if he was going to say something but left through the kitchen and out the back door. "Maybe you should talk with him," Alice suggested. I excused myself and followed Danny to the back porch. We sat on the stoop for a few minutes, watching moths flutter around the bare porch light bulb. Danny absentmindedly twirled Corey's ring on his finger.

"Sorry you had to hear that," he offered.

"Hear what?" I said, as consoling as I could.

"We have that conversation about once a week," Danny explained. "Dad was a Marine. My uncles were Marines. Corey is a Marine. So I'll be a Marine. No questions, no discussion. It's the O'Neal way. The enlistment papers are upstairs, just waiting for my signature."

"What's wrong with the Marines?" I asked. "Might be better to enlist than take your chances on getting drafted into who knows what."

"Nothing's wrong with the Marines, if you're going to serve. I just haven't decided if I want to. It used to be so simple and now it's so damn confusing. You hear so much about how bad it is over there, how we're wasting lives, how even the Vietnamese don't want us there. Then you think, this is my country, right or wrong. Somebody in Washington must know what he's doing."

"That's a big assumption," I offered.

"Don't get me wrong. I'm not a hippie or Yippie or whatever they call themselves. If I'm drafted, I'll serve, but volunteering is another story."

"You've got options even with the draft. Ever considered taking an extra long vacation in Canada?"

"Canada? Well, there's an idea." Danny replied, smiling. I knew he wasn't serious. Danny becoming a draft dodger would have killed his father and it just wasn't in Danny's character. I didn't know Danny all that well at the time but I knew that much. He wasn't one to walk out on an obligation, whether he liked it or not.

"Well, there's always a student deferment," I suggested.

"What, me go to college?" Danny asked. "That would take both brains and money, neither of which I have in abundance."

"You could easily get an athletic scholarship," I surmised. "You're good enough to get an offer or two. Run in college for four years and maybe the war will be over by the time you graduate." This must not have been a new idea to Danny. There must have been a stack of offer letters from college coaches from across the country sitting on his desk.

"You know, Michael," Danny admitted, "I don't work any harder than Shaun or Billy or Carl. Yes, I may put in the miles and run intervals around that track for hours at a stretch, but so do they. It just doesn't seem fair. They work just as hard as I do, maybe harder. But I'm the one who'll end up getting a scholarship and a deferment, and they'll end up getting drafted."

"Life's not fair, Danny. You're gifted. You do something other people can't. Sometimes you get rewarded for your gifts. Sometimes you don't. There's no shame in taking what's offered to you." Danny let this sink in a bit.

"Getting killed in some jungle 10,000 miles from home shouldn't depend on how fast you can or can't run around a track."

CHAPTER 6

My first day at Barrel High School was memorable for many reasons, but mostly for meeting Coach Frank Dillon. It was before classes, and the cross country team was congregated in front of Danny's hall locker. If they weren't running or in class or eating burgers at Mabel's, that's where you were likely to find them, in front of Danny's locker. The Hawks staked out that territory as theirs and few argued with them.

Danny enjoyed those pre-class gatherings because he enjoyed the company of his teammates. He usually stood silently, listening to the banter, while holding hands with Shelly, his girlfriend since junior high. Shelly was the type of girl that small town parents dream of their sons marrying. Girls like Shelly, pretty, organized, proper, devoted and devout, were seemingly content in their small world of Barrel, Illinois. They would shun the women's liberation movement of the coming decade as something as foreign and distasteful as the Vietnamese they watched on the evening news. They would be content marrying their high school sweethearts, keeping their homes tidy and taking care of their children. It would be only later in life, after opportunities had passed them by, when they would wish for there to be more in their lives. But for now Shelly was passionate about only a few things, and Danny was first on that short list.

Carl surprisingly had a girlfriend too. Candy was as bright and pretty as Shelly but a world apart in what she wanted in life. What Candy saw in Carl was a mystery to me from day one. Where Carl was short and unkempt, Candy was tall and tailored. Where Carl was a man of few words, Candy was a chatterbox. Where Carl had resigned himself to sift through the dregs of life, Candy had ambitions for him that she had yet to even find words for. It was only years later that I came to realize that Candy may have had as large a hand in saving my life as Danny did, for it was Candy who nurtured Carl to that single day of greatness.

Shaun, in spite of his well-documented exploits with the fairer sex of Barrel High, only occasionally showed up at Danny's locker with a girl by his side. If only a tiny fraction of what was rumored to be true about Shaun's amorous adventures was actually true, there would one day be a prize named after him. Shaun spent most of the time before classes swapping lies with Billy about one girl or another doing one thing or another to him in the back seat of one car or another. Billy, on the other hand, was never seen without a girl on his arm or lipstick on his cheek. The Hawks kept a calendar on the inside of Danny's locker on which they recorded the girls Billy appeared with draped over his arm. If only his parents knew. So much for being a choirboy.

Amos, for all his extraordinary good looks, impeccable manners and muscle-bound chest, had probably never actually gone out on a date. It wasn't that he didn't like girls or girls didn't like him. He was an Adonis who was the topic of more girls' locker room chatter than you could imagine. It was a matter of size. There wasn't a girl in the county who was within 12 inches in height or a hundred pounds in weight of Amos. I think they were all deathly afraid of what might happen if Amos rolled over on top of them.

Danny and Shelly, Carl and Candy, Billy and his girl of the day, Shaun and Amos, and now me. We were the Hawks of Barrel High and their camp followers. It was over this brood that Coach Frank Dillon presided.

My first glimpse of Coach Dillon was through a crowded hallway as he wound his way through the jabbering clumps of girls and boys. One of the most popular teachers in school, it was difficult for him to progress more than even a few feet through the hallway before one student or another asked for his attention. The coach was never too busy to lend advice, ask about a sick brother or joke about Principal Milo's latest inexplicable edicts. Though he never admitted it, it was a well-known secret that Coach Dillon dug into his own wallet on a regular basis to buy lunch for students who had the misfortune of living on the wrong side of the tracks. Coach Dillon might not be first in line for sainthood but he was far from being last in line.

Coach Dillon was a moderately tall man with the leanness and sometimes gauntness of a former runner. His hairline was just beginning to recede and the creases around his eyes were just beginning to deepen, both at odds with the youthfulness of his disposition. It was only as he maneuvered through the last clump of students before Danny's locker that I saw he walked with a cane that only partly canceled the bobbing of his limp. The poorly hidden grimace on Coach Dillon face when he twisted in response to a student's call told me that his injury was still fresh even though, as I later learned, it had been decades. Coach Dillon walked right up to me and extended his hand.

"Michael, I'm Coach Dillon. Welcome to Barrel High. Danny told me all about you." I'd been in Barrel barely 24 hours. When did that happen? "I'm thrilled you're going to be on the team this year. We can use a runner like you."

"Nice to meet you, Coach." I barely had a chance to reply. Coach Dillon continued to pump my right hand while he hooked his cane on his belt, pulled an envelope out of his pocket and thrust it into my other hand.

"Here's your schedule. I took the liberty of registering you early. You haven't taken Government yet, right? Practice is at 2:30. Check in with Donald at the gym to get a locker. See you then." And with that he was off, disappearing into the throngs of students. Little did I know then that I had just met another man who would have a hand in saving my life.

My first day of classes at Barrel High was memorable for one additional reason, how miserable it was. The high school was built as a WPA project during the depression, a legacy that yielded marble-walled toilet stalls in the boys' room, gargoyles perched on the parapets and Grapes-of-Wrath murals in the auditorium.

You couldn't say the building lacked character but it did lack air conditioning, an unthinkable luxury for the Barrel Unified School District. Some time during third period, the sun was sufficiently high overhead and the breezes sufficiently absent that the mugginess of the late summer day oozed through the cracked plaster into the classrooms. It was the sort of day when writing paper sucked up so much humidity that pencils pushed through their surface like sharp needles. Teachers sprouted sweat rings simply sitting at their desks.

Thanks to Coach Dillon, there was at least one Hawk or his girlfriend in every one of my classes, strategically seated next to me to ease my transition and make me feel welcome. As the bell to start fourth period stopped clanging, Amos hurried into class and squeezed into the empty desk beside me. He passed me a copy of the *Barrel Gazette*, the town paper that had just hit the newsstand, pointing to a front-page story below the fold. I couldn't tell if it was sweat or tears that had fallen from his cheeks and stained the paper. The headline made me think tears.

"Former Barrel High School Cross Country Runner Killed in Vietnam." The accompanying photograph must have been a senior class picture. The caption simply read "Frederick H. Delisle." He was a handsome kid, smiling at an unseen camera, proudly wearing his letterman jacket, an unpredictable future awaiting him. Who would have predicted this?

Freddy had graduated from Barrel High two years before, when Danny and the rest of the Hawks were sophomores. Freddy was their team captain, third man to Danny and Corey, and the salt of the earth. Freddy was a role model to the meandering, a brother to the brotherless, and an inspiration to the unmotivated. He was the boy mothers wished their daughters would date and, if God smiled down in them, marry. Freddy was senior class treasurer and 4H Club president. He finished eleventh in the state cross country finals. Freddy volunteered at the VA hospital and looked after his sisters when his mother worked the swing shift. He enlisted because that's what his dad had done, a man he cherished and who had worked himself into an early grave.

Now Freddy Delisle was dead. He was just one more fatality in a war that, with every passing day, fewer and fewer seemed too enthusiastic about. I never knew Freddy but I knew his death had to have been a waste. The article didn't give any details, only that he was killed in action. Maybe the lack of detail was for the best. Sometimes there are things that are best not known. There would be a memorial service, a funeral and another name etched on a plaque in Holden Park.

Coach Dillon arranged for me to have a study hall the period before practice and so I wandered the halls on the way to the gym. As ornate as the aging classroom building of Barrel High was, the gymnasium was a lesson in making the best of a bad situation. Imagine a Quonset hut on steroids and you have a good mental picture of the Barrel High School Gymnasium. The entrance lobby was not unlike a railroad switchyard. The track to the right led to the boys' locker room, the track to the left to the girls' locker room and the track straight ahead to the gym proper. The coaches' offices were upstairs. Coach Dillon's office was directly over the entrance to the gym. I remember many times leaving the gym in the dark after long practices and glancing upwards to see Coach Dillon fatherly looking down over his wards. He never went home before we did.

The small lobby to the gym also held the crown jewels and historical documents of Barrel High. It was where the trophy case and athletic record boards could be found. It was no less true for Barrel High School than any other small town, downstate high school in the 1960s; their pride and bragging rights were embodied in the tarnishing trophies and plaques that adorned these cases. Thousands of forgotten students traipsed through the hallowed halls of Barrel High School with nary an ounce of remembrance or recognition. But the boys and girls whose names were carved on those trophies, whose names were listed on the record boards, would live forever in truth and legend.

As a stranger to Barrel High the names had little meaning to me, but as I scanned over the collection, a single trophy caught my attention. The loving cup was perhaps the largest and its two accompanying photographs the most cherished. The cup was engraved with "Barrel High School State Cross Country Champions, 1942," and there, listed as a team member, was Frank Dillon. The photograph to the left was of a young Frank Dillon finishing first in the state cross country finals, grabbing his stick with a "1" clearly visible as his powerful stride carried him into the chute. Directly behind him was his Hawk teammate, Peter Lorenzo, finishing second only a step to the rear. The image to the right of the trophy was a team photo: seven fantastically happy boys huddled around the very same trophy, each holding up his finishing stick. Coach Dillon held one handle of the trophy and Pete Lorenzo held the other. The Hawks of 1942 were the first and only Barrel High School team to win a state championship. Frank Dillon and Pete Lorenzo would forever be frozen in time in those photographs as innocent boys at the apex of their youth. If you looked carefully into the eyes of those two boys, barely discernable in the graininess of the photographs, you would also see their unfathomable commitment to duty to country and to each other, both of which would grow to a tragic crescendo.

I dressed for practice in the company of sadness. Every Hawk had known and cherished the company of Freddy Delisle. He would be missed no less than a brother. The Hawks spoke little but communicated volumes by the hurt in their eyes. Only a few years before, Freddy sat on these same benches, exchanged the same worn-out stories and shared the same comradeship of being a Hawk. And now he was gone, nothing left but his memory in their hearts and a soon-to-be inscription on a plaque in Holden Park. The same thought rattled through the mind of each Hawk that afternoon: Was Freddy's fate awaiting me?

Coach Dillon limped into the locker room, his cane hooked on his belt as he flipped through a stack of papers on his clipboard. There was no reason to the shuffling of the papers. It merely provided a means for the coach to focus his attention. He motioned us all together and we grouped around him.

"Freddy Delisle was no less dear to me than had he been my son," Coach Dillon began, "just as each of you have become an inseparable part of me. You cannot share what we experience together without forging such a bond. It is for that reason I have to believe that Freddy died for a purpose. It would be too much to bear if his life was wasted." Coach Dillon paused, as if debating his next words. "Each of you will be soon face the decision of your lifetimes, whether to follow in Freddy's footsteps or to choose a different way. I wish the good Lord had given me the power to protect you from having to make that decision."

Coach's expression suddenly became very distant, as though he was part of another conversation, oblivious to our company. A tear streaked down his cheek. "The Hawks have paid too dearly for what others enjoy." Coach Dillon unhooked his cane and walked to the door leading to the track. Glancing at his watch he said without looking back, "Today's workout is intervals on the track. Take a two-mile warm-up. We'll start in 30 minutes."

CHAPTER 7

Cross country running is all about endurance and all about speed. You need endurance to finish the race. You need speed to win the race. Training to be a cross country runner is a delicate balance between building the endurance that gets you around the course and refining the speed that enables you to grab the winning stick. If you have it in your mind to be a champion, one is worthless without the other. I wish I had a dollar for every freshman boy who, nearly blinded by visions of Olympic gold, innocently presented himself at the first day of practice. After four years of unspeakable dedication, he would grow to have endurance or speed, but not both. When it comes to the championship race, you call those runners spectators. Now, even years later, the unfairness of those outcomes still breaks my heart.

The more achievable part of the equation is building endurance. If you have the fortitude to spend endless hours on the roads, pounding out mile after mile, no matter how hot the weather or how high your own temperature, you will become fit and you will build endurance. With each mile you run, your conditioning will improve and you will become that much better prepared for the next mile. A running friend of mine once said that you have to spend enough hours on the roads so that when you finally get to a race it seems short in comparison. He's right. Your fate is in your own hands because endurance is something you have control over. If you are willing to put in the miles, your endurance will improve.

On the other hand, speed is God-given. You either have the potential for being fast or not. That's all there is to it. Case closed. It has something to do with how many fast twitch fibers and how many slow twitch fibers you have in your muscles, and that was determined the day you were conceived. Just how fast you might ever hope to run may have been decided in the back seat of a 1946 Ford convertible. The gotcha is that we don't know what that upper bound to our speed is. It could be a 5:30 mile; it could be a 3:50 mile. You just can't know ahead of time. The process you must survive to discover that limit is the unbearable torture called intervals.

Interval training is done on the track and consists of sets and combinations of quarter-miles, half-miles or miles. You run a quarter-mile, once around a 440-yard track, at a set pace, rest a bit by walking to the turn and back, and then run another quarter-mile. This might go on for 20 quarters, followed by maybe four or five half-miles or a set of mile repeats, topped off with another 20 quarters. This can go on for hours, and usually does. Interval training makes the track your own personal circular hell, an endless path of exhaustion with no beginning and no end. It is a rite of passage through which all runners who aspire to greatness must pass.

My first day of intervals on my first afternoon as a Hawk at Barrel High School is an experience that is seared into my being and, like a bad tattoo, I carry that experience with me wherever I go. And like that tattoo, as time passes, the sharp edges may blur but the memory is forever. The Hawks jogged a few miles at Coach Dillon's direction to warm up for the intervals, a needless exercise considering the temperature was nearly 100 and the humidity not much less. When we lined up at the start-finish line of the track to begin our intervals, we were already drenched in sweat. We had long since abandoned our shirts and had long since stopped trying to guess what Coach had in mind for us. We feared being right as much as we feared being wrong.

Coach Dillon stood on the inside grass, stopwatch and clipboard in hand, eyeing us as if making some final mental calculations. Just how much was he going to be able to throw at us before we begged for mercy? After a few moments he announced our sentence and the intervals began. "Twenty quarters. Ten in 75 seconds, five in 70 and five in 65...Go!"

We surged forward and began running into the first turn. The Hawks' unsaid hierarchy became immediately apparent. Danny went into the lead, followed by Billy and Shaun. I tucked in behind Shaun. A gap quickly formed as Amos and Carl just as quickly lagged behind. By the time we reached the 220-yard pole, we were strung out over 20 yards. "36, 37, 38...." Coach Dillon called out across the track giving us our half-way splits. "Establish a pace!" Now, 75 seconds is not terribly fast for a quarter-mile. It is only a five-minute mile pace. But in the heat and humidity of that first day of intervals, even a 75-second pace was enough to be taxing.

By the time we rounded the turn into the last 110 yard straight-away, our breathing was heavy and our hearts were pounding. The salt from our sweat stung our eyes like wet needles. "Power it in!" Coach Dillon yelled. "Don't let the pace slow!" We lifted our legs and rotated onto the balls of our feet to keep the pace up to the finish. Looking ahead as I approached the start-finish line, I was impressed with Danny's style. Smooth, efficient, consistent. Without Danny to compare to, Billy and Shaun might have also impressed me, but next to him, they looked like hacks. Glancing back, it was almost painful to look at the pounding gait of Amos. With each step, his tree-trunk legs hit the track like pile drivers, rattling distant windows, his bulging chest nearly straight up and down, an Adonis-like pose. He left footprints in the rock-hard track. Carl, on the other hand, was grotesque in his lack of style. His tiny, choppy steps seemed to make little progress, his face so contorted as to make Emil Zotapek seem handsome. Yet he never faltered, not once, not ever.

"72, 73, 74...." Coach Dillon read from his stopwatch as the first group of Danny, Billy, Shaun and I finished. "78, 79, 80..." he called as Amos and Carl finished. Coach Dillon jotted lines into a small notebook on the clipboard.

With hands on our hips and the sun beating on our sweaty backs, we began slowly walking the curve of the track. "Jog the interval!" Coach Dillon commanded, and we all obediently began jogging.

"That wasn't so bad," I said to no one in particular. Billy turned to look back at me.

"Praise the Lord," he mocked, "We've been blessed with an optimist."

"This is going to be a real ball buster," Shaun lamented. "I can't believe we're doing intervals on the first day of practice in this heat."

"There'll be plenty of time to complain later," Danny said with captain-like authority. "Let's just concentrate on the workout."

"What does the Coach write in that notebook?" I asked.

"Nobody knows," Amos answered.

We looped around the 110-yard pole and jogged back to the start-finish line across the infield grass. I glanced at the grandstands overlooking the backstretch and noticed that Candy and Shelly had taken up quarters in the top corner under the shade of an overhanging tree. They spread out their books, opened bottles of soda as though they were at the local diner and settled into busily doing homework. Nobody else seemed to notice, so I assumed this was standard operating procedure.

As soon as we were grouped together at the start-finish line, Coach Dillon said "Another in 75…Go!" and off we went around the track. We quickly fell into our set order: Danny, Billy, Shaun, me, Amos and Carl. This time, the heavy breathing and the stinging sweat began before we finished the first turn. "36, 37, 38…" Coach Dillon called as we passed the 220 pole under the occasional glances of Shelly and Candy. Our legs were more than just a little heavy as we powered into the finish. "73, 74, 75…" Coach Dillon announced as the first group finished. "78, 79, 80," as Amos and Carl finished. "Don't let the pace lag, Amos. It's too early to be suffering, Carl", he said. "Jog the interval!" And for quarter-mile after quarter-mile, we labored to keep the pace. Our legs grew heavier, our breathing more labored, the stinging sweat in our eyes more painful. Shelly and Candy also became more watchful, occasionally timing a quarter with their wristwatches and buzzing between themselves about the time. By the eighth quarter, the interval seemed to disappear. There was simply no recovering between quarters. We began the next quarter still breathing hard and with our legs emptied of reserves from the previous circuit.

We had all but forgotten the menu of the workout when for the eleventh quarter Coach Dillon said, "Well, gentlemen, the pace is now 70. Turn it up a notch...Go!" The prospect of running five seconds faster each lap seemed an impossible undertaking. We were barely able to claw our way through the thick air to make a 75-second pace. A 70-second pace was beyond comprehension.

Danny seemed unfazed by the new pace. He simply reset his inner metronome and took off around the track, the sun reflecting off Corey's ring, giving notice of his faster cadence. The outcome was a lot less certain for the rest of us mere mortals. My throat was already sore from trying to suck in enough air to keep my body in motion and my calves were already red-hot centers of pain. Billy and Shaun didn't look too much better as we rounded the first turn. Their arms no longer swept smooth arcs at their sides, but were held tightly by their chest. The gap between us and Danny began to widen. "33, 34..." Coach Dillon called as Danny crossed the 220 pole. "36, 37...Pick it up!" he yelled as Billy, Shaun and I crossed. "38, 39..." as Amos and Carl passed by.

Thirty-six seconds was too slow, and with an effort I can't now explain, I dug down, recklessly increased my pace, passed Billy and Shaun, and settled in behind Danny. And as simple as that, there was a new hierarchy for the Hawks. I had become second man. Danny and I finished the quarter together in 69 seconds. Billy and Shaun finished in 72, Amos and Carl in 78. Coach and Danny both gave me quizzical looks for having made my bold move but said nothing. For the next four quarters, Danny led the workout and I labored to make pace only steps behind him. Each quarter was miraculously only a second different from the one before, 69, 70, 71. Without Danny, I would have never come close to making pace. I just mentally hooked myself to the rear of his running trunks and let him pull me through each quarter. It was a strategy that served me well.

At the end of 15 quarters, we were a battle-scarred group. Conversation had long since evaporated. The effort of jogging the interval nearly exceeded that to finish the quarters. The sun just nicked the top of the stands and threw the first shadow across the track when we lined up for the next quarter-mile.

"Gentlemen, the pace is now 65 seconds." The mind has a wonderful defense mechanism. Hide and deny that which you have no power to change, and hope for the best. Deep down in the recesses of my subconscious, I knew that the last five quarters would be at 65 seconds, but I chose not to concede that knowledge. Suddenly, reality showed its ugly face. I looked to my right at Shaun at the start-finish line. He was staring intently at the ground ahead of him. To my left, Danny seemed almost content as he fingered Corey's ring. "Go!" Coach Dillon commanded, and we set off around the turn.

It was at that instant that I understood the difference between Danny and the rest of us. Danny just changed the setting on his internal clock and turned his legs over that much faster to meet the new pace. I tried to follow him but my body refused. I was already on the balls of my feet by the 110-yard pole, pumping my arms, fighting the pain in my calves, gasping for air, yet Danny continued to pull away. I glanced behind me. Billy and Shaun were fighting their own demons. Amos and Carl were laboring just to move their legs. As Danny passed the 220 pole, Frank called out, "31, 32... That's the pace, Danny. Let's go, Michael...33, 34...Shaun, Billy, don't lose contact...36, 37...Amos, lean forward!...39." Shelly and Candy were standing against the grandstand rail, intently watching the proceedings.

Danny finished that quarter-mile in 63 seconds with as even a pace as the first quarter. I can't remember my time. I must have finished because the next thing I knew we were lined up for the next quarter. That quarter blurred into the next, which was indistinguishable from the one that followed. With each quarter, the gap between Danny and the rest of us widened. As Danny powered around the track, we degenerated into survival mode. We were no longer running for pace. We were just trying to finish without shaming ourselves in front of Coach and the girls.

The last quarter-mile we ran that afternoon nearly ended my life. I knew that all I had to do was to make it around the track one more time and I would have survived the ordeal. I just had to lift my legs through another 440 yards and it would be over. I made promises to God to just let me finish. We might have to take a four- or five-mile cool down run after that last quarter, but the set of quarters would be done with. The pain in my legs was bearable only because the end was in sight. There was only one quarter-mile dash left.

We lined up at the start-finish line mentally blocking what we would likely have to endure in the next minute. "Remember, gentlemen," Coach Dillon reminded us, "the pace is 65 seconds... Go!" We took off around the curve with unbelievable vigor. You can run one more of almost anything if it's the last one, and this was the last quarter. We would survive. We worked our way around the track, draining every ounce of energy out of our bodies, confident with the knowledge that this was the last quarter.

Danny was about 50 yards ahead of me as he approached the start-finish line when the Coach began rotating his arm like a windmill. "Go around, go around," he yelled. Instead of finishing, Danny just kept on going around the curve into another lap. I began to slow as I neared the start-finish line when Coach Dillon's arm started windmilling again. "Go around, go around," he yelled, and not knowing exactly what to do, I followed Danny around the track. What was I doing? My breathing came in short gulps, my body not even able to process the air before asking for more. My legs called out for mercy. Sweat rivered down my legs and saturated my socks. I glanced behind me. Billy and Shaun, like Gemini twins, labored around the turn after me, their closeness somehow feeding the other. Amos, his pace unchanged for the last 10 quarters, stoically plodded into the turn. Carl's grimace, yards behind, made his face unrecognizable.

We were in the midst of a dreaded Coach Dillon "go-around." At any moment during an interval workout, Coach was liable to yell "Go around!" and instead of finishing, we would keep going around the track. I can't explain the terror that pulsed through my body when Danny approached the start-finish line at the end of his second go-around lap and Coach's arm started windmilling again. "Go around! Go around," he yelled. Danny seemed almost to enjoy the challenge. I couldn't believe it was happening. We were going around a third time. I would have been happy if I was only exhausted. Whatever is three stages beyond exhaustion could only start to describe how I felt. Danny was more than 100 yards ahead of me as I crossed the start-finish line, passing by the wind-milling Frank Dillon, his mouth moving but his words not penetrating my ears. I tried to lift my legs but the track was like flypaper, grabbing at the soles of my shoes, making each step a superhuman effort.

The sun was directly in our eyes as we rounded the last turn to the start-finish line. Danny, now 150 yards ahead, was only beginning to labor. Coach Dillon, looking at his stopwatch, called out "3:15" as Danny crossed the start-finish line. Shelly and Candy exchanged whispers in the stands. Random football players who had been tossing a ball on the infield stopped to watch. Danny kept on running into his fourth lap as the Coach's arm windmilled and the words "Go around!" wafted back to me. As I approached the start-finish line, Coach Dillon's arm stopped rotating. It was clear from Coach Dillon's expression and motionless arm that the rest of us were mercifully done. As each of us crossed the finish line, we staggered only a few steps before collapsing onto the track, our chests heaving for air, our sweat making pools on the bumpy track beneath us.

Danny passed the 220-yard pole before I realized what was happening. This was perhaps the greatest display of high school running I had ever witnessed. Every eye in the stadium followed Danny as he entered the final turn. Danny lapped Carl and then Amos before he passed the 330-yard pole. Danny rolled up onto the balls of his feet and began pumping his arms, lifting his legs, kicking in the last 110 yards like an Olympic finalist. He powered across the finish line as Coach Dillon calmly called out "4:18." Shaun, Billy and I looked at each other in disbelief. After 19 quarters of brutal intervals on what may have been the hottest, most humid day of the decade, Danny ran a 4:18 mile on the tail end of a Coach Dillon go-around. We had witnessed greatness. There is no category in the record books for such an awe-inspiring performance, but had there been, Danny deserved to be at the top of the list.

Danny was jogging the turn long before Amos and Carl finished their third lap. Candy and Shelly calmly gathered their things, took down their little encampment and started their walks home. The football players waved to Danny in respect. Coach Dillon made entries into his little notebook. "Good start to the season," he said to us, "Finish up with an easy five-miler. I'll see you all tomorrow." And with that, he grabbed his cane and hobbled across the track to the gymnasium.

"Shit, did you see that?" Billy asked.

"Unbelievable," Amos said. "That time would have won state a few years ago."

"It could be a long season," Shaun concluded as he rubbed his calves. As Danny jogged on the other side of the track, Carl looked up from where he lay prostrate on the track and said his first words of the afternoon.

"Hard workout."

The boy had a way with words.

CHAPTER 8

Frank Dillon was born in Barrel, Illinois in 1925. His family owned a small market on Main Street, a pubescent version of a 7-11. Their motto was "Open When You Need Us," which meant most of the time. If you needed a quart of milk at 3 a.m. or hot dog buns on the 4th of July, Dillon's Grocery would be open and at your service.

Frank wasn't a terribly impressive boy and was easily lost among his six brothers and sisters. He was the middle child, not so much ignored as overlooked. Frank wasn't the best-looking boy you might happen upon and he wasn't the smartest either. It seemed that his only distinguishing quality was that he could run far and he could run fast. Had it not been for a chance encounter with the girl who would one day become his wife, Frank Dillon may have lived a life of obscurity, one more worker on the assembly line in the factory that gave Barrel a reason for being, cranking out transmissions, tank treads and rifles.

Diane Dillon began her life as Diane Miller, and by high school she was a plain but poised-to-bloom young woman, ready to take on the world. Diane was the smartest girl in school, president of the honor society and desperately lonely. It was 1940 and few boys dated plain, smart-as-a-whip girls who wore glasses, and so Diane spent most of her Saturday nights alone.

Diane was also a keen observer of human nature. She observed Frank Dillon and his sidekick Pete Lorenzo as they labored over homework in the library, both happy to get an occasional B and relieved not to get D's. She observed that Frank and Pete were inseparable, both overlooked by their families and nearly invisible to their classmates. She observed that Frank and Pete were comrades in arms, as unlikely as that might have been. Where Frank was tall, Pete was stocky. Where Frank was Scandinavian white and blond, Pete was Sicilian olive and dark. How this unlikely pair came to be fast friends was a mystery, but they were beyond brothers in their closeness. They fed on each other and were growing into fine young men.

Diane knew Frank was the one his family tasked with manning the store through long, nearly customerless weekend and holiday nights, seeing to the occasional insomniac's needs. She also noted that Pete kept Frank company more nights than not. Diane admired Pete's loyalty. She pondered on why Frank and Pete ran lap after lap on the Barrel High School track every morning as dawn brightened the field. Frank was always to the front and Pete was always one step behind, an arrangement both seemed to be comfortable with.

Diane left Frank his only Valentine when she observed his box was empty.

The evening of Thanksgiving 1940, Diane's mother sent her to Dillon's Market for a can of cranberries that had been remarkably forgotten. Diane found Frank tending the little market alone, studying behind the counter, waiting for the forgetful customer. It was then they had their first conversation. She was surprised at Frank's eloquence. He was somehow able to string together simple words that expressed complex thoughts. It took Diane only moments to realize that Frank Dillon was an unusual boy who would one day become a remarkable man.

It was Diane who dragged Coach Dickerson to the Barrel High School track one dark morning so he could watch Frank and Pete grind out their speedy circuits. It was Diane who convinced Frank and Pete that they should accept Coach Dickerson's offer to join the track and cross country teams. It was Diane who came to every practice, doing her homework in the stands, as Frank, Pete and their teammates trained on the Barrel High School track through humid late summer days and frigid early spring afternoons. It was Diane who massaged Frank's sore legs, consoled him through his losses and cheered for his victories. It was Diane who opened the door for Frank to become a champion.

Frank stepped through that door full of confidence and purpose. He became the leader that Barrel High School athletics had never before been blessed with, a record-setting runner with victories too numerous to recount. And through this remarkable transformation, Pete Lorenzo was his shadow, content and in some ways proud to be a perpetual second place to Frank. As Frank matured as an athlete and young man, so did Pete, and neither would have been successful without the other. They trained together, ate together and went to class together. They would become champions together.

Frank, Diane and Pete were an inseparable trio. Finding one meant that you found them all. When not at school or training, they were camped out at the last table by the rear door at Mabel's Diner, studying, fantasizing about life after Barrel or holding court to Frank's increasing cadre of fans. They were rarely alone at Mabel's because Frank's cross country teammates were never far away. The camaraderie of the team that nucleated around Frank created unspoken bonds of devotion. It was the respect and friendship between young men that evolves into the character required of champions.

And champions they became.

The cross country season of 1942 was like no other for Barrel High School. Frank and Pete were unstoppable. The team plowed ahead, victory after victory, like a juggernaut of human ambition. Frank won every cross country meet that fall, with the Hawks being victorious 15-50 more often than not. Pete was Frank's shadow through every finish chute, grabbing the number 2 stick only seconds after Frank's victory. There were those who speculated that Pete was the better runner and it was only his devotion to Frank that placed him in his shadow. The old-timers at the barber shop still argue that point.

The Hawks of 1942 swept the conference final and downstate regionals, feats never before and never since accomplished. They were unstoppable in the state finals. Frank and Pete led their team to the first state championship ever bestowed upon Barrel High School. The faded photograph in the trophy case is to this day still testimony of their achievements. The celebration in Barrel for their victory was memorable in the light of the growing conflicts in Europe and the Pacific. It honored seven boys who together trained their way from obscurity to become champions. It was both the crowning event of their youth and the end of it.

The day after the state finals, five of the champion Hawks of Barrel High School met at the recruiting office on Main Street and enlisted in the United States Army. War had once again called upon the young men of Barrel and they answered the call to duty with pride and purpose. Frank was the first to sign his enlistment papers and Pete Lorenzo the second. It was the second time that Frank had signed his name that day. The first was on the marriage license that wed him to Diane.

CHAPTER 9

Sid Benson was a walking contradiction. Years later, he might have been described as a Jabba-the-Hut look-alike. He was obese beyond description. His walk was more of a waddle and his thinning hair had not seen a comb in a decade. He was vulgar in the company of ladies and an incessant cigar smoker. The contradiction was that Sid Benson was also the best college cross country and track coach in the Midwest. He coached Illinois State's cross country team to 22 NCAA Division III titles in a span of 30 years. His track team produced more All Americans than any other small college in the country. Sid Benson was a legend in his own time and in his own mind.

Sid shouldn't have been successful as a coach. He didn't so much mentor his athletes to greatness as intimidate them. He had never run a competitive step nor once put a shot or thrown a javelin. What he knew of coaching he learned by watching or stole from others. Sid Benson's success as a cross country and track coach was an unintended artifact of his fear of flying. His lack of punctuality caused him to miss the first and only flight he was ever scheduled on. That fateful bit of tardiness saved Sid Benson's life as his missed flight crashed on takeoff, killing all aboard. The experience for Sid was no different than seeing God. He vowed to never again step on the grounds of an airport, let alone board an airplane.

As a result, Sid never recruited athletes more than driving distance from the Illinois State campus. Instead, he built his reputation on his uncanny ability to scoop up talent off the farms and from the small towns of downstate Illinois, talent that big-time universities chose to ignore. These were solid, no-nonsense boys raised to respect their elders, follow directions and work hard when told to. They also had untapped athletic talent. It was a combination that not even Sid Benson could avoid but be successful with. The boys that Sid Benson recruited knew little of the outside world and the prospect of attending college on athletic scholarships, even at the dregs of Illinois State, was beyond their wildest dreams.

Sid sat in the Dillons' kitchen waiting for Frank to return home the evening after the first practice of the season. Sid rudely filled the kitchen with cigar smoke while telling off-color jokes to Diane as she busily prepared dinner between gasps for air. Frank stood on the back porch watching Sid through the screen door, almost fearing to enter his own home, but finally and reluctantly opened the door and stepped into his kitchen.

"Do you know what I despise, Frank?" Sid Benson asked as he watched his smoke-rings float towards the ceiling.

"No, Sid, what do you despise?"

"A missed opportunity. It's a Goddamned sin," Sid answered. "Every time an opportunity walks away, it's like you're sticking a hot poker up my ass." Diane gave Frank a kiss on the cheek as he sat at the kitchen table with Sid, placing his cane between them as a symbolic barrier. Sid picked up the cane and twirled it like a baton.

"A missed opportunity is never a good thing, Sid," Frank reluctantly agreed.

"You could've been the best, Frank. I could've made you the best, maybe break four minutes in the mile 10 years before that candy-ass Roger Bannister did it. I begged you to come run for me at Illinois State, and you laughed in my face and walked away from a scholarship," Sid painfully recounted. "What a wasted opportunity. You could've been the best. It makes my cheeks pucker just thinking about it."

"I didn't laugh in your face," Frank corrected. "I enlisted. We were at war, if you recall."

"Another hero-boy. When are you going to grow up? With you or without you, the war would have been the same. And if you'd run for me at Illinois state, maybe you wouldn't need this," Sid countered, pushing Frank's cane back across the table. Frank began to answer but thought better of it.

"What do you want, Sid?" Frank finally asked.

"That boy, Danny whatever."

"Danny O'Neal. His name is Danny O'Neal."

"Another fucking Irishman. Yeah, I want O'Neal to run for me at Illinois State. He's the best there's been since you, Frank. He could be the best ever." Diane was carefully observing.

"You don't need my permission, Sid. Go talk to him," Frank admonished.

"Yeah, I do. O'Neal's too much like you, Frank. He parrots you like a trained chimp. He's liable to enlist just because you did. Turns out he's from a family of Goddamned rednecks who enlist because they think it's fun. Christ, another wasted opportunity. You've got to talk him into running for me at Illinois State. I'm his all-expense ticket out of that trumped-up war in Vietnam, a full-ride scholarship complete with a 2S student deferment. Without me, he's dead meat. He'll never make it to college otherwise." Frank gave Sid a long calculated look before grabbing his cane and standing, almost hovering, over the older coach.

"I'll talk to him, Sid, but not for you," Frank said and he left the room. Sid turned his attention to Diane.

"Make certain he talks to the boy, Diane."

"Take it easy on Frank. The memories are still fresh. I know it's been years, but they're still fresh," she said, wiping her hands on a towel. "It's to the point that he's almost afraid to open the paper, afraid he'll read about another one of his boys dying a soldier's death." Sid gathered his hulk up, like a crane lifting a wounded elephant, and began his waddle across the room. He squeezed through while Diane held back the screen door.

"He can't save the world," Sid said over his shoulder, walking down the porch steps. "Only a fool would try."

"Someone has to," Diane said, more to herself than to Sid.

CHAPTER 10

Dawn comes early in the morning in Barrel, just as in the real world. The glow in the eastern sky was just becoming visible when Danny appeared a block away, running down the center of the otherwise deserted street. His sun-greeting arrival was becoming part of my new routine. The Hawks of Barrel High School ran two-a-day workouts, each mile bringing us closer to an unspoken goal. After a week of classes and indescribably difficult workouts, I was tired in both mind and body. My brain ached just about as much as my calves. The former might not recover but the latter was responding to hot whirlpools. Danny slowed to a jog as he approached my front steps, where I sat tying my shoes.

"Up and at them," Danny cheerfully said, a difficult thing to do at such an early hour.

"It is only because I am a gentlemen," I said, pushing myself off the stairs, "that I don't tell you to screw yourself."

"I appreciate that," Danny replied, as we both cranked up to speed, running down the middle of the street. We ran in silence for a few blocks on our way to Carl's house. As we neared his home, the neighborhood began to slowly decay into the poverty that so distinguished his side of the tracks. Streetlamps went unreplaced, cracked sidewalks went unrepaired, and potholes were perpetually unfilled. Most homes were neat but in disrepair, a sign that their inhabitants had pride but no money.

"This is a mean-looking neighborhood," I commented. "It makes the places I've lived look not so crappy."

"Not mean," Danny corrected, "misunderstood. These people work as hard as any of us do but for some reason life has left them behind." It was more than just happenstance. It seemed more like a Machiavellian plot. Why the rich side of Barrel got its potholes filled and the poor side didn't always puzzled me. It was the same town, but crossing over into the low-rent district was still a chassis-jarring experience.

Carl's home was a house in name only, perhaps better described as a multi-room shack. Its roof swayed so badly it looked like an old nag's back. Carl sat on the porch waiting for our arrival while Mrs. Hager stood in the doorway. She was a saint of a woman trapped in a shapeless body covered by a shapeless smock. The years she wore on her creased face were multiplied by the sorrow she had experienced. She lost a brother in World War II and a husband in the Korean conflict. Both of their names are etched on the plaques in Holden Park. All she had left in the world was Carl, and she was not about to have three inscriptions on those plaques.

"Morning, Mrs. Hager." Danny waved as we slowed so Carl could join us.

"See you tonight?" she yelled.

"Wouldn't miss it," I returned as the three of us ran off. It was Carl's birthday and Mrs. Hager was having the team over, a party she could ill afford.

Only a few blocks away, Amos stood at an intersection, stretching his tree-trunks legs, bare-chested in spite of the surprising morning chill. Amos ran in from his farm a mile or so down the road. He quickly assumed his position at the back of our growing pack.

"You look tired," Danny commented as Amos stifled a yawn.

"I was up all night helping deliver a calf," he explained. "It wasn't pretty. I can't remember the last time I talked hours straight to a cow."

"I never pictured you as an animal lover," I said, "more of an animal eater."

"Dr. Doolittle," Carl of few words concluded.

When Shaun and Billy joined us in another few blocks, our assembly was complete. We ran with purpose. Yes, it was only a morning workout, but there was a purpose for us being there. We ran to the edge of Barrel, and when the town ended we continued on county roads. It had rained the night before but the water that pooled in the depressions of the bumpy pavement was not an obstacle as we splashed through the puddles. The pace intensified, not out of competition but out of the sheer pleasure of running among comrades in the untainted air of a new day. Breathing became more labored and the pack strung out as our knees came up and our arms began pumping. It was simply too good a morning to waste.

Danny reached the two-mile turn-around point, a T-intersection, in a little more than 12 minutes, a very good pace for so early in the morning. I became very used to watching Danny from behind. It wasn't that Danny didn't enjoy running with the rest of the Hawks. More days than not, our morning runs were more for conversation than becoming fit, a way to share time with friends, and Danny was as talkative as the rest. On some days, though, Danny would start a run in the midst of the pack of Hawks, silently move toward the front and then begin fidgeting as though he was being held against his will. Then, with little fanfare, he would simply start pulling away. His uneven fidgeting pace would morph into the style I had come to admire, the slight swing of his arms, the tuned rolling from heel to toe, the slight tip of his head.

When Danny arrived at the T-intersection, he jogged in place, waiting for the rest of the Hawks to catch up while absent-mindedly fingering Corey's class ring. I soon arrived with Shaun and Billy at my sides and jogged little circles waiting for Carl and Amos, who arrived a minute later. The deed having been done, the run back would be for conversation.

"Now, let me tell you about my date last night," Billy began. This was a morning ritual. We really didn't believe Billy had a date nearly every night nor that his exploits had occurred in any world other than his own mind, but his tales were entertaining. "Let it be known that Susan McClain knows more about male anatomy than a urologist, and uses that knowledge well!"

"This should be good," Shaun interrupted, "I taught Susan McClain everything she knows about male anatomy!"

"It's okay to say cock, you sissies," Amos taunted. That almost ended the conversation until Carl's second utterance of the morning.

"Cock."

And that pretty much put everyone into stitches, everyone but Danny. Billy and Shaun continued to exchange lies about poor Susan McClain to the delight of themselves and Amos and Carl while the pack ran back into Barrel. Danny and I fell behind to talk among ourselves.

"Anything bothering you?" Danny didn't answer right away.

"Coach wants to see me before classes this morning."

"You know why?" I asked.

"Yeah, he wants to save my life."

"Save your life?"

"Yes, because he couldn't save Pete Lorenzo's life." I gave a Danny a puzzled look. "You don't know much about Coach, do you?" Danny asked. I shrugged.

"He won the state championship in '42 and was wounded in the war," I summarized.

"That barely scratches the surface," and Danny told me the story.

CHAPTER 11

The Hawks cross country team of 1942 won the state championship by placing five runners in the top 15. It was a feat never before accomplished and never since approached. The vitality of those young runners was extraordinary. None came from wealth, none came from privilege and none ran for the prospect of reward. They worked their jobs, did their chores, studied their courses, went to their parties and ran their miles. They lived their youth to the fullest because they knew their futures held dangers in distant lands.

When Frank Dillon won the state championship with Pete Lorenzo at his heels, their innocent youth ended with the grabbing of their finishing sticks. Their country was at war and the young men of Barrel responded in droves. Frank and Pete, and his Hawk teammates, were no different. The day after the state championship, in the company of family, friends and half the student body of Barrel High School, five members of that championship team enlisted in the United States Army to fight in World War II. They signed their enlistment papers with the pride of knowing they were doing the right thing. There were no questions. There was no need for a debate. That's just the way it was. Finishing school could wait. The six long months that it would have taken them to finish high school meant six months of frustration, watching their older brothers answering the call to duty that they could not. The thought that there was danger in this decision, that their own self-preservation might counsel them to wait, did not deter them. Our nation survived the peril of World War II because of boys like the Hawks of 1942.

Of the five championship runners who enlisted that day, the day after the greatest triumph of their youth, only Frank Dillon returned from the war. He returned as a broken casualty of the war and even that was miraculous. The other four members of the champion Hawks joined the many other young men of Barrel who fell in battle during World War II, boys who gave their lives for their country and are now immortalized by engravings on plaques in Holden Memorial Park.

Stuart Barnett, third man on the Hawks' cross country team, fifth in the state championship and the youngest high school runner in the state of Illinois to break two minutes for the half-mile, was a tail gunner on a B-17. Stuart had 13 confirmed Messerschmitt kills and three probables. His plane, limping home to its landing field in England on only two smoking engines, was shot down over Holland. No chutes were seen as the plane spiraled into the ground, trailing flame behind it. Stuart was only a hundred miles from being a member of the first crew to finish 25 missions and so claim his ticket home. It was an honor that the crew of the *Memphis Belle* earned only months later.

Eddie Gilbert was the fourth man on the team, ninth at state and Barrel High School's first steeple chaser. His legs ended just under his chin, enabling Eddie to almost walk over the steeple chase barriers. His father was a pacifist minister and only allowed Eddie to enlist if he became a medic and didn't carry a gun. Eddie carried out that mission with indescribable heroism. He earned a silver star and bronze star with two clusters while weaponlessly tending to the wounds of his comrades in the midst of battles on one forsaken Pacific island after another. His landing craft took a direct artillery hit assaulting the beach on Okinawa and exploded into tiny shards that fell back into the water. Not a soldier survived.

Craig Wilson, fifth man and fifteenth at state, was a sprinter at heart. Craig could run a 440 in under 52 seconds, a blazing achievement for a high school runner in 1942. He ran cross country simply for the pleasure of the company of his teammates and as a way to keep in shape for track. His mind was as quick as his 440 time. Craig was plucked out of basic training and sent to Officer Candidate School, his record jacket fudged to show him as a high school graduate. He was captain of a tank company and a veteran of the Sicily Invasion when he was tasked to become the spearhead of the 3rd Army as General Patton sliced across Europe toward Berlin. When General Bradley gave Patton's fuel to Field Marshall Montgomery, it was Craig's tanks that ran dry. Craig and his tank platoon fought valiantly to the last man, occupying enough of the enemy that the remainder of their battalion could escape with their lives. Craig Wilson was incinerated in his immobilized tank.

Frank Dillon and Pete Lorenzo pledged to enlist together, they pledged to go through basic training together, they pledged to fight together and they pledged to be responsible for each other. Those pledges sustained the transformation of two brave but innocent high school boys into the hardened, professional soldiers they became. They fought as infantry grunts in North Africa, their leadership earning them corporal and sergeant chevrons. Frank and Pete led their men up the mountains of the Italian backbone, accumulating experience and expertise in the art of warfare. They learned that the value of their lives was measured by the accuracy of their fire and the willingness of the soldiers they led to risk their lives for each other. Those men would risk their lives only for comrades who had earned their respect and loyalty. Frank and Pete had done so in spades and set the example for others. Their success as leaders of men took them back to England into the inner sanctum of Operation Overlord to train even younger and more idealistic men in the art of surviving a beach landing.

Even the most skilled and observant of soldiers survives in part by being luckier than the enemy. Frank and Pete knew that undeniable fact while they huddled in the bottom of a gyrating landing craft headed toward the beaches of Normandy on the morning of June 6, 1944. They dared not share that knowledge with the green troops they commanded, fodder from the heartland of the America. Those young boys were untested in battle, but they were also so unaware and unafraid of their mortality that they would follow Frank and Pete anywhere. When the front of the landing craft swung open and their platoon spilled out into the surf, it would be the lucky few who made it across the beach into the debatable safety at the base of the cliffs.

At the appointed time, Frank and Pete jumped out of the landing craft into the water and into a barrage of enemy fire that could not have been predicted or, perhaps worse, was predicted but ignored. A dozen of their platoon members' combat careers lasted only seconds as they were gunned down rushing out the maw of the landing craft. In spite of having told their soldiers to leave the wounded behind and unceasingly fight their way through the surf and across the beach, Frank and Pete disobeyed their own orders and pulled wounded soldier after wounded soldier out of the water, carrying them forward onto the beach and into precarious safety behind the tank traps.

These were actions of unspeakable courage, actions that saved the lives of a dozen wounded soldiers, actions that mere medals could never appropriately reward, but they were also actions that tempted fate. With each return into the water to rescue the wounded, the odds of Frank and Pete themselves surviving the trip diminished to vanishingly small proportions. The intensity of the German machine gun fire raining down from the top of the cliffs ensured that the luck of even the most skilled soldier had its limits.

Pete, second to Frank for their entire friendship, was tragically the first to be hit that heroic morning. In chest-deep water, he had just hoisted a wounded soldier onto his shoulder when a shell fragment pierced his throat. Frank, wading back into the water from the beach to rescue yet another fallen soldier, locked eyes with his friend at that same instant. The image of blood spurting from Pete's neck and his slipping backwards, bobbing like a reddening cork, scorched Frank's retina. It was then that Frank knew why he was allowed to survive the countless battles and skirmishes he had fought in. He knew the purpose of his having run those endless miles, building strength in his legs beyond the average mortal. The hidden motive was now revealed. It was to prepare Frank to rescue his cross country teammate from drowning in the cold and reddening waters of that Normandy beach. It was to give Frank the strength and will to save his best friend's life. It could not have been any clearer.

Frank ran through the deepening surf toward Pete, pushing back the water with the intensity of his strides. He instinctively moved left and then right, a zigzag that provided meager protection against the enemy gunners. Bullets zipped into the water all around him like pulsating fountains. Frank was only yards from reaching Pete, his destiny nearly fulfilled, when the first bullet pierced his lower back. The second bullet shattered his right femur. Perhaps it was Frank's forward momentum that allowed his outstretched hand to brush against Pete's foot, one last contact with his pledge brother, before darkness overcame Frank and he slipped beneath the waves.

Frank awoke a week later in a hospital in England. Pete's body was never found.

CHAPTER 12

Danny arrived for his meeting with Coach Dillon early and sat on the oak bench next to the trophy case, his book-bag at his feet, to wait for his mentor. He passed the time by inspecting the photographs in the trophy cases and absent-mindedly spinning Corey's ring. He imagined what it must have been like to be a Hawk on the '42 championship team, knowing that the championship race would be his last, knowing that he would be in the service of his country in a matter of only days. The shuffle of Coach Dillon's gait interrupted Danny's thoughts.

"Morning, Coach," Danny said, gathering up his book bag.

"Good morning, Danny," Coach replied.

Danny followed Coach Dillon up the stairs and waited while he unlocked his office door. Frank's office was an unkempt eclectic mix of the past and present. The walls were covered with photographs of all the teams Frank had coached, framed newspaper clippings telling of their triumphs and losses, faded ribbons from forgotten meets and schedules from long since completed seasons. As Frank busied himself with his first-to-the-office rituals, Danny pushed back a stack of folders to look at the hidden framed articles behind. The stack of folders had been there for years, perhaps decades, and each generation of Hawk cross country runners passed on the knowledge of what lay behind. The frame contained two now yellowed newspaper clippings. The first featured a large picture of Frank Dillon grabbing the number-one stick at the 1942 cross country champions below the headline "Hawk Cross Country Champion Wounded at Normandy." The second was a small photograph of Pete Lorenzo in uniform above a short obituary. Danny carefully replaced the stack of folders that hid the picture frame and sat in front of Coach Dillon's desk.

"Danny," the Coach said, handing over an official looking envelope, "Sid Benson came to see me a few days ago. Do you know who Sid Benson is?"

"He's the coach at Illinois State," Danny answered.

"He came to talk about you."

"Me?"

"You."

"What about?"

"It's in the letter." Danny opened the letter and began reading as Frank explained. "It's a full scholarship, Danny. Sid wants you to run for him at Illinois State. This is a great opportunity."

"How great?"

"It's a full ride. You won't have to pay a cent and knowing Sid, you'll probably make a few dollars along the way." Frank paused as Danny finished the letter.

"My grades aren't very good. They probably wouldn't accept me."

"Danny, if Sid wants you at Illinois State, they'll accept you. It's the way of the world," Frank explained. "Take the offer, Danny. This is the chance of a lifetime." Danny carefully folded the letter as though it was made of ancient parchment and returned it to the envelope.

"I don't know if I can," Danny began. "My father expects me to enlist." Frank was ready for this. He hitched himself up in his seat and leaned across the table as if preparing to reveal state secrets.

"This scholarship comes with a 2S deferment, Danny. That means no draft, no Vietnam and no need to enlist. By the time you graduate, the war and the draft will be over. Vietnam will be a long forgotten memory."

"What about Corey?" Danny asked.

"What about him?"

"Corey enlisted. My dad enlisted. Every male in my family has enlisted. It's what we do." Frank leaned closer.

"Is it what you want to do?" Danny began to answer but didn't. He turned to gaze out the window onto the track. The first period girls' PE class was beginning to assemble on the infield.

"You enlisted," Danny finally answered. "Sid Benson offered you a scholarship. You could have gone to college but you enlisted instead. So did Pete Lorenzo." Frank fell back in his chair as though punched in the face.

"Those were different times, Danny. It was a different war. It was a just war. Don't pass this opportunity up to enlist just because..." The phone rang expectedly, interrupting Frank. "That'll be Sid." Frank answered the phone. Danny fingered Corey's ring as he watched a small group of girls slowly jog around the track, their mouths fluttering with unheard conversations. "Danny, Coach Benson wants to talk to you." Danny took the receiver and held it to his ear with both hands.

"Danny, you there, Danny? Goddamn it boy, speak up!"

"This is Danny O'Neal, Coach Benson."

"Frank tells me you got the letter, boy. You're one lucky son-of-a-bitch, you are. I'm not making many offers this year but you're getting one of them. All you got to do is sign that letter and get your old man to sign. Come next fall, you'll be on scholarship at Illinois State. Hot damn, kid, it'll be great."

"Thank you, sir."

"Thank you, sir? What the hell does that mean? Does that mean yes?"

"It means I've got to talk this over with my father."

"Goddamn it, O'Neal, what's to talk over? This is your ticket out of that hell-hole of a town you live in and your get-out-of-the-draft deferment. It means no Vietnam, no coming home in a body bag. I'll make you a champion, boy. You know I will. You'll be the champion Frank never was. Only I can do that for you, boy. Ask your coach." Frank, hearing Sid Benson's bark even across the desk, watched Danny intently. Danny glanced up at his coach.

"It's more complicated than that, sir" he said into the mouthpiece while looking at Coach Dillon. "You see, my father and my brother Corey..."

"Son, don't be a damned fool," Sid interrupted. "Just because your old man sucker-punched your brother into enlisting into that farce of a war doesn't mean…" Danny ripped the receiver from his ear as though it had suddenly become hot and handed it to Frank. He grabbed his book bag, leaving the letter on Frank's desk.

"See you at practice, Coach," he said meekly and left the office. Sid's voice leaked out the receiver in Frank's hand.

"O'Neal, you there? Goddamn it, say something!" Frank thought a few moments before speaking.

"Sid, it's Frank."

"What the hell's going on there? What's wrong with that kid? Doesn't he know…"

"Sid, take it easy. I'll talk to him."

CHAPTER 13

Consistency is important, very important. Ron Clarke, one of the greatest distance runners of all-time, once wrote that the difference between running every day of the week and resting one day is wasting your time the other six. Before becoming so enlightened I rationalized that missing a day of running every once in a while was good for your body, letting it recover from days of hard workouts. How could I have been so naïve? Missing a day of running is as unforgivable as lifting money out of the Sunday collection plate. Nobody may know but you and God, but that doesn't make it any less of a sin. There were times when I lay in bed, not having run that day, listening to the accusing tick of my alarm clock as its hands approached midnight. I tried to fight off the obsession but failed no less than a drug addict surrendering to his addiction. I grabbed my shoes and burst out of the house onto the dark streets to get in my quota of running before the bewitching hour passed. There are tales of runners not having missed a day of running in decades. To the uncaring and uninformed, they are obsessed lunatics. To the initiated among us, the dirt beneath their footsteps is hallowed ground.

After a lifetime of running, of not missing days, of obsessing beyond reason, of enduring practice and competition, the days begin to blur together. I think there is at least one decade that I couldn't give you a single detail about a single run that I took, even though I didn't miss more than a day or two of running in those 10 years. It's sort of like going to work. You do it every day and on any given day, what you do can be panic-stricken or it can be boring. But as time passes, thinking back, each day pretty much looks like the rest. Any given day is not particularly memorable, but in the aggregate there is meaning and purpose. I endured hundreds of interval workouts and thousands of gut-busting long runs that I couldn't recount even one step to you. But that first workout on the hill is something that I will never forget. I could play back every minute of that workout to you in widescreen Technicolor.

Monday workouts were usually intervals on the track and I thought that that Monday would be no different. I got to the gym a little late and by the time I changed, all of the Hawks were already lying on the infield of the track, waiting for Coach Dillon to command them to their feet and into the interval workout. Billy was entertaining the group with yet another story of his exploits. Amos was doing sit-ups. Carl was counting blades of grass. It was a suicidally hot and humid day. My tank-top was already clinging to my back and all I'd done was walk out of the gym. It was not a good omen. The running gods would be cruel that day.

"How's it going, Mike?" Shaun asked as I jogged across the track.

"Trigonometry is going to kill me," I answered.

"Who you got?"

"Miss Anderson."

"A bitter old woman. I'll bet she's never been laid," Shaun surmised. That got the Hawks laughing, just what he wanted.

"Who'd want to?" Amos asked. We all laughed again. Carl looked up from his blade counting appearing a bit annoyed. We stopped our chatter, waiting to hear Carl's quota of few spoken words of the day.

"She's lonely." Carl spoke from experience.

That pretty much ended the conversation.

Within a minute or two, Coach Dillon appeared at the doorway to the locker room. He had his cane and notebook in hand. His stopwatch swung from a lanyard around his neck and he wore a Hawks baseball cap. His car keys dangled from a loop on his belt. A starting pistol swung from a loop on the other side. Coach Dillon checked his attire and equipment like a Ranger parachute jumper standing in the open doorway of a DC-3. Satisfied with the results of his inspection, he walked onto the track. Amos was the first to notice.

"Shit, he's got his car keys and the pistol," Amos said.

"No, it's too early," Shaun wished. "Maybe he just forgot he had them."

"Not likely," Amos surmised.

"We knew it was coming eventually," Danny advised.

"Yeah, just not this soon," Billy said.

"What're you guys talking about?" I asked. Nobody answered, as though they were sharing a secret.

"You've been there already, Michael," Danny explained, though his explanation didn't do much good. I'd been a lot of places. Coach Dillon stopped in the first lane of the track.

"Men," he started, "we've got two weeks until our first cross country meet. It's against the Spartans." Billy howled a disapproving boo.

"We'll kick their butts," Shaun said.

"Like they kicked our butts last year?" Coach retorted. "The Spartans are defending state champions. They may be a bunch of jerks and you may not like them, but you have to respect them. I suspect the Spartans may be amateur human beings but they're talented runners." Being an amateur human being was one of Coach Dillon's worst put-downs. It was even worse than being called a weenie. "If we're going to beat the Spartans, we've got to start running seriously. We've got to do more than just go through the motions during a workout."

"But we..." I wanted to explain that we had been giving it our all, but Danny touched my shoulder and shook his head, signaling me to be quiet. Coach continued without missing a beat.

"Why are we here?" he asked.

"We're here to become champions," Billy answered.

"...and who do we have to beat to be champions?"

"The Spartans!" we all replied in chorus.

"Do you trust me?" Coach asked.

"With our lives!" the Hawks echoed. This all seemed to be well-rehearsed. Sometimes I felt as though I needed a script.

"Okay. Okay. Jog out to the hill. I'll see you in 30 minutes." With that, Coach shuffled off to his car, his cane raising periodic puffs of dust from the track, climbed inside and roared off, leaving the Hawks to bemoan their fates.

"Let's go," Danny said as he started running towards the exit from the track.

"The hill?" I asked.

"The hill," Danny answered.

"You mean, the hill we…"

"Yep, that hill."

"Shit."

The run out to the hill was largely in contemplative silence, like six condemned prisoners on their way to the execution chambers. As we passed the outskirts of town and spilled onto the county roads, it all began to look familiar, and then it really hit me. The hill. We were going to work out on the hill I first met Danny on. I tried to conjure up an image of the hill. All I could remember was that it was long and steep, and that was not a good sign. The sweat dripping onto my eye glasses quickly evaporated, leaving streaks of encrusted salt.

When we arrived at the base of the hill, Coach Dillon stood by his car waiting for us. We gathered around him.

"Most of you know this but we have a new member of the team, so bear with me," Coach Dillon began. He turned to face the hill, gazing up toward the summit, and paused before continuing as though caught up with old memories. He pointed his cane toward the summit. "This hill is 1050 yards long and has 350 feet elevation gain from the base to the crest…"

"That's about an 11% grade," Amos whispered in my ear.

"…It is the highest point in the county. There are trees with white crosses painted on them at the one-third and two-third points. We will use them to mark our transitions." Coach Dillon turned to face us and seemed to be looking straight at me. "Twenty-five years of Hawks have trained on this hill. Champions have been made on this hill. Character has been tested on this hill. Having been tested, some of those unwilling to face the challenge again have quit the Hawks. Those who have returned to face the hill again have done so with pride. Conquering the hill made them the runners they thought they could never be." He paused. "Any questions?"

There were none.

"Leave your doubts behind and put your faith in me. I will not betray you. Is that understood?"

Our heads bobbed yes in unison. We had just signed away our souls.

"Okay, gentlemen, you will run 10 repetitions this afternoon. The first will be build, sustain, build to full pace. Listen for the pistol." Coach Dillon got in his car and disappeared in a cloud of dust to the crest of the hill.

We stood at a line that Amos scratched across the road like it was the beginning of a race. There wasn't even a sliver of a wind. Sweat poured off us just standing there. The sun had been baking the road for the entire day and its surface radiated back humid heat no less than a sauna. I could feel its warmth through the soles of my shoes. The crack of Coach Dillon's starting pistol from the unseen crest of the hill wafted down to us and we leapt forward up the hill.

We built the pace steadily as we began our climb. A hill that steep cannot be run; it has to be assaulted. Within a few steps, we were on the balls of our feet, leaning forward into the hill, struggling to bring our knees high enough to plant them on the road before falling into the slope. Our arms were pumping in an exaggerated effort to will ourselves up the grade. Running up stairs is child's play in comparison. Stairs are cooperative, predictable and in the shade. The hill fought us on every step, throwing obstacles in our way, while conspiring with the sun. Every third or fourth stride, the rocky gravel loosened under our steps and our shoes slipped to the rear instead of propelling us ahead. All the while, the sun baked our backs.

The pack quickly strung out. Danny went to the front. His stride was even and rhythmic as though he was still on the flat. I fixed my gaze on his calves, which were just about at the same height as my head. I tried to time my footsteps with his, using the planting of his steps as a metronome. Billy and Shaun were a few yards behind me. I could already hear their heavy breathing and we were only halfway to the first marker tree. I risked looking behind. Amos, shirtless with the sun reflecting off his sweat-glistening shoulders, scaled the hill by brute force. His arms were nearly motionless, his trunk-like legs carving steps out of the slope like chopping wood chips from a log. Carl was already lagging far behind, his face completely hidden by his unkempt hair hanging over his bowed head, like vines off a cliff, as he leaned into the hill. His legs were too short to do much more than scurry up the incline.

My calves were already burning and my Achilles tendons were already stretched to their limit when I reached the first marker tree, a sad lightning-struck oak with generations of X's spray-painted on its trunk. Sweat rivered into my eyes and dripped onto the inside surfaces of my glasses. My sight was obscured by the salty trails left behind, like drippings down the side of a can of paint. The sweat pouring off my back had long since saturated my running trunks and already was beginning to moisten my socks.

Just after the first marker tree, the road flattened a bit, giving us an opportunity to recover for a few paces, shake out our arms and look up from the road. I jogged only a few yards of flat before the road lifted into its steepness again. Danny never missed a beat and was another five or 10 yards ahead of me. I leaned into the hill, began pumping my arms, lifting my knees, telling myself the pace was to be steady and not to be a hero. But even a steady pace required a burgeoning effort as the heat sapped my strength and the heaviness of the air conspired to keep precious oxygen from my bloodstream. The soreness of my calves intensified into sharp pain, my thighs were in a constant state of tightness. My steps shortened as the effort of bringing my knees high on the steepening slope exceeded my abilities. I gave up trying to mimic Danny. I was in a survival mode.

I brought my head up, looking for the next marker tree. Had I missed it? Was I actually running so strongly that it had swept by without notice? That must have been it because as I looked ahead, there was the summit. A summit, yes, but a false one. As I crested it, the marker tree laughed by the side of the road, taunting me that I yet had another third of the hill to climb.

The Coach had said build-steady-build, and so as I passed the marker tree, I obediently made an honest effort to start increasing the pace. It was a gallant but utterly unsuccessful attempt. The run up the hill had degenerated into just surviving the experience. My breathing was harsh and raspy, my arms beginning to flail. Not able to stay on the balls of my feet I landed on the mid-soles, which only intensified the slipping. My eyes were shut half the time, trying to keep out the stinging sweat.

The hill steepened once more to an inhumane slope. I was ready to admit defeat and walk a few steps when glancing ahead, I saw Coach Dillon standing at the summit, his stopwatch in hand. Danny had already finished. He was recovering by jogging small circles, his hands on his hips. I was new enough that impressing the Coach was still important to me, so I willed my knees higher and somehow managed to accelerate into the finish. The grimace on my face must have been frightening. As I crested the hill and passed the Coach, he yelled out "3:34."

I came to a halt and lay on the ground, back down and knees up, my chest heaving. My heart pounded so loudly that birds flitted away. The sweat streaming off my chest pooled between the gravel. Danny jogged over and pulled me up. "Keep moving," he said, "we have nine more of these."

"What was your time?"

"3:05." Danny looked stressed but he wasn't exhausted, and 3:05 was an incredible time. A moment later Billy and Shaun's heads popped into view, bobbing like corks as they pumped their way up the last few yards to the crest. Billy finished first and melted to the ground as soon as he crossed Coach. Shaun did the same.

"3:52." I helped them both up. Amos crested next, his pace seemingly unchanged from the bottom.

"4:21." Amos came to an immediate stop and stood statue-like, just letting the sweat stream off. He looked skyward as though seeking heavenly strength. There was no sign of God and no sign of Carl.

I relearned a forgotten lesson during that first assault up the hill. The last time I ran the hill on my first day in Barrel, it was a leisurely jaunt during a leisurely afternoon run. That experience was a world away compared to what Coach Dillon was putting us through. There's running, then there's training and then there's racing. The level of effort from one to the next just can't be compared.

"Okay, gentlemen, that's one. Jog down to the bottom and listen for the gun. This next one is steady 'til the second tree, then 90% pace 'til the end." We began to slowly shuffle down the hill. "Jog the interval!" Coach Dillon barked, and so we picked up the pace into what passed for jogging. The sun was at our backs as we proceeded down the hill. I could feel the sunburn beginning on my neck. We went about 30 yards when we passed Carl still on his way up.

"That's the way," Danny encouraged, "only a few more yards."

"Hot," Carl said, his little steps chopping away at the hill. We continued down the hill.

"This stinks," Billy complained. "This has to be the hottest day of the year, and he has us doing intervals up this mountain."

"I can think of other things I'd rather be doing," Shaun said.

"I'd like to see him run this hill even once."

"Unfair," I interjected, not thinking it necessary to point out the obvious.

"You know there's a reason for everything the Coach asks us to do," Danny broke in, "and he isn't asking us to do anything that he hasn't done himself a zillion times before. You forget he was the first Hawk to train on this hill."

"Yeah, 25 years ago. I wasn't even born yet," Billy said. Amos had been listening silently.

"You've got to trust someone," he surmised. We reached the

bottom and turned to face the hill as Carl appeared jogging down the hill. The road went due west, directly into the sun, which had begun its downward trek. The east side of the crest was barely beginning to cast a shadow. As soon as Carl reached the bottom, we heard the crack of the pistol.

"Up and at them," Danny yelled, and we started up the hill again. The second climb made the first seem like a relaxing stroll, like holding hands before the big date. From the very first step, my calves ached, my thighs burned and my breathing was labored. The jog down simply hadn't been long enough to recover. We quickly strung out, Danny to the front, Carl to the rear. Sweat pooled in my shoes and I could feel a blister starting to form in the steam bath my shoes had become. It was a struggle from the start. Making it to the second tree was an accomplishment of sheer courage.

I was only steps behind Danny at the second tree. "It's 90% from here," I heard him toss over his shoulder to me and then he accelerated up the hill. I sent a message to my legs to turn over faster, to kick into another gear, but the message was ignored. It was all I could do to keep from slowing down. I finished at a pace that any other day I would have been ashamed of. That day, I was beginning not to be so proud. "4:01," Coach Dillon called out. I just couldn't seem to catch my breath. I stood folded over, my hands on my knees. The drip of sweat from my chin was like a leaky faucet. Danny pulled me upright.

"Walk around. Just keep your legs moving," he counseled.

"You. How fast?" I managed to ask.

"3:01" He ran the second faster than the first. Incredible.

Billy, Shaun and Amos appeared one-by-one, conversation having melted away into exhaustion. Carl was still deep into his climb.

For another eight repetitions, we jogged to the bottom, waited for the crack of the pistol and assaulted the hill. With each climb, our legs protested louder, the air grew heavier, the gravel slipped quicker beneath or feet. The hill seemingly grew steeper, bolder and more cunning with each run, adding yards and creating false summits, playing with our minds as expertly as a sideshow conjurer. My father would have been proud of the deception. With each climb to the summit, the sun fell closer to the horizon and the hill acquired longer shadows that provided our only respite.

I had my doubts that I'd be able to finish the last repetition. Billy passed me 20 yards from the summit, somehow willing more out of his body than I could. Danny stood at the crest, yelling encouragement while he fingered Corey's ring. With his arrival at the summit, each Hawk fell to the ground, recovering in silence, thankful that the workout was over. This continued until all the Hawks but Carl were on the summit. We lapped Carl somewhere around the eighth repetition, and he was still on his ninth climb.

"That's 10," Coach Dillon said, and wrote something in his little notebook. He surveyed the team sprawled on the gravel. "On your feet, gentlemen," Coach Dillon said, "don't let those legs get stiff." We helped each other up. "That was a good effort, but I know you can give me more. This is as much a mental exercise as a physical one. Don't think about the next repetition and don't dwell on the last one. Keep focused on the task at hand. The only limits you have are those you place on yourself, and most of those limits are mental." At that moment, Carl appeared, struggling the last few yards to the summit, finishing his ninth repetition. He crested and almost without slowing turned around and started his jog to the bottom. "Carl, that's all for today," Coach offered. Carl looked almost hurt.

"One more," he said, and continued to the bottom. Coach smiled.

"Okay, one more," Coach said. Carl nodded and disappeared down the hill. Coach watched Carl for a moment before continuing. "You all could learn something from Carl. He's never given in to the pain." We stared at our shoes sheepishly. Coach was right.

"Don't worry, Coach," Billy offered. "We'll be ready for the Spartans."

"Do you know why the Spartans are good?" Frank asked. Nobody answered. "The Spartans are good because they know they're good. They've mastered the mental game. Do you think they're sitting around saying 'Oh, my gosh, we're running against the Hawks in a couple weeks?' No, they're confident in their abilities. They're saying, 'We're going to kick the Hawks' asses.' We need to have that same confidence." Another pause. "Any questions?" We had none. "Okay, run back to the gym by way of the water tower and I'll see you tomorrow." That was an eight-mile route.

"What about Carl?" Danny asked.

"I'll wait for Carl. You all start your run back."

The run back to the gym was on wobbly legs and sore calves. We finished in darkness. As I rode my bicycle home, I passed Carl three miles from the gym. He was jogging but a fast stroller would have easily passed him. "Want a ride in?" I asked. He shook his head no.

"Ice cream later," Carl said.

CHAPTER 14

By the time Danny arrived home, dinner had already started. He parked his bike in the garage and entered through the side kitchen door. The letter from Sid Benson lay open on the kitchen table. Danny dropped his backpack and picked up the letter, reading it as though for the first time. Danny's mind began to analyze the situation. The opportunity it represented called for a decision, the sooner the better. He read the letter again and then again. He probably wouldn't get to college any other way, Danny surmised. His grades were shaky and his family's finances would be of no help.

What were his other options, Danny asked himself? A job on the assembly line at the rifle factory waiting out the months before getting drafted? Following in the footsteps of his uncles, father and brother, and enlisting? Danny knew that accepting the scholarship would get him a deferment and place him out of harm's way for at least four years. Maybe the war in Vietnam would be over by then, he thought. He would have dodged the bullet by studying Kant. But where was the fairness in that, Danny asked himself? The kid across the aisle in history gets drafted and shipped to Vietnam because he can't run two miles in under 10 minutes while Danny gets a full-ride scholarship and a deferment because he can? Danny sat at the kitchen table, staring at the letter as these thoughts filled his mind.

The war in Vietnam was a sham anyway, Danny rationalized to himself. Everyone knew it. Campuses were fermenting with antiwar protests. The government was beginning to lie about battle outcomes and body counts. Our allies were backing away from a situation that was not going to improve any time soon. Why risk getting killed for nothing, Danny wondered? Shouldn't I think of myself first?

Danny looked up from the letter, directly into the service portrait of Corey hanging on the kitchen wall. Corey, his precious brother Corey, enlisted in the Marines a week out of high school, just like his father. What would Corey think of me, Danny asked himself? He smiled. The portrait showed Corey to be the handsome kid he was. The creases in Corey's dress blues were razor-sharp, his new corporal chevrons bursting with pride off his sleeves, his expert marksman badge bright and shining on his chest, his Vietnam service ribbon front and center. Corey's expression could not be faked. He was a soldier, serving his country and proud to be doing so. Corey must have decided that duty to country was greater than duty to self, Danny concluded. Danny was unconvinced of the wisdom of that decision but he accepted it because he loved Corey.

The clink of dishes and muffled voices drifted in from the dining room. Danny carefully placed the letter back in its envelope and put the envelope in his book bag. He cautiously entered through the swinging door to the dining room. His mother looked up and smiled. Hannah looked up and made a face.

"You're late," Hannah said. "He's late."

"I'm sorry," Danny said as he took his seat.

"Long workout?" Alice asked.

"The longest," Danny answered.

"He's late," Hannah insisted again. Danny's father did not acknowledge his presence as his mother began filling a plate.

"Not too much, Mom. I'm going over to Carl's in a bit. It's his birthday." Danny's father pushed away his plate as he spoke to his wife.

"What was it that Dillon said when he brought over that letter? A great opportunity? An automatic student deferment? We ought to be proud? Damned coward. He should have had the balls to be honest and say what he really thought. 'Get Danny to sign on the dotted line so he can ignore his duty and embarrass his father.'" Ben was getting more upset by the second. "When were you going to tell us about this?" he asked, finally turning to Danny.

"Soon, I was going to tell you soon," Danny answered. "I had to think about it first." Ben pointed a finger at Danny.

"This has already been decided. I have decided. You will not use this, this, trap door as a means to shirk your duty. Hiding in college for four years while those who know their duty serve in your place; it's no better than being a draft dodger. You might as well go to Canada."

"He'd be getting the education you wish you had," Alice explained. "What could be bad about that?" Ben turned his finger toward his wife.

"There's time for that after he serves."

"He might not have a scholarship then."

"I could do ROTC. I was thinking I could do ROTC," Danny offered.

"You an officer? Not likely," Ben bellowed and then started laughing. It was then that I pushed the doorbell.

"That'll be Michael," Danny said, "I've got to go."

CHAPTER 15

Danny and I walked the few blocks to Shelly's house and he told me about the scholarship.

"So you'll take it, right?" I asked.

"I don't know. It's complicated."

"Doesn't seem so complicated to me," I surmised. "Take the scholarship, get a free education and get a deferment. Don't take the scholarship and get drafted or enlist, and maybe get your ass shot off in Vietnam. Doesn't take a genius to figure this one out. Take the scholarship."

"There's my father..." Danny began.

"It's your life," I interrupted.

"...and Corey..."

"Like I said, it's your life."

"...and my duty." Danny was fingering Corey's ring.

Shelly was waiting on her porch and the three of us began the walk to Carl's. Danny and Shelly made a good-looking couple. She put her arms around his and leaned on his shoulder. She was in love. I wasn't so sure about Danny.

"Did you tell Michael?" she asked.

"Just now."

"Isn't it wonderful?" she asked me. "Now Danny and I can both go to college, get married, live in one of those little apartments, just like we planned." Shelly was a pretty smart girl; misguided, but smart. She'd be accepted to almost any college without a problem. She lived in the second biggest house in Barrel so I had to assume her folks could afford the tuition. She didn't seem like the type who would, who could work her way through college waiting on tables or turning tricks.

"Are you two engaged?" I asked.

"Not yet," Shelly answered, taking Danny's hand, "but we will be." Danny seemed not to have an opinion on that subject. Everyone was already at Carl's house when we arrived. Mrs. Hager greeted us at the door, carrying a tray of lemonade and scoops of rapidly melting ice cream.

"Come on in. You're the last to arrive," she said, propping open the door with a foot. "Help yourself." Danny, Shelly and I obeyed, and entered the small home with drinks and desserts in hand.

The inside of the Hager household was about as shabby as the outside. The furniture was well-worn and patched. The television was so ancient its tube was round. The shelves were almost devoid of books. The walls held prints of Whistler's Mother and The Last Supper, which had at best been procured at the five-and-dime, and at worst came from the back of cereal boxes. The only image of quality was a dated portrait of a soldier who I correctly assumed was Carl's father.

The Hawks and their girlfriends sat on the sparse furniture and floor while enjoying each other's company. Candy sat next to Carl, cradling his hand. Shaun brought a girl whom I had never met before and never saw again. She was oh-my-God pretty and wore a skirt that showed more thigh than I remember ever having seen before. She was in conversation with Amos, our Adonis, who could have had any girl in school but showed up alone, again. Billy, our Don Juan and also uncharacteristically alone, amused us with yet more stories of his romantic conquests, occasionally glancing at his watch, fearful of missing a later planned rendezvous. Shelly began talking with Mrs. Hager, a woman who was deathly serious about life but somehow managed to be cheerful at the same time. I joined swapping lies with my teammates.

It was only Danny who sat alone and silent across the room. His gaze went from conversation to conversation, as though he was telepathically gathering data. When his gaze fell on Shelly, she sensed it, turned his way and smiled the smile of a girl in love. When Billy came to a punch line and we all laughed, Danny smiled, nodded and raised his empty lemonade glass in a salute. Nobody was much bothered or concerned by Danny's retreat into silence.

While the rest of the Hawks busied themselves with the small cake Mrs. Hager produced, I brought a piece across the room to Danny. We sat on the floor together and ate in silence for a few minutes.

"This is what it's all about," Danny finally said. "This is what being a Hawk is all about."

"Cake and ice cream?" I asked. He smiled.

"No, being in the company of friends," Danny explained while he fingered Corey's ring. "We're a team. We train together, we sweat together and if that's all there was to it, we would go home at night and not give each other a thought until the next day. Instead, here we are, the same guys and girls we spend the whole day with, listening to the same stories we've heard a dozen times before, and we're enjoying ourselves. You know, the Hawks have been doing this for 25 years."

"Maybe nothing's good on television tonight," I joked.

"I don't deserve any better than any of them," Danny said.

"Deserve what?" I asked, but before Danny could answer, a chorus of "Happy Birthday" erupted, led by the duo of Shelly and Candy with their surprisingly good voices. Carl, clearly embarrassed by the attention, rose to his feet and spoke his rationed words for the evening.

"Thank you."

CHAPTER 16

The next week passed slowly. Classes were excruciating. Bouncing around from school to school for nearly a dozen years made me an expert in not looking conspicuous when a teacher asked a question, but it didn't provide me with much of an education. Even a crappy school like Barrel High was a challenge for me. The problem was that Coach Dillon's workouts were even more challenging. We were back on the hill twice before the end of the week. Coach must have had a plan but it wasn't clear to us what it was. There wasn't a hilly course in the conference, but there we were training on one.

I think it was Thursday. We were on the return leg of our morning ritual, running easily in a group when Billy glanced to the rear.

"Damn," he said, "there she is again."

"Who?" Shaun asked.

"Her," Billy answered, jerking a thumb to point behind him. About a block away, trailing us like a bad detective, was a girl running. She was tall, thin, with a girl-next-door look to her. Her long blond hair was pulled back into a ponytail that bounced on her back. Her running style was more boy-like than girl-like, a quality that did not at all detract from her sparkling looks. "She was there yesterday and the day before too." Leave it to Billy to notice a girl a block away that the rest of us didn't have a clue about. "I thought it was just a coincidence but three days in a row…I think she's stalking us."

"You're nuts," Shaun concluded.

"She's not bad-looking," Amos observed. Danny began to drift to the back until he was trailing the group by a few yards. I was about to ask what he was doing when by a wave of his hand he let it be known that we should go on without him.

Danny slowed until he was just about walking when the mystery girl caught up with him. Danny matched pace with her and they ran together for a few blocks. Danny glanced to his side more than a few times. She was not a bad-looking girl at all, he concluded. She did her fair share of glancing as well.

"I'm Danny O'Neal," he finally said.

"Yeah, I know. There aren't many students at Barrel High who don't know who you are."

"So you go to Barrel High?"

"Yep."

"Why haven't I seen you before?"

"I haven't been there for too long."

"Do you have a name?"

"Yep." She wasn't making it easy for Danny. They ran for a few more blocks.

"Why were you following us?" he finally asked.

"Rather not be seen with you," she said, dead serious. But then with a smile she added, "Well, rather not be seen with some of them," pointing toward the Hawks.

"They do take a bit of getting used to," Danny said, dead serious, but then with a smile added, "just like you."

"Yep." After another block of silence, she asked, "It's about a half-mile to the gym, right?"

"Yeah, about that," Danny answered.

"Race you!" and with that, the blond-haired girl lit off in a burst of speed. Danny let her get a few yards away before picking up his pace and calling to her.

"You're on!" Danny thought he would make short shrift of this smartass but pretty runner. He increased his speed, but she wasn't getting any closer. So Danny turned it up another notch, and she still wasn't getting any closer. Danny was beginning to sweat and breathe a bit harder. Her form was nearly as flawless as Danny's. Her arms swung only forward, her gait landed on the balls of her feet with a light touch to the ground. She wasted not a single motion. Her ponytail bounced only up-and-down, not side-to-side, testimony to her efficiency. This was not at all lost on Danny. There were only a few blocks to go and Danny still hadn't caught her. He was on the balls of his feet, lifting his knees, his cadence at sprint speed, and only then did the distance between them begin to close. With the gym only yards away, Danny was within a step of catching her when she took a sharp right turn and ran through the arch leading to the track.

Danny wasn't ready for her move, and before he could react, she had opened a gap again. By the time Danny got to the infield grass, she was already there, standing with her hands on her hips and a smile on her face, breathing hard and sweating in an almost amorous way. Danny was almost more out of breath than she was.

"Not a bad finish, not bad at all," he managed to say between breaths. "So are you going to tell me your name now?"

"I don't think so. You can't even beat a girl," she said, and began jogging off.

"You surprised me," was all Danny could think of saying.

"And you've got a girlfriend," she called back as she left the track, "but I bet she can't run like me."

Danny had to admit she was right.

CHAPTER 17

Corporal Corey O'Neal's squad had separated from his platoon during the morning's battle. With the lieutenant nowhere to be found, Corporal O'Neal took command. He peered through the steady pinging of the monsoon rain trying to discern whether the trail was safe ahead. Three of his squad members were only days from completing their tours. Corporal O'Neal was not going to allow carelessness to keep them from climbing on a transport plane that would take them back to the real world. After their surviving a year of bloody and sometimes senseless war, Corey vowed that no harm would come to them. That was his mission.

Corporal O'Neal pulled a laminated map from his chest pocket, unfolded it and tried to find his position. His squad was strung out on the trail behind him, crouching and hugging the bush to one side for what scant protection it could provide. A soldier moved up to Corey's side. Corey pointed to an intersection on the map. The soldier shrugged and pointed to another intersection. The maps were a decade out of date and the trails were only months old, a bad combination by any measure. The low hanging clouds were at canopy level and made taking any bearings impossible.

Corey's squad carried wounded. They had been in a fierce firefight only a few hours before. His squad performed well as measured by the body count but the casualties they carried were the price of the victory. Corey called for a Medevac chopper every 15 minutes but not even the bravest of pilots would risk a pickup in this weather. It would be suicide to even try. Corey did not begrudge them their decision to opt out of such a dangerous mission, but he hoped there was at least one hero in the bunch. There seemed not to be even one.

Without knowing what lay ahead or knowing exactly where they were, moving his squad along the trail was dangerous at best. They could be walking into an ambush. Corey thought about hunkering down to wait for better weather but knew that at least a few of his wounded soldiers would bleed out before the clouds cleared away. He had to make a decision and it was a life or death one. They could wait for better weather and a Medevac to save one or two of the wounded but sacrifice the others. Or they could venture forward with the hope of saving all of the wounded while putting the entire squad at risk. Corey hated having to make the choice. He was beginning to hate the war. Had the cause clearly been just, he could have easily rationalized to himself the worth of the sacrifices that either decision might produce. He would have done so with the comfort of knowing that sacrifices are sometimes the outcome of serving your country in war. But with each passing day, it was becoming more difficult for Corey to make that rationalization. The senselessness of being in Vietnam was compounding like a high-yield bond.

Corey crouched back along the trail, saying encouraging words to each soldier in his squad and giving words of comfort to the wounded. He looked into the eyes of each soldier. Was he ready to move forward into the danger ahead? Would he be up to the challenge if they had to do battle again? Would fatigue mitigate his training? It had been an exhausting, four-day patrol, all of it in rain, none of it out of danger. One of the wounded soldiers grabbed Corey's hand from his litter as Corey crouched by him.

"Leave me," he said, barely audibly. "I'm just holding you back." Corey put his hand on the soldier's chest and looked deeply into his eyes. Was there still an ember of survival instinct left burning in his soul? Would it be worth putting his squad at risk to save him? Corey leaned over the boy.

"We all stay together or we all go together," Corey whispered. "Besides, you owe me money." The soldier smiled. Corey brushed the soldier's hair out of his eyes as though they were brothers. In a way they were. Although strangers up until only a few weeks before, they had lived lifetimes together since. Corey had seen this soldier's expression before. It told of an almost serene realization of mortality as life bled out of him, an acceptance of what he could not prevent. Corey knew the soldier would not live through the night if they waited for better weather. He had to try to bring him home regardless of the cost. It was the Marine way. It was Corey's way.

Corey made his decision. He motioned the squad to their feet. The litters were lifted off the trail. All eyes were on him, their leader, their beacon, their brother, their hope. Corey took the point and began carefully moving along the trail. His squad followed obediently and in doing so placed their lives in his hands. They comforted themselves with the knowledge that Corey made the only choice he could have made as a Marine. If they were lying on the litters instead, Corey would have made the same decision. They lived for each other and they died for each other. It was the Marine way. It was Corey's way.

Half a world away, students marched on college campuses and protested the war Corey and his squad fought on their behalf. Politicians and newscasters questioned the morality of their decisions. Hippies called them baby killers and spat on those lucky enough to make it home alive. Movie stars visited and gave comfort to their enemies. Shirking the call to duty became the cause du jour. Service became a dirty word.

The endless debate on the war in Vietnam being conducted at that very moment by his former high school classmates in the safety and comfort of a university library was less than unimportant to Corey. Did Dante's Inferno foretell the conflict in Vietnam, they asked? All that concerned Corey at that very moment was saving the lives of as many of his soldiers as he could. That was Corey's reality, not the abstractness of Kant or the ranting of Fonda. Ankle-deep in mud on an unidentified trail in a jungle on the Mekong Delta of Vietnam, only yards from an unseen enemy bent on killing them, Corey's next action would mean life or death to his men. The importance of deciding what elective to take next semester paled in comparison.

The squad crept cautiously along the trail, alert to every raindrop splashing on leaves and every wind-driven rustle of vines, trying to separate these sounds from the footsteps of an unseen enemy. Without warning, a mortar round slammed into a tree only yards from Corey. An instant later, a second round plowed into the ground, splitting the trail and splintering his squad. The deafening sound and blinding flash knocked Corey off his feet. He instinctively hugged the ground, his training kicking in without him having to think. He scurried to cover as small arms fire began raking through the foliage around him. His attention was immediately on his squad as he began crawling backwards through the gunfire to their aid. Two of his soldiers were sprawled grotesquely on the trail. The only motion from them was the blood leaking from their bodies. The rest of the squad had already let their training dictate their actions, finding whatever protection they could against the enemy's fire, and returning that fire wherever they thought the enemy had hidden. There was little Corey could immediately do for the dead, wounded or living so he turned his attention to the enemy.

Corey surveyed the scene quickly, rising as high as he dared to better his view. Bullets ripped the foliage around him. A slight motion, perhaps a brushed branch among the jungle vines, gave away the enemy's position. Corey shouldered his M16 and began firing. He hit his target and one stream of enemy bullets was silenced. He shifted his attention to the muzzle flashes to his left. Gunfire seemed to be coming from both directions now. Corey emptied another clip, silencing a second stream of bullets while yet another erupted from a few yards away. His squad was bracketed. They had no choice but to retreat back into the jungle. Corey yelled to his squad, motioning them backwards into the thick vegetation and they quickly obeyed. They dragged the wounded with them. They would come back for their dead after the battle.

Corey took one last look back to the trail, now barely visible through the unrelenting rain. One of the shattered soldiers he was certain had been killed and so left lying on the trail inexplicably opened his eyes. Corey was dumbfounded as to how life could still emanate from a body whose entrails spilled onto the trail, but life there was. The soldier stared at Corey, silently pleading his case for survival. The soldier's bloodied hand made a fist and then opened, made a fist and then opened, as if recording his slowing heartbeat.

Corey knew his duty then just as he knew his duty when he enlisted. It was his decision that had plunged his squad into this crisis and it was his duty to remedy it. Corey motioned his squad to continue their retreat, turned around and crawled back to the wounded soldier. They exchanged a lifetime of experiences in the instant they touched, their fates now bound together no differently than when Coach Dillon went back into the water to rescue Pete Lorenzo. Corey grabbed the soldier by the collar and began dragging him to safety through the mud of the trail. The soldier feebly pushed at the mud to help them along. Corey had run thousands of miles in the company of his Hawk teammates. He had enjoyed the accolades of hundreds of friends and fans. But now Corey's world was only as wide as the few yards between him and safety, and was populated by only himself and the soldier whose life he was trying to save. Nothing else mattered. Nothing else could matter.

The torrents of rain were so loud against the leaves of the bushes that Corey did not hear nor did he see the line of automatic rifle fire that worked its way down the center of the trail toward him, creating fence-like posts of miniature geysers in the puddles. He felt only the first of the half-dozen bullets that pierced his chest. Corey fell lifeless onto the trail, his hand still gripping the collar of the soldier he so valiantly tried to save.

A half a world away the debate on the meaning of *Dante's Inferno* concluded and Corey's former classmates went out for a beer, congratulating themselves on having braved such a difficult assignment.

CHAPTER 18

There are certain days in our lives we will never forget. The day President Kennedy was shot. The day Neil Armstrong set foot on the moon. The day Danny committed himself to saving my life.

Mabel's Diner is a relic of the 1930s, a long, railroad car-like restaurant housing a Formica counter with red plastic-covered stools, and a row of six-person booths. Mabel's blue-plate specials were predictably delicious and the apple pie was warm whenever you wanted it. Mabel's was the only place open after 10:30 p.m. in Barrel and so was a magnet for high school students testing their parents' patience, and for graveyard workers looking for a quick mid-shift meal. Mabel's was as comfortable as a broken-in La-Z-boy. The music that piped from the ancient jukebox was peppered by rock-and-roll and ballads of lost love.

There must have actually been a Mabel at one time or another because her timeless photograph hangs behind the cash register even to this day, though no one that I knew remembered her. In my high school days, the madam of Mabel's Diner was Dorothy, a housemother to decades of students and the confidante of dozens of Hawk cross country teams. And like those teams before us, Mabel's Diner was a second home. If you needed to locate the Hawks, the first place to look was Mabel's, and there you would find us doing our homework, debating the war or just watching the world go by through the large plate glass windows.

It was the Sunday before our first cross country meet of the year against the hated Spartans. It was a rainy, gloomy afternoon. Danny, Shelly and I were in the middle booth at Mabel's, nursing the remains of onion rings, French fries and long-melted real-ice-cream-milkshakes. We were friends just passing the time. I flipped through the latest issue of *Distance Running News* and Shelly was going on about the apartment she and Danny would rent at college. They were predicting that Derek Clayton would set the world's marathon record at Fukuoka in December. What an animal! Shelly thought that yellow drapes in the kitchen would make the room brighter.

Danny was gazing out the window while fingering Corey's ring, seemingly uninterested in neither new marathon records nor new drapes. Something caught his attention as he was looking behind me. Danny stiffened his posture, his gaze intent. I looked over my shoulder. There was the mystery runner girl we had encountered a few mornings before, the one Danny has lost his pride to. She was striding through the light rain, her pace steady, the wet strands of her hair clumping together, her t-shirt clinging to her body. She seemed not to notice us watching her through the large windows when, for no apparent reason at all, she looked across the street straight at Danny. At first he didn't respond but she gave him the tiniest of waves and Danny nodded. She kept her pace going and soon disappeared from sight.

"Is that who I think it is?" I asked.

"Yep," Danny answered.

"And that would be?" Shelly asked, her soliloquy on the apartment drapes interrupted.

"Just a friend." Shelly seemed unconvinced. I was unconvinced as well.

It wasn't more than a minute later when Shelly pointed out the window. "Carl certainly looks to be in a hurry." We followed her finger toward Carl running down the middle of the street, his legs carrying him faster than we had ever seen before. A cloudburst filled the street with water that Carl splashed through. He was barefoot but in his school clothes. Wherever he had come from, he left in a hurry. He headed straight for the stairs to Mabel's, taking them two at a time, slipping on their slick surface and bursting into the diner, nearly colliding with Dorothy.

"Whoa, there, Carl, what's the hurry?" she asked.

"Danny. Danny," is all Carl could manage to say between gasps for air. Dorothy pointed our way and Carl ran the short distance to our table. He stood in front of us, water dripping off his nose, his bare feet covered in mud.

"What is it?" Shelly asked.

Carl had been crying. His eyes were bloodshot and his nose was running. He tried to speak. His mouth was open but words would not come out. He choked down a sob and stared at Danny.

"You Okay?" I asked. Danny got out of the booth and crouched in front of his much shorter friend. He took Carl by the shoulders and looked him in the eyes.

"Oh, God," Carl finally said. "Oh, God."

"Tell me," Danny commanded. "Tell me." Dorothy hovered a few feet away. The old men at the counter turned to look. The family two booths down stopped talking. Rain pelted on the window. I think Danny already knew what Carl had come to tell him. Carl slipped from Danny's grasp, sat on the floor and began crying, choking out the words.

"There's a Navy chaplain at your house."

Danny stood and looked out the window expressionlessly while fingering Corey's ring, intent on the patterns of the water streaming down the panes.

"There's a Navy chaplain at your house," Carl said again, this time barely audible while staring at the floor. Danny stood motionless. Shelly threw her arms around Danny's neck, already beginning to cry.

"Is it Corey?" Shelly asked. Danny said nothing while Carl nodded, still looking at the floor. I began to get up, wanting to say something but unable to think of the right words. What can you say?

"Danny..." I began when he turned his head as if slapped across the face and looked at me, and then Carl. His expression changed to that of a father with concern for a son in danger.

"This will not happen to you," Danny said to me, with a

conviction I had never heard before or since. He turned to Carl. "And it will not happen to you either," Danny repeated. "I promise." Gently pulling Shelly off his neck, Danny walked out of Mabel's. Through the windows we could see him running through the rain in the direction of Coach Dillon's house.

Danny crossed a threshold none of us could imagine. Events in his life were beginning to spiral out of control, creating instability that, with only a small push, could send him careening in one direction or the other. He was being pulled apart by the conflicts of his loyalties and the demands of friends and family, all of whom seemed to view him as a commodity, all making decisions for him that were in their own best interest. Danny had to take control. He had to have a goal with unquestionable merit that would cease the debate in his mind.

Danny was drenched as he slowed to a halt at Coach Dillon's house. He pounded on the front door. Diane opened the door, surprised to see Danny silhouetted through the screen mesh. The sight of him, soaked to the skin, was unexpected.

"Danny, come in out of the rain" she pleaded.

"I've got to talk to Coach," Danny said calmly. Coach Dillon appeared behind Diane before she had a chance to call him.

"I'm here," he said, already having heard about Corey.

"Set up a meeting with Coach Benson," Danny commanded. The Coach nodded and Danny ran back into the rain.

CHAPTER 19

Corey O'Neal's funeral was only unusual in the intensity of the emotion it evoked. Barrel was no stranger to the funerals of the young men it sent to war. The filled and filling plaques in Holden Park were testimony to that. Corey O'Neal's funeral was in some ways a turning point in Barrel's tolerance for the sacrifices it persuaded its youth to make. Corey was symbolic of the best Barrel had to offer: an athlete, a scholar, a leader, a patriot. He was a young man who was admired by all and loved by most, and who would have returned to Barrel to make it a better place in whatever he chose to do. Now, that promise would be unfulfilled and the potential would never be realized. Had the better good been served? Did the sacrifice of the few create benefit for the many? We will likely never know.

Shops were closed and classes were canceled so their proprietors and students could attend Corey's funeral. The friends and strangers at the crowded gravesite spoke volumes in their silence, their mere attendance saying more than words could convey. The 21-gun salute and taps offered by the Marine honor guard reminded them that Corey's funeral would likely not be the last. There were many more of Barrel's young men in harm's way in distant lands. The odds being what they were meant that the report of the 21-gun salute would soon be heard in Barrel again. The oversized plaques in Holden Park demanded it.

Ben O'Neal stood stoically proud at the gravesite, perhaps the only person in attendance convinced of the worth of the price Corey had paid. Alice, Hannah and Danny stood huddled together at his side. Alice accepted the triangularly folded flag with the grace and pride that O'Neal women instinctively had or developed to survive.

It took an hour for the crowd to disperse. The line of those paying their respects to Corey's family stretched longer than a football field. Danny remembered few of the hundreds that passed by, shaking his hand, saying kind words, kissing his cheek in sympathy. Danny still wore Corey's ring, perhaps in denial of what he knew to be true or perhaps because it gave him strength and comfort. Danny's teammates, the Hawks of Barrel High, felt a loss as deep as the O'Neals. They were all there. Amos, dressed in a hand-me-down suit that ill-fitted his large frame, led a small procession of his parents and siblings. Carl and his mother followed, their small family of two being no less welcome. Shaun, his parents and sisters, and Billy with his father, created an extended family that grieved with Danny in a way that only the Hawks could appreciate for its depth of devotion. I stood alone at the fringe of that family, my father too absorbed in his own schemes to be a comfort to strangers, and my mother too devoted to him to tell him he was wrong.

When the long procession of neighbors, friends and strangers finally finished their condolences, the O'Neals walked to their waiting car with their arms around each other. Danny noticed one last mourner who had stayed behind, awkwardly standing alone among the headstones. "I'll see you at home," Danny told his family and he walked to her. Danny had never seen her in anything other than running shorts and they previously had exchanged only a scant few words. Even so, seeing her there that afternoon gave Danny more comfort than he expected.

"I'm sorry," she said. "I didn't know Corey, but I know you, and if your brother was anything like you...what a terrible loss."

"I'm glad you came," Danny said, both of them suddenly realizing he didn't know her name.

"Jill. My name is Jill Burke."

"I'm glad you came, Jill."

She put her arms around him and they held each other.

CHAPTER 20

The first cross country meet against the Spartans was only two days away when Sid Benson unexpectedly showed up at the Barrel High School track. The Hawks were finishing a grueling interval workout in the midst of a stifling hot and sticky afternoon. Sid sat in the first row of the grandstands and lit up a cigar. The plank seats, bending under his weight, were barely able to accommodate his girth. Sid sweated profusely just sitting in the grandstands as the effort of simply pumping blood through his huge mass taxed his body.

As the Hawks ran by, Sid alternated between smiling with satisfaction and shaking his head with incredulous doubt. Sid Benson was in his realm. He could watch athletes perform for hours on end, no matter how talented or untalented they might be. As the Hawks lapped the track, Sid did the mental arithmetic of what it might take to transform these young runners into college class athletes and maybe national champions. He had no interest in anyone but Danny but Sid couldn't keep himself from plying his craft, turning high school boys into hardened college athletes. That's what Sid did better than almost any coach in the country. It was an unlikely destiny for a man whose own personal athletic achievements peaked at picking up towels in the boys' locker room. The rocky running tracks of small town America provided the grist that enabled Coach Benson to be the success that he was. He was a sculptor of young athletes but he needed clay to work with. Sitting on bending grandstand planks of countless stadiums in the most forgettable of small towns of downstate Illinois is how Sid Benson scouted the future runners who would be his clay.

The workout soon ended. Danny and Frank stood aside, talking between themselves while the rest of the Hawks were sent off on a cool-down run. Frank waved to Sid, letting him know that Danny and he would be with him in a short while. Sid sat back to wait, patiently chewing on his cigar as sweat dripped off his brow, staining the tobacco. The Hawks' curiosity about the mysterious goings on with the infamous Coach Benson was piqued to a frenzy. I left the field with the Hawks but ran only a block before turning back to the track. I took a seat in the stands on the other side of the field from Coach Benson, able to see what was going on but not looking too obvious.

Sid leaned on the railing, thoughtfully watching Danny and Frank's discussion across the track. Sid Benson could size up a situation with the skill of a small town con man and that quality served him well. They must be discussing some strategy, Sid surmised. That meant they wanted something. Danny and Frank were up to something, Sid was sure of that, but he just didn't know what. So he had to prepare for the unexpected. A few minutes passed before Danny and Frank seemed satisfied with the outcome of their discussion and walked the short distance across the track to join Sid in the stands.

"Kid, I don't come south twice for the same reason too often," Sid greeted them, his cigar firmly clenched between his teeth. "Count yourself fortunate."

"Thanks for coming, Coach," Danny replied.

"Always a pleasure to see you, Sid," Frank added.

"Let's cut the crap and get to business." Sid was, if anything, a businessman. He used a pinky finger to remove a sliver of tobacco from between his teeth and spat it out. "You signed the offer letter yet?" he asked Danny.

"No."

"What?"

"No. I haven't signed the letter."

"Then what the hell am I doing here?" Sid asked, feigning annoyance. "Frank, what's going on here?"

"We have a proposition for you," Frank explained. Sid shifted his weight on the bench. His suspicions were correct. This would be a negotiation, he thought. "We have something you want and you have something we want."

"And what might that be?" Sid asked.

"You want Danny and we want scholarships," Frank went on.

"Did you say scholarships, like than more than one?" Sid hadn't expected this.

"Yes. Six of them."

"Holy shit, Frank," Sid exclaimed, "and who are these six scholarships for?"

"One's for Danny," Frank answered.

"And the rest are for the Hawks," Danny said. Sid let out a guffawing laugh.

"Well, I gotta admit you got a shit-pot full of nerve, kid," he offered. "Why should I want to waste scholarships on your teammates?"

"Because," Danny said, his voice quivering as he fingered Corey's ring, "we're a package deal. If you want me, you've got to give scholarships to all the Hawks." Sid was taken by surprise. Advantage Danny, but Sid was ready to return the next serve.

"Frank, you got something to do with this?" Sid asked, but he didn't wait for an answer before turning back to Danny. "There's not chance in hell I'm going to waste scholarships on those loser teammates of yours, and here's why." Sid sat back on the bench and removed the cigar from his clenched teeth. "First, you've got a kid who's slower than my dead grandmother and can't string a dozen words together. Then there's that Paul Bunyan look-alike who should be throwing a javelin instead of running. And then you've got two guys who might be better than average but all they can think about is getting laid. And finally, there's the Jew, and everyone knows Jews can't run."

Sid paused to reinsert his cigar and take a puff. He pointed a finger at Danny. "Kid, you're playing a losing hand. You gotta know when to hold 'em and when to fold 'em. My original offer's still on the table. Take it or leave..."

"There's good reason why you should be offering us those scholarships," Frank interrupted.

"Oh?" Sid responded, shifting his weight to softer spot on the bench. "Enlighten me."

"The Hawks are going to win the state cross country championship," Danny said.

"They're what?"

"We're going to win state," Frank concurred. "Listen, Sid, we're offering you a deal. If we win state, you give the Hawks scholarships. If we don't win state..." Sid shook his head and looked at the sky.

"Frank, you're just about as big a dreamer as the kid," he said. "The Spartans won state by 20 points last year and they've got their whole team coming back. Your guys barely made it to the finals and took last, and you've got no one worth shit coming back except for Danny. Don't you know the finals are going to be at Pioneer Park? You'll never win on that course."

Frank looked surprised but didn't say anything as he let Sid calm down a bit. Sid stared at Frank, twirling the cigar in his mouth. "So how do you plan on winning state?" Sid finally asked.

"The how isn't important, Sid. What's important is the why," Frank said. It suddenly dawned on Sid what the plan was.

"It's the deferments, isn't it, Frank? It's the Goddamned deferments," Sid spat. "You couldn't give a shit about the state title or the scholarships. All you want is for the kids to get deferments so they won't get drafted and end up in some crap hole in Vietnam. You're selling your soul for a handful of 2S's. Shit, Frank, you gotta stop trying to save the world. You haven't changed in 25 years."

"What does that matter, Sid?" Frank asked. "You say you're a businessman, start thinking like a businessman."

"What do you have to lose, Coach Benson?" Danny added. "If we win state, we get six scholarships, and you get a championship team. If we lose state, it costs you nothing, and we get nothing."

Sid crossed his arms, gave a careful look at Danny and began thinking this through. Danny was running scared; Sid knew that. After what happened to his brother, no way Danny would enlist, no matter what his old man said. He'd probably do anything to get out of being drafted. I've got him on the ropes, Sid concluded. So why waste the other scholarships? Sid scratched his chin and shifted his enormous bottom on the bench again. So if I've got Danny hooked, Sid asked himself, what's the best way to reel him in? Sid looked at Frank and shook his head. Frank Dillon, out to save the world, he thought, and he's dragging the kid down with him. What a pair.

Sid looked across the track and seemed to stare right at me. He got up, stretched his legs and leaned up against the railing. Then it came to him. Play on their weakness, Sid concluded. If Danny is so bent on saving his teammates from getting their asses shot off in Vietnam, then let him think he's doing it. Offer the scholarships and get Danny hooked on coming to Illinois State. There's no risk to me, Sid convinced himself. There's no way the Hawks are going to win the state championship, not with the Spartans standing in their way and not on the Pioneer Park course. Offer them the scholarships and then look sorry when the Spartans whip their butts. Danny would love him for having made the offer and take a scholarship to save himself.

Sid let a smile creep onto his face and nodded with satisfaction. He had his plan. But he was still a businessman and businessmen bargain. He couldn't just accept Danny's proposal. It would have been too obvious and probably would have killed Sid to do it. Sid was going to bargain.

"Okay," Sid said, turning to face Danny and Frank, "I'll play your game. If the Hawks win state, I'll give you your scholarships and with them you'll get your precious deferments." Danny's eyes widened like a kid opening gifts on Christmas morning. Frank began smiling like I'd never seen before.

"That's great, Sid," Frank said, "just great."

"I can't thank you enough," Danny began.

"But there'll be only five scholarships," Sid interrupted. Frank's smile left as quickly as it arrived.

"There're six runners on the team. We've got to have six scholarships," Frank protested.

"It's out of my hands, Frank," Sid explained. "Conference rules. I've already made two offers and I can't give more than seven scholarships in any one year. You're getting all I've got to give." Sid was lying. It would be years before the NCAA began making such rules, but Sid was a conniver and he couldn't agree to a first offer. It just wasn't in his genes. Besides, Sid knew the Hawks almost as intimately as Frank did. Who would he lose by providing only five scholarships? Only Carl and that wouldn't be a great loss.

Frank sank slowly to the bench. Victory had been nearly within his grasp and it scampered away like a scared cat.

"But there are six runners," Frank repeated.

"Nothing I can do about it, Frank," Sid insisted. "Can't get blood out of a turnip."

"I don't know," Frank stammered.

"We'll take the five scholarships," Danny quickly said.

"You sure about this, kid?" Sid asked.

"Yes, I'm sure. You wait and see. We'll win state," Danny said, perhaps more to convince himself than Coach Benson.

"I'm sure you will, kid," Coach Benson said, "I'm sure you will. I'll send the papers over in the morning, Frank." Coach Benson threw the stub of his cigar onto the track and began waddling in the direction of his car.

"What's so special about Pioneer Park?" Danny asked the Coach.

"Think of the hill, Danny. Think of the hill."

As I watched the scene unfold from across the track, I somehow sensed my life would never be the same.

CHAPTER 21

Barrel, Illinois was a football town. No matter how good or bad the team, the stands at the Barrel High School stadium would always be full for a Friday night football game. The town only had a population of 12,400, but somehow a stadium with 25,000 seats was filled with screaming fans week after week. I could never quite figure that out. It could have been that there wasn't all that much to do in Barrel and the towns within 50 miles on a Friday night, and going to a football game was better than watching whatever happened to be on TV. It could have also been the case that the road to fame in Barrel made a beeline through the football locker room. To be a football player was to be at the top of the food chain. There were new uniforms every season and cheerleading squads of the prettiest girls in school who passed you their phone number and let you grab their bottoms. There were brass bands that announced your entrance onto the football field, free milk shakes at Mabel's and a blind eye to your fake ID at Larry's Liquor Emporium. And until Principal Milo ferreted out the perpetrators, the answers to your midterms appeared in your locker the morning of the exam. There wasn't much more you could ask for than to be a football player when your world was bounded by the city limits of Barrel, Illinois.

The members of the cross country team were not so blessed. Our locker room was in the sub-basement of the gymnasium, a space shared with the boiler and assorted vermin. We paid for our milkshakes at Mabel's and Larry inspected our IDs like they were passports at Checkpoint Charlie. Our team budget was, well, there wasn't any budget. Whatever it took to get the team from meet to meet probably came out of Coach Dillon's back pocket. Our team's transport was Coach Dillon's 1953 Chevy station wagon. Our mismatched sweats were a collection of football castoffs and our running singlets were basketball hand-me-downs that Diane patched before every season. The ice cold Coca-Colas that waited for us at the end of brutal workouts came out the Dillons' refrigerator. At the beginning of each season, Frank loaded up the team into his wagon and we drove to the Adidas outlet in Peoria. Every Hawk got a new pair of running shoes and it never cost them a cent. It was only years later that I learned that Diane did the shop's books for free in exchange for the shoes.

The boisterous crowds that filled the stands at the football games were painfully absent from our cross country meets. Shelly, Candy and Diane could always be counted on to be in attendance. So could Mrs. Hager and Shaun's father when they could get off of work. My parents came once, but only so my father could size up a deal. Once in a while, a former Hawk would find his way to the meet, or one of Billy's or Shaun's girlfriends would come by, but otherwise, the crowds were pretty thin. Diane was the official timer, calling out splits and finishing times. One of the girls handed out sticks while the other recorded places and times. Clearly, it was a family affair.

Our home course wound its way through Dillard Park a few miles from campus. The course was three laps around a one-mile loop that circled the lake. It was picturesque, if not imaginative. The course was fast and mostly flat but still required the astute runner to pay attention to race tactics. The first quarter-mile of each loop was a gentle slope through an open field that ended in a 90-degree left turn leading into a narrow path. The path entered the woods, following the contour of the lake, before making a jog to the right up a steep but short incline onto a paved service road. The course followed the road for another quarter-mile, turned left back down the incline into the woods and threaded its way along the lake until the course spilled back into the meadow. Generations of Hawks ran to fame and victory, or obscurity and defeat, looping the lake at Dillard Park.

On the afternoon of our first cross country meet of the 1967 season, we jogged over to Dillard Park, full of the confidence that graces the untested. The fall had yet to bring the dry coolness that runners so look forward to. The race would be contested as much against the heat and humidity as against the Spartans. Coach Dillon, Diane and the girls drove over earlier, and were busying themselves with setting up the finishing chute, setting poles that marked the turns in the course, and laying down the white-chalk arrows that pointed the way around the course.

We were stretching near the starting line when the Spartans arrived with the fanfare of a presidential motorcade. Their bus was enormous, like one of those mobile-mansions used by touring country music stars. When the doors opened and the Spartans filed out, it was like watching an assembly of a squadron of Hitler Youth. They were seven identically tall, blond, muscular and good-looking specimens that could have only been the result of genetic engineering. They looked like clones from some eugenics experiment gone amiss. The Spartans were attired in uniforms of gleaming polyester sweats with matching baseball caps and shoulder bags with "The Spartans" embroidered on their side. We looked at their uniforms and then at our mismatched castoffs, and then at each other.

"They're awfully snazzy-looking," Amos finally commented.

"Yeah, snazzy-looking like pansies," Billy said.

"Sort of makes you want to be a pansy," Shaun admitted.

We knew most of the Spartans. They had abused us on more than one cross country course on more than one occasion. Their first runner was Denton Bentley, last year's individual state champion. He was a good-looking kid with the sort of brash, naive personality that results from being over-privileged. He was good and he knew it. Denton was destined to be a senator or a convict or both. Their second runner was Kyle Mandy. Kyle, whose compassion made Denton look like a saint, was known to throw an elbow or two. He finished fourth at state last year. His speed came naturally and not from hard work, and that was his weakness. Kyle could be beaten. The Spartans' third runner was Brian Vardy, fifth at state last year.

Brian had miler speed and his race was best in the first mile-and-a-half. He was the one who pulled the Spartans' opponents through a pace they couldn't sustain, and then let Denton and Kyle clean up the pieces. Brian was rumored to have spent a year at military school, a judge's offer in lieu of serving time at juvenile hall. We were guessing arson before we saw Brian's blade. The Spartans' fourth man, David Washington, was the quiet one. Taller than the rest by at least a few inches, he intimidated the competition simply by staring them down.

A dozen of the prettiest cheerleaders I've ever seen filed out of the bus after the Spartans. We instantly and speechlessly fell under their spell. The Sirens bade us to crash upon their rocks.

"Holy shit, will you look at them?" Shaun finally managed to say.

"I think I'm getting a hard-on," Billy groaned.

"They do travel in good company," Danny commented, trying to keep his composure.

"Don't look too hard," Billy taunted. "Shelly might catch you!"

We tried to keep from staring but the cheerleaders' spell was strong and binding. The tops of their long, incredibly smooth legs disappeared under their insanely short skirts. Their halter tops barely contained their braless breasts. We had to do something to gain their attention. We waved to no avail.

"Amos," I said, "take off your shirt." Amos pulled off his top and flexed his Herculean frame. A few of the cheerleaders glanced in our direction but their attention was short-lived.

"Hmmm. If Amos doesn't get to them, they've got to be lesbians," Shaun concluded. Carl stood, looked at the Spartans and then the cheerleaders.

"Pretty girls," he said.

As we were lusting at the Spartans' cheerleaders, a small caravan of cars arrived. Dozens of students, parents and teachers, Spartan supporters all, poured out. Amazing. They were able to put together almost as many fans for an away cross country meet as we assembled for a football game.

The Spartans left to jog around the course as Coach Dillon limped toward us with Diane and the girls at his side. He leaned heavily on his cane. The effort of setting up the course was as telling in his stride. The pain was a constant reminder to Frank of the beaches of Normandy and the day he failed to save Pete Lorenzo's life. It was like a ringing in his ears that would never go away, the buzzing of a fly that could not be shooed. The tinnitus of guilt. Coach Dillon motioned us to a nearby picnic table and we gathered around him. It was clear he had something more to tell us than the usual pep talk.

"This is the first meet of a special season," Coach Dillon began. "We are facing the best team in the state, or so they think. They're good, but so are we. On any given day, any team can beat any other team. It will be a test of just how much we want to win. The team that wants to win more usually does."

"We'll cream 'em, Coach," Shaun said.

"These guys may look slick, but looks don't make hay," Amos offered.

Frank smiled and then became very serious. Frank was about to go back into the water.

"There's something more I need to tell you," and Frank told us about Sid Benson, about the scholarships and about winning the state championship. He told us of the deferments that would allow us to dodge the call to duty with the air of a scholar instead of the stink of traitor. With Frank's carefully chosen words, our worldviews instantly changed. Each of us knew just what Frank's words meant. The memories of Freddy Delisle and Corey O'Neal were still too fresh for us not to understand. We were being offered a way out, a way to avoid their fates, a trap door out of Vietnam: an education, a deferment, a better life, no risk of coming home in a body bag. This was all suddenly within our grasp. It was like being mailed a winning lottery ticket. All we needed to do was cash it in.

But Frank was not committing a selfless act. The plan was his way of atoning for having failed to save Pete Lorenzo's life on the beaches of Normandy. Frank was going back into the water to save lives once again, but this time, he couldn't do it alone. He could throw us a life preserver but it was up to us to grab it and swim ashore. Frank made us the masters of our own destinies, masters of our own fates. All we had to do was win state.

But something was left unsaid.

We all looked at each other, and then at ourselves. Doubt raced through our minds. Would this be a fool's errand? Had Coach Dillon set us up for a sucker punch? Did the Hawks have a chance of winning state? I looked at my teammates. Carl, as innocent, dedicated and likeable as he was, would be of no help. As much as we adored him, Carl was not championship material. Amos had the constitution of a lion and the physique of a body builder, but at best he was an average runner. Billy and Shaun were solid, dependable and competitive runners, the heart of the lineup. You could count on them to slap a double or triple to the opposite field when the chips were down but I wasn't sure of either of them being able to knock it out of the park. I was good. I knew that, but I didn't know if I was good enough.

And then there was Danny. If we were going to win state, Danny was going to have to win the race. He was the key to our salvation. He would be our Christ. We would be his disciples. But even with Danny, we had only four really competitive runners. We were going to need a better fifth man or we'd be digging foxholes in Vietnam within the year.

"Men," Coach Dillon said, "let's have a good race." We all put our hands together and began the Hawks cheer.

"Hawks, Hawks, Hawks! Go Hawks!" We were the Hawks and always would be. We were brothers and comrades. We would go back into the water for each other, just as Frank had gone back into water for Pete Lorenzo and now was doing for us.

As we took off our sweats and moved in the direction of the starting line, it suddenly hit me. I knew what had been unsaid. I ran over to Danny.

"You did this," I accused of him.

"Did what?"

"The scholarships. This was your doing as much as Frank's." Danny looked the other way, twirling Corey's ring, but I put myself in front of him. "That night at Mabel's, what you said to Carl and me. You said what happened to Corey wouldn't happen to us. You made a promise. And then that day at the track with Coach Benson. You made a deal." I looked into his eyes and saw only commitment. Danny said nothing and jogged toward the starting line. I was about to run after him but decided to let Danny be. I knew what the truth was even if Danny wouldn't admit it.

Diane pulled Frank aside as he walked toward the starting line. "You didn't tell them there would be only five scholarships," she whispered.

"They don't need to know. I'll find a way," Frank replied.

"And what if you don't? How do you choose? They deserve to know."

"I'll find a way."

We lined up on the chalk starting line, alternating between Spartans and Hawks. The Spartan cheerleaders were lined up to one side, yelling, gyrating and showing their assets in support of their team. The Spartan fans unfurled banners espousing the greatness of their team, "Spartans—State Champions 1966!" Our cheering section had grown by two: Sid Benson, who waddled toward the starting line as though he was a new landlord who had come to inspect the premises, and Jill Burke, who just seemed to appear out of nowhere.

The contrast between the Spartans and Hawks could not have been greater, the bold and the beautiful versus the meek and the mindful. Danny stood between Denton and Kyle, fingering Corey's ring, ignoring his opponents. He was deep in thought, playing the upcoming race over in his mind. Danny surveyed the course before him glancing at the small crowd assembled to the side. A shot of adrenaline pulsed through him when he caught sight of Jill. He couldn't help but let his eyes soak in her freshness and enjoy the surprise of seeing her there. He gave Jill a smile and a small wave that she returned with a wink. Danny didn't see Shelly's glare as she intercepted this unspoken exchange.

Frank, Sid Benson and the Spartans' coach were busily discussing the details of the race when David Washington's voice broke Danny's concentration.

"Out of my way, runt," he yelled, and with a shove sent Carl sprawling onto the grass. "That place is for a Spartan." Amos gently helped Carl to his feet and, being the only Hawk close in height to David, glowered at him.

"Touch that boy again and I'll punch your lights out."

"He can talk!" Brian Vardy said, "I didn't think shit-kickers had the brains." Amos went chest to chest with Brian.

"Let it go," Danny advised Amos. "He's just trying to rile you. Just concentrate on the race."

"Yeah," Denton taunted, "just think about how bad we're gonna stomp on you guys." Kyle, a good six inches taller than me, grabbed me by my jersey.

"Is this the Jew?" he asked his teammates, who broke out laughing. Danny pulled Kyle's hand off me and shoved him away."

"Back off, asshole," Danny commanded.

"Who are you, his bodyguard?" Kyle asked, turning to Denton. "Too bad he didn't do the same for his dead brother. What was that jerk's name, Carly?" Danny hesitated for an instant and then began to take a swing at Kyle. Billy caught his arm before he could connect a punch.

"Like you said, Danny, let it go," Billy advised. Coach Dillon's voice ended the confrontation.

"Okay, let's settle down. The course is three loops. Keep the poles to your left at all times and there will be no cutting the corners. You'll get mile and two-mile splits. Is everything understood?" The line of Hawks and Spartans nodded their reply. "Are there any questions before we start?" There were none. "Okay, to your marks." We all brought our feet to the chalk line and tensed waiting for the start. Our singlets were already soaked and sweat dripped off us even though we had yet to start the race. Frank raised the starting pistol and with a crack and a puff of smoke, the first race of the most important season of our lives began.

In an instant the Spartans were off the line and into their strides. I'd never seen such big runners move so quickly in unison. They may have been assholes, but they were well-trained and good runners. They were professionals. Within only a few yards, all seven Spartans were ahead of the Hawks as we ran up the gentle slope through the open meadow toward the first turn. The Spartans kept a tight nucleus as they powered ahead. The Hawks trailed in a single line. Danny soon began moving up and penetrating into the group of Spartans. I followed Danny the best I could. I could feel Shaun's and Billy's efforts behind me.

The first turn came quickly. It was a 90-degree dogleg to the left. The wide meadow funneled into a two-runner-wide gap between a guide pole and a massive oak tree. Denton and Kyle were in the lead and negotiated the turn easily. A step or two later, David followed them, with Danny tucked in behind him. I had just caught Brian as we began to lean into the turn. The next thing I knew Brian's hand was on my shoulder and I was careening into the tree. I was momentarily stunned by the impact. Before I could recover, all the Spartans had negotiated the turn and had nearly disappeared into the woods. Amos passed by before I could rejoin the race. Carl was behind me.

The path through the woods was so narrow that passing was nearly impossible. Low hanging branches had to be pushed aside or they whipped across your face. Kyle and Denton kept a steady pace through the trees. Danny slipped by David before the path got too narrow and slotted in behind the two leaders. Six Spartans were ahead of Shaun and Billy. I followed Amos into the woods. Sensing my approach, he moved to the side to let me pass. I couldn't see farther ahead than the backsides of Shaun and Billy. We were already in trouble.

The path burst out of the woods and crossed a small creek before taking a turn to the right up the steep incline to the road. The tall Spartans and Danny were able to stride over the water. I could see splashes as Shaun and Billy caught the edge of the creek. I did the same, soaking one foot. The path widened enough going up to the road that I passed Billy and Shaun. The three of us ran together in a small pack, turning left onto the road. The relative cool shade of the woods was replaced by glare of the afternoon sun and heat radiating off the pavement. After baking for the day, the tarred road felt gooey beneath our feet. The course straightened out enough that I could look ahead. Denton, Kyle and Danny, the lead group, had opened a gap over the trailing cluster of four Spartans. I led Billy and Shaun and the last Spartan. I glanced back. Amos just popped onto the road from the path. Carl was nowhere to be seen. We had to break into the Spartan pack soon. Otherwise we would lose contact, and the Spartans were too good to let that happen.

We kept these positions until the half-mile marker, just before turning left onto the trail back into the woods. I passed two Spartans just before the turn and powered down the incline. I was just behind Brian. He glanced back at me and gave an evil grin. I suddenly felt the pace slow as the lead group and David moved ahead. What's going on here, I thought? Why is this asshole slowing down? Then it struck me. He was bottling up the rest of the Hawks behind him. If he didn't want me to pass him on the narrow path, I wasn't going to be able to do it without eating another tree. This was not good, not good at all. I moved up to his shoulder. We were literally touching as we jockeyed for position. I tried to squeeze by.

"Let me pass," I said between breaths.

"Eat shit," he said, and pushed me aside again. This time I kept my balance and with a small widening in the trail, I slipped by him.

The sun focused into my eyes as we burst onto the meadow. I wiped the sweat that was streaking down my forehead and stinging my eyes. Denton, Kyle and Danny were still in a tight group and David was about five yards behind. I lagged David by about 10 yards, with Brian at my heels. Shaun and Billy were locked in a pack with the other three Spartans another 10 yards behind. Amos lumbered behind them. Carl was still in the woods. We swung around into the starting straightaway, completing the first loop. Coach Dillon was poised to call out the first mile splits as we passed.

"4:48, 4:48, 4:50..." he yelled as the lead group passed, barely audible over the din of the Spartan cheerleaders. Diane jotted down the times onto a clipboard. They were good splits.

"You're way behind on points," Sid Benson yelled over the crowd.

"It's early," Frank countered.

Shelly and Candy stood on the picnic table.

"Go get 'em, Danny!" Shelly screamed.

"Go Hawks!" Candy yelled.

Danny let his concentration falter for a moment as he scanned the small crowd, hoping to catch a glimpse of Jill. She wasn't to be seen.

"4:55, 4:56, 4:57," Coach Dillon yelled as Brian and I passed. 4:55 was an okay split, but cross country meets were first about placing well and only second about times. I did the mental arithmetic. I had to join the lead group if the Hawks had any chance of winning this race. I allowed myself a quick look to the rear. Shaun and Billy would have to leave their Spartan shadows behind, and then it would be up to Amos to have at least a Spartan or two behind him.

We were back on the slope of the meadow in our second loop, approaching the first turn. I passed David, tied a mental rope to the back of Kyle and began pulling myself into the lead group a yard at a time. My breathing began to get labored. That raspy, I-can't-get-enough-air sound began coming out of my throat. The sun was cooking the back of my neck. We still had nearly two miles to go. I had to pace myself.

Denton shot ahead of Danny as they approached the turn. Danny knew he couldn't let Denton open a gap. You could feel the conscious effort that Danny made to turn the dial up a notch to match Denton's pace, but a small gap had opened and Danny had to deal with it. Kyle began falling behind the leaders as they accelerated ahead. I now had my target. I had to finish ahead of Kyle. Denton and Danny reached the turn nearly together, with Denton a few steps ahead. They took the turn so sharply that they both scraped against the tree. A girl's voice suddenly came out of the ether.

"Go with him, Danny! Don't let him get away!" It was Jill at the edge of the woods. Danny looked up at her. "Dig down!" she yelled. Danny obeyed and turned up the pace another notch, closing the gap with Denton as they entered the woods. Denton and Danny were all business. There were no antics; there was no shoving. No matter what they may have felt about each other off the course, they were runners who took their sport seriously. The one who crossed the finish line first would do so because he ran the better race, not because he was the bigger jerk.

We kept our places through the woods and up onto the road. I worked my way forward and was now at Kyle's heels. I looked over my shoulder. About 20 yards behind me, Shaun shadowed David. Another 10 yards back and Billy led a pack of three Spartans. Amos and Carl were yet on the road. We weren't winning this race by a good stretch. The gravel and tar road had softened into a spongy mush under the afternoon sun. You could feel the heat through your shoes. Small rocks occasionally sprung out of the matrix and careened backwards as a shoe sought traction. Singlets were drenched in sweat. I could hear Kyle taking deep breaths ahead of me. The soreness of my calves from the week's workouts suddenly cried out.

Danny focused on keeping contact with the leader. Denton was a gifted runner. You couldn't be state champion without having some God-given talent. Danny had also been so blessed. But there was something not so subtly different between Denton and Danny. The Spartan ran from the front as though the position was his birthright, a confidence that might crumble if too strongly challenged, but it served him well. Danny worked his way to the front as though leading a race was a privilege granted to the diligent, and valued that privilege because of its sanctity.

Danny had raced on this course dozens of times. But his most vivid memories were as a junior high school boy watching Corey win his races when he was a Hawk. Corey, the popular young running phenomenon, easily outdistanced his older, more experienced opponents. Danny used to position himself in these same woods, waiting for Corey to come by, cheering his brother to victory.

Letting these memories bubble to the surface, Danny's eyes began to water, not with sweat but with the first tears Danny had shed for his brother.

A branch scratched against Danny's face, startling him back to the present. He and Denton were already in the woods. He had allowed the memories of his brother to interfere with his concentration and Denton opened a five-yard gap as they burst into the meadow. Danny would not let that happen again. He wiped the combination of sweat and tears from his eyes, raised his knees and moved up the pace. He was even with Denton at the two-mile mark.

"9:42, 9:43, 9:44," Frank called as they passed, barely to be heard above the shouts of the Spartan cheerleaders and fans. Diane stood closer to Frank so she could jot down the splits.

"That's the way, Danny" Shelly yelled. Sid poked Frank in the back.

"Good second mile."

Kyle and I were even as we too burst out of the woods and onto the flat. The glare of the sun was unwelcome in most ways, but one: Big runners don't do well in the heat, too much volume, not enough surface area. Kyle was beginning to suffer as the humidity took its toll. I pulled just ahead of him as we passed the two-mile point.

"9:52, 9:53, 9:54," Frank yelled. We had slowed a bit on the second loop, not to be unexpected given the heat. This was my chance. I had a quarter-mile in the sun and on the flat meadow to put some distance between Kyle and me. I'd never started my kick a mile out in a race, but there was always a first time. I jumped ahead of Kyle and powered down the straightaway trying to open a gap before entering the woods. If I could get 15 or 20 yards, I would be out of sight in the trees and that's always a good thing.

Ahead of us, Danny and Denton were running side-by-side, their pace visibly quicker than only a few minutes before. Neither intended for the other to finish first. Both of their singlets were soaked through, as was mine. My eyes stung as sweat sluiced down my forehead. I'd have to take off my glasses to wipe them and so I didn't risk it. As I navigated the first turn, I glanced behind me.

Kyle was only about 10 yards behind but not looking very well. Another 20 yards behind Kyle was a group of four strung out in a line. Shaun and Billy, bracketed by Spartans, mirrored each other's stride. As I gained a little elevation moving up the hill, I could see the last three Spartans, comfortably running in a group with Amos trailing them, his metronome cadence chewing up the landscape, gaining imperceptibly on the slightly slowing Spartans with each step. If these races were 10 miles long, Amos might be first man. Carl was another 20 yards behind.

I quickly added up the points. What's the best case? Danny wins, I'm third, Shaun or Billy fifth, the other seventh. Maybe Amos beats one Spartan for eleventh. That's 27-29 and we win, but everyone has to come through.

Danny took the lead going into the woods. His countless hours of training during the stifling heat of the summer were beginning to show. He let his stride lengthen. He rolled up onto the balls of his feet, lowered his arms, and began to pull away. He burst out of the woods and without even an inch loss of stride, powered up the incline and onto the road. That torridly hot surface was enough to cook our feet but its openness compensated for its discomfort by providing an unbridled opportunity to speed to victory. If you were fit, if you trained with the focused intensity that comes with unquestioned dedication, if you can ignore the piercing pain in your calves, if you can put aside the tightening of oxygen-starved muscles, then you can grab that opportunity, make your legs move faster and taste the possibility of winning. There is an inexplicable high when you make this transition and pass the test of willpower, knowing that you could easily fail by succumbing to the temptation of not inflicting more pain on yourself.

As I reached the road I sensed that Danny had passed through that threshold. He made the commitment that he would win this race. As Danny powered ahead, Denton's stride shortened and he glanced behind to see where I was. Danny had broken him. Denton's glance over his shoulder was to assure himself he could still salvage second place. It was my cue to run that asshole down. I was feeling alright and he was slowing down. If the race was long enough, I could catch him. Making the turn down into the woods, I looked behind. David and Brian were still ahead of Shaun and Billy.

The woods were treacherous. Only a half-mile to the finish, the barely one-lane-wide trail snaked between the massive trunks of hundred-year-old oaks. Passing was dicey as roots jumped out of the soil to grab at your feet. Branches lurked around corners to scratch at your face. The stream-laden gully that cut across the trail had to be jumped just right or you would be eating mud. If more than a few yards separated you from your opponent, the winding curves in the trail hid him from view.

Worse than that, the woods held memories and ghosts. The woods were a refuge where Danny and Corey hid from the expectations of their father. When no place seemed safe for them to be just boys, the woods were their haven. Corey and Danny ran the trail together countless times, fantasizing about grabbing the number-one stick in front of cheering crowds. They played hide-and-seek among the trees as children. When Danny's first girlfriend dumped him, Corey knew he could find his brother sitting in the woods alone in his misery.

As Danny ran into the woods only a half-mile from the finish, almost certain of victory, these memories assaulted him. The depth of Corey's loss enveloped him, depriving him of air no less than had he been wrapped in Saran Wrap. In the few days since that frightening afternoon at Mabel's Diner, Danny had been unable to accept that Corey would never again come to the woods. Running through the tunnel-like trail of the woods that afternoon, the realization finally came to Danny and the grief was unbearable. He stumbled on a trail-crossing root, his balance weakened by the weight of that grief. His cadence could not recover. His breathing became sporadic through his choking sobs. Denton took advantage of Danny's grief. He caught and passed him.

I saw Danny only yards before I too passed him as we left the woods a few hundred yards from the finish. I had no way to know what had happened to him but I also had no time to figure it out. I looked ahead at Denton only 30 yards in front of me. Maybe I could catch him. I started my sprint into the finish. My arms pumped, my legs flew, the gap to Denton closed. I saw Candy at the end of the chute, waving the number-one stick. The cheerleaders were gyrating, the Spartan fans were yelling. Somewhere through the din I heard Jill screaming. Even Sid Benson was yelling. I attached my rope to Denton and began pulling him in. But even as tired as Denton was, an athlete of his caliber doesn't let himself be caught in the chute, and his raw talent kept him inches ahead of me as we crossed the finish line. "14:40," Frank yelled as we passed and Diane recorded the same time for both Denton and me. She wrote "4:48 last mile" by my name. I fell to the ground as I grabbed my second-place stick. I felt hands under my arms, pulling me up as Danny crossed the finish line, his face contorted by his grief and the pain of his failure. Kyle was at his heels.

I ran to the sidelines and cheered the rest of the Hawks in. The Spartan David powered across the line a few yards ahead of a lurching Shaun, who dived for the finish line in a futile attempt to best his rival. "15:10" Frank called out. The same scene played out in reverse as Billy edged out Brian. "15:16." Two more Spartans finished before Amos, the beauty of his perfect physique giving poor testimony to the effort he had expended, crossed into the chute.

The Spartan crowd had already pulled away from the sidelines before Carl finished. I couldn't help but be captivated by the intensity of Carl's effort. Dead last, yet pushing himself beyond the limits of any of any of his teammates or opponents. His character exceeded his stature and athletic ability by immeasurable bounds, not unlike his mother nor, I suspect, his late father. The essence of Carl's determination, disguised to most by the pain of his efforts, should have been bottled and sold. Mere drops of the elixir would have made gods of mere mortals. Candy was Carl's only greeter as he crossed into the chute. She handed him the thirteenth place stick with an enthusiasm that is usually reserved for first place finishers. Candy's joy in spite of his having finished so poorly was not in recognition of Carl's place but in acknowledgement of her faith in him.

Coach Dillon and the Spartan coach retired to a picnic table, each having gathered their team's finishing sticks, to officially tally the score. In cross country the sticks tell the story, as no visual record could hope to contain the same tradition. There are no replays. There are no style points. There are no Russian judges jimmying their scores. There is only the undeniable reality of who grabs their sticks first. There is only the indisputable tally of points as told by the numbers the sticks carry. A small crowd of students, cheerleaders, fans and Sid Benson stood around the picnic table to watch the tally in near silence, whispering among themselves out of respect for the proceedings. Waiting for white smoke at the Vatican garners less reverence. The Spartans sticks were laid out on one side of Frank's clipboard and the Hawks on the other, so that all could see and validate the tally. The sweat stained tongue depressors, veterans of a dozen seasons, told the tale.

Spartans; 1, 4, 5, 8, 9, 10, 12.

Hawks; 2, 3, 6, 7, 11, 13.

Spartans 27, Hawks 29.

Sid Benson eyed Frank, shook his head and waddled away to his car, not belying his satisfaction that his plan was already working. Sid complimented himself on his cleverness. He would never have to make good on his offer of five scholarships for the Hawks. It was only the first meet of the year and already the Hawks had lost to the reigning state champs. What had happened to Danny was a mystery to him but not anything Sid would worry about. Danny was just a kid but good raw material. Sid would mold the clay when Danny delivered himself to his door at Illinois State to save himself from Vietnam and his brother's fate, while the rest of his teammates got shipped off to war.

The Spartans and their entourage finished a short back-slapping celebration and began to depart. The runners loaded themselves onto their bus while they grabbed at their cheerleaders' bottoms and congratulated themselves on their victory while deep down knowing they had barely squeezed by. They were vulnerable.

Danny sat on the grass with his back to a tree. Shelly was by his side, her arm around him while saying consoling words, something she was unpracticed at doing. Jill and I arrived from different directions at about the same time. I had never seen Danny so disheartened, suffering the double whammy of finally grieving for Corey while blaming himself for the loss to the Spartans and maybe the premature loss of our scholarships. His eyes betrayed the tears he had shed.

"You all right, Danny?" I asked.

"He'll be okay," Shelly answered. "He just needs some time to himself." I sat on the grass next to Danny.

"What is it? Are you hurt?" Danny shook his head no while staring at his feet and fingering Corey's ring. "Did that asshole Denton foul you?" Danny shook his head again. "Were you whipped from the workouts? I know my legs were tired." Shelly gave me a dirty look, not appreciating the inquisition. Then Danny looked up, and I could see everything I needed to know in his eyes. They were the eyes of his brother. Danny had aged a decade in the span of an afternoon.

"Good race," Danny said, barely managing a supporting grin. "It's been a long time since I've been second man on this team."

"Don't get used to it. I'm not that good."

Jill sat down in front of Danny and put her hand on his arm. Somehow she seemed to know intuitively what Shelly didn't even think to ask about.

"We can't take Corey's place," she said, "but we're here if you need us, anytime, anyplace." Shelly brushed her hand aside, as though an annoying bug.

"I can take care of him," Shelly insisted. I had doubts about that but I didn't say anything.

"Go to the team," Danny commanded of me. "Tell them I'm sorry."

The Hawks had just started jogging their mandatory cool-down along the course, and I easily caught them. The conversation was already intense.

"We're screwed already," Billy complained. "If we can't even beat the Spartans in a dual meet, how're we going to win state?"

"It was a wet dream, anyway," Shaun said, "Do any of you think Benson would fork over scholarships to this bunch? Look at us. The only one of us worth a scholarship is Danny. There's something else going on."

"And Michael," Amos corrected. "He almost won today." Amos gave me a congratulatory nod of the head.

"Yeah, but only because Danny screwed up. Maybe we would have won if he hadn't shut down," Billy surmised.

"That's unfair. Any of us moving up a place or two would have won that race. Do the numbers," I said. "Billy, fourth instead of sixth would have won us the race." Billy winced.

"Well I wasn't supposed to finish fourth but Danny was supposed to have won."

"Amos, knocking off a few would have done it." Amos nodded in agreement. He wasn't one to dispute the facts. "It's no one's fault and everyone's fault," I tried to explain. "This is a team sport. We win as a team and we lose as a team."

"Well, it still stinks." Shaun was maybe the unhappiest of the group. "For about an hour I thought maybe I wouldn't be going to 'Nam. Now, it looks like I am. Viet-fucking-Nam. It didn't do Corey much good." We ran in silence for a while. I looked around at my teammates. These were good kids, young men, who loved each other like brothers. But a dream dangled in front of them and maybe snatched away, all in a single afternoon, was enough to sour even the most devoted. I don't think they were looking forward to serving, but only a few hours before, they would have stoically accepted their duty without question, and probably done so with a bit of pride, no matter where that service took them. Now, that same service would be tainted by what could have been. If not for a few yards, a few seconds a mile, their futures could have been free of the danger of service. Now, their futures might be immersed in that same danger. Amos would accept that danger, Billy would tolerate it and Shaun would fear it. But what of Carl? The silent one, always to the rear;

the taken-for-granted friend who could always be depended on to put out his own version of super-human effort but whose toil never made the grade. The danger would consume Carl.

They had all judged Danny, their benefactor, unfairly. They wouldn't know the truth unless I told them.

"It was Corey," I finally said. "A half-mile from the finish, Corey came to Danny and he couldn't deal with it, or maybe he did deal with it. It was the first time I've seen him cry over Corey."

"What do you mean, came to him, like a ghost?" Billy asked. I didn't try to explain.

"It's not over," I said. "We've still got a chance. The top two teams in the conference go to the state prelims. If we win the rest of our meets, we'll be second in the conference and we'll go to state. We'll get the Spartans there. Those scholarships are still within reach."

"Okay, we'll do it then," Amos offered.

"Right," Billy concurred.

"Okay, we do it to them at the finals." Shaun began to get fired up. "We'll kick their asses from here to St. Louis. After all, we're the Hawks!"

Frank and Danny waited for us at the picnic table when we finished the cool-down lap. Diane, Candy and Shelly kept a discrete distance. Jill was nowhere to be found. She vanished as quickly as she had appeared, like smoke dissipating in the wind. We gathered around Frank. He looked uncharacteristically rattled.

"Gentlemen," he began with a bit of a stammer, "you made a good effort today. The Spartans are a good team. There is no shame in nearly beating the defending state champions so early in the season. It is unfortunate we met the Spartans this first meet. Do you know why?"

We answered with only questioning stares.

"Because as the season goes on, the Spartans will get no better, but we will. We will get better because there is greater purpose to what we do. Maybe the Spartans run to impress their girlfriends, maybe they run for the glory of winning another championship.

Whatever their purpose it pales to my purpose..." Frank caught himself. "...to our purpose."

That Freudian slip caught our attention no less than an atomic attack.

"Winning the state championship may bring you glory, but it will also bring you scholarships and those scholarships will free you from having to go to war. None of you will have to watch your best friend bleed to death in the surf..." Another slip. We had never seen Frank like this. "Sorry, I didn't mean that. This is not about me. This is about you."

"We all know what it means," Billy said, "and we know how hard we're going to have to work. When it comes time to beat the Spartans, we'll do it."

"I know you will. All of you will. Anything more to say?" Frank asked us. Nobody had anything more to say. It was clear that Frank was in this as deep as we were. "Okay, go long on Saturday and Sunday, maybe 10 or 15 miles, and we'll be on the track on Monday." We all nodded our agreement and began jogging back to the gym. All of us except for Carl. Carl, who hadn't said a word since the race ended, stood as though his feet were staked to the ground. We seemed to all notice at the same time.

"Corey will help us," he said, and began running back to the gym.

How could he have known?

CHAPTER 22

I didn't see Danny or the rest of the Hawks until Monday. I made a flimsy excuse about having to do some yard work instead of running with the team on Sunday. I needed some time to myself, and that meant going out to run on the county roads alone. The days were just beginning to get shorter, the mornings cooler and the nights more sleepable. Fall was coming and there wouldn't be many more weekends to revel in the heat and humidity of a summer's afternoon run. I needed that revelry no less than an addict needs his drugs. Stepping out of my house into the glaring sauna of that afternoon, anxiously anticipating the sweat-drenching run in front of me was a catharsis more effective than a hundred Hail Marys.

I headed west on an out-and-back course, deliberately choosing to run into the wind on the outbound leg in order to increase the enjoyment of the return leg. To some, the uniform grids of county roads might add boredom to the effort of the run. To me, it eliminated ambiguity. With every intersection I crossed, another mile could be confidently tallied, the total to be recorded that evening in my logbook. Runners brag about the miles they've run no differently than golfers brag about their tee-shots. Outrageous claims of the length of hero runs are met with no less skepticism than boasts about 300-yard drives. But most such claims by devoted runners are made out of enthusiasm and not for deception. Runners, if nothing else, are as honest with each other as they are with themselves.

The harvest was well underway. As I ran by, the fields alternated between bursting under the weight of thousands of bushels of feed corn and being shaved clean of their bounty, a moon-like wasteland of cornstalk stubble. Combines, nearly the size of houses, lumbered across the fields, sucking in the fruits of the farmers' labor and spewing out the kernels into a waiting truck-bed. Runners and farmers share an unspoken respect, exchanging waves and nods as they pass each other on the crowns of the county roads. They both appreciate the other's largely unobserved efforts, both knowing that, at the end of the day, they can rely only on themselves.

I have never taken a run on county roads, no matter the time of the day or the day of year, on which I failed to observe a farmer hard at work. In even the dead of winter, there are animals to be fed and repairs to be made, an endless stream of tasks to be attended to in quest of that one additional bushel per acre. And so it is with the runner. There will always be more miles to run, more effort to expend. No matter how swift your time, with more effort you could perhaps run faster, and so you run that extra mile, in quest of those fleeting seconds.

I paused at the T-intersection that marked my turn-around point and looked back at my return route. The flatness of the landscape was impressive, endless fields sliced by a ribbon of a road that undulated only because of the swelling of the tar-and-gravel in the summer heat. Its straightness was attributable to an uncompromising surveyor of a hundred years ago whose pride in his work was evident in its results. I read somewhere that the horizon lay six miles away from the height of an average man on the flatness of the ocean. That day, I had run out of the city of Barrel, beyond its horizon and into the innocence of the American heartland. On my return leg, I would leave that innocence behind and be consumed once again by Barrel.

As the miles began to tick away behind me and with the wind at my back, my rhythm coalesced and my pace quickened. My arms began that subtle side-to-side cadence that served Jim Ryun so well, and with that cadence my legs felt light and my speed increased. The wind rustling through the dry corn stalks became the cheers of the street-lining crowds who came to admire my form and whisper about my unbelievable speed. My feet barely scraped the gravel as I propelled myself forward, each step swifter than the last. Where were the timekeepers when you needed them? Surely records would fall if only my pace could be recorded. I felt the will to be whoever I wanted to be, to be wherever I wanted to be. It was my day to dream. It was a runner's freedom.

I suddenly found myself in the lead pack of the 1968 Olympic Marathon. My high altitude training of so many years gave me advantage in the thin air of Mexico City over my sea-level brethren. As we passed 24 miles, the stadium came into view. The first runner through marathon tunnel and across the finish line would live forever in the Olympic annals. They may break your records and they may steal your titles but they can never take away your medals. The lead pack thinned as we began our grueling kick toward Olympic Stadium. The inspiring cheers of the crowd were deafening. I moved deftly to the front of the pack and soon my only challenger was Abebe Bikila, back to vie for a third marathon gold medal. His bare feet were nearly noiseless as they pushed the ground behind him. With effort that I mined from years of training, I stayed on his shoulder. We didn't dare look at each other out of fear of revealing how close we were to giving in to the other's intensity. In some ways, we didn't need to, as we sensed each other's effort through the ether.

We entered marathon tunnel racing stride for stride and burst into the blinding lights of the stadium. Only 400 meters, one lap around the track, separated one of us from an Olympic victory. Abebe pulled ahead as we rounded the first turn. The deafening noise of the crowd masked my footsteps from his notice as I caught him at 300 meters and gained a step and then another. My legs turned over at a phenomenal pace, the air whipped by so quickly it tore tears from my eyes. The finish tape lay only meters ahead, beckoning me, teasing me with victory.

Suddenly, the voices of the cheering crowd sharpened into a shrill monotone that hurt my ears. Then, there were no voices; only the baying of a horn.

A horn? I turned my head to look behind. The stadium diffused from my mind into the stubble of a cornfield. The Tartan track morphed into the tar and gravel of the county road. Abebe Bikila vanished back into my imagination. Instead, an ancient Ford station wagon full of children, a tired mother at the wheel, bleated its horn at me. I moved to the side of the road to let it pass, jolted back to the afternoon's reality. A little girl in the back seat stuck her tongue out at me, as though mocking my flight of fantasy, for it was only in the theater of an afternoon's run on the back roads leading into Barrel that I would ever share the company of Abebe Bikila, let alone nearly defeat him for Olympic gold. Perhaps I would finish that race some other time, I thought, as I resumed my run toward Barrel.

Or would I? The time for frivolity seemed to be rapidly passing and with it, innocence was slipping away.

As I slowed my pace approaching the Barrel city limits, I realized that everything was now different. Only a few weeks ago, I ran because it fulfilled some inner need. I enjoyed outracing my imagined opponents as well as beating the real ones. But now there was unimaginable purpose to my training. With each second I improved, with each second my teammates grew swifter, the promise of the scholarships came a step closer. And with those scholarships came the priceless deferments that made service to our country and Vietnam another boy's duty. This was now very serious business.

A truck overloaded with the afternoon's harvest rumbled by on a crossroad. A weathered ancient farmer was at the helm. A boy, perhaps 11 or 12 years old, maybe his grandson, gazed out the passenger side window and waved at me. I returned his wave as the truck jolted over a pothole, shaking loose handfuls of corn onto the roadbed. I bent over to pick up a few kernels. It suddenly struck me. The sacrifices in war of my friends and my friends' brothers began to make sense. Young men are called to duty by their country to protect the children and the elders who provide the bounty that makes this country the great place it is. The system relies on there being an unlimited supply of those willing to serve, who accept their obligations, so that the children can grow to be men, the old can live out their years, and the bounty can be harvested. And it is the children and the elders and the bounty that make this country great. Without the sacrifices of those who serve, we are without the children, the elders and the bounty.

I ran by Holden Park on my way through town. Children were playing hide-and-seek among the monuments as though they were trees in the forest, testing the boundaries of what to them were new and exciting discoveries. I could not argue against the worthiness of protecting these unknowing children, these innocents, from whatever threatened them. But what threat were they being protected from in Vietnam? Hitler and Hirohito threatened our very way of life. Had I been of age, I would have gladly served in World War II. But how do illiterate peasants scratching out a meager existence in the rice paddies of Vietnam present a threat to us? They certainly don't threaten me, so why should I risk my life to kill them?

Train hard. Run hard. Race hard. Pray that Shaun and Billy, the Gemini Hawks, have the race of their lives. Pray that Danny leads us to victory. Pray that someone else fights the endless, meaningless battles in our places.

CHAPTER 23

The *Barrel Gazette*, the town's only publication, was never in danger of winning a Pulitzer Prize. At best, the *Gazette* reprinted the newswire stories without introducing many new errors. At worst the paper glorified war and so inspired the naïve and uninformed to become the fodder that wars require.

In many ways, the *Barrel Gazette* was competing way out of its league. Any news of national or international importance was better heard about on television or read about in the *Chicago Tribune*, and we got the *Trib* only a day late. What the *Gazette* did excel at was small-town news. It chronicled the day-to-day comings and goings that were so important to the citizens of Barrel and so painfully unimportant to anyone else. Birth announcements and obituaries, shop openings and bankruptcies, high school graduations and parole hearings, the *Gazette* told the story of the cycle of life in Barrel.

The *Gazette* also covered high school sports with the enthusiasm of a cub reporter on his first assignment. If there was anything to be passionate about in Barrel, Illinois it was high school sports. A good high school athlete in Barrel appeared in the *Gazette* more often than the President. I doubt the *New York Times* has ever devoted 10 column inches to a high school cross country meet, but that's just what the *Gazette* did every week. It didn't hurt that the sports and grain futures editor (most did double duty) was one of Frank's former runners.

By the time we got to school on Monday morning, Frank had already posted Saturday's *Gazette* articles on Barrel High's wins and losses on the sports bulletin board. Football had miraculously won and water polo had also uncharacteristically squeaked out a victory. Cross country had sadly lost. The tales were in the headlines.

"Hawks Harriers Season Opener Spoiled by Spartans." Sometimes the truth hurt. There was no disputing ink on paper. If it appears in the *Gazette* it must be true.

The Hawks were gathered around the bulletin board when I arrived.

"Hey, they don't say much about me," Billy complained.

"We lost, dummy," Shaun countered. "Maybe you don't want to be mentioned too much."

"Hey, this is how my new squeezes find me. Better by a whole lot than the personals."

"Maybe you should start being a bit more discriminating."

"Why?"

"In Hollywood, they say there's no such thing as bad publicity," Shelly offered, her arms wrapped around Danny's.

"Right, I guess that's what axe murderers say on the way to the electric chair," Danny said. Amos was scrutinizing the article.

"I don't know if I like being referred to as the 'stalwart Amos Danforth.'"

"Why not?" Shelly asked.

"Don't know what it means."

Carl stood on his toes to read the article. His finger traced every line, pausing at the names of his teammates. His expression telegraphed his disappointment.

"Doesn't mention me," he said, but no one heard.

"I know what tomorrow's headline is going to say," Danny offered. "'Hawks Get Asses Kicked in Workout!' It's going to be a tough one. The whole week's going to be tough." Friday's meet would be against the Tolono Tigers. They were an alright team but nothing we couldn't handle, so we all expected Coach Dillon to work us hard right through the meet. We would have been happy to be surprised with an easy week but we weren't holding our breaths.

Our expectations were met in spades. We were on the track Monday so late they had to turn on the stadium lights for us to finish the workout. Tuesday, we ran the hill 15 times. Wednesday, it was back on the track, four sets of mile ladders. Thursday, it was out on the roads for a 20-miler. Coach Dillon was ruthless. The pace for every quarter was faster than the last. Mile repeats were doled out like candy on Halloween. Go-arounds were as commonplace as dandelions in the grass. Frank went hoarse yelling times across the track. He was the last out of the locker room every evening, massaging our sore muscles, prepping the whirlpool to just the right temperature, saying encouraging words when our spirits were down. Frank even started posting workouts for us to do in the morning. No more of that take-it-easy-for-the-morning-run-because-it-doesn't-really-mean-anything routine. Now, every step was meaningful.

Classes weren't getting any easier either. Barrel High might not have been much to look at but it tried to be serious about education, and that meant going to class and paying attention. Principal Milo's claim to fame came from disbanding the notorious ATS, the Athlete's Testing Society. There was a good reason why most athletes, and all football players, used to take their hard classes late in the day. That way, tests and answers from first and second period classes could be in the hands of athletes hours before they walked into the exam room, compliments of the ATS. The truth be told, most teachers turned a blind eye to the practice and some were known to have left copies of exams in unlocked drawers just to make it convenient for the ATS. Before the intrepid and sometimes anal investigations of Principal Milo, there had never been an athlete academically ineligible at Barrel High School. After the demise of the ATS, athletes were suddenly on their own.

The cross country team did its best to take care of its own, and Mabel's was the place we did it. Shelly and Candy were godsends. Hardly a school night went by that they didn't set up shop in the corner booth at Mabel's Diner to tutor the Hawks over the rough spots in their classes. Trust me, there were a lot of rough spots. Although the Hawks were dedicated runners and the best friends a boy could ask for, they were in no danger of winning a Nobel Prize. Not only were Shelly and Candy godsends for the cross country team, they weren't very discriminating in choosing their clientele and so were godsends to all of Barrel High's athletes. The wayward water polo player, the hopelessly lost basketball forward and the occasional tight end would sheepishly present himself to the girls and embarrassingly mumble his request for help. Ask and ye shall receive, and receive they did. Glory hallelujah!

The Thursday night before the Tolono Tiger meet was not that unusual for a Thursday night at Mabel's. Candy and Shelly were well into their second hour of explaining the intricacies of algebra to Carl, much to their growing frustration. Amos, Billy and Shaun were nursing the remains of burgers and fries in the next booth, their occasional raucous laughter echoing through the diner in response to one of Billy's doubtfully true but always humorous stories of sexual conquest. Danny and I sat at a third booth. Candy's patient but tense voice wafted toward our booth between the laughter of our teammates.

"No, Carl, sweetie, you add 'x' to each side."

"X?"

"Yes, honey, 'x.' You add 'x' to each side."

"Where does 'x' come from?"

"It's just there, Carl, honey. If you add it to each side, nothing changes since the equation's still balanced."

"Then why do it if nothing changes?" I had to smile. Carl may not be at the top of the class, but he did have a knack for stating the obvious with clarity. Danny caught my smile and the reason why.

"You better hope Candy is able to perform miracles," he advised.

"Why is that?"

"Because if Carl doesn't pass algebra, then he's not eligible to run and we're down to five men."

"Carl's a nice guy," I replied, "but it's not as though we've been counting on him to lead us to victory." Danny leaned over as though ready to divulge a secret.

"If one of us twists an ankle and can't run, Carl's suddenly our fifth man. Carl not passing algebra could mean the difference between our spending the next four years at Illinois State or sitting in the bottom of foxhole in Vietnam trying not to get our asses shot off." Suddenly Candy's tutoring skills took on added importance. I twisted around to check on her progress.

"I wonder if she needs any help?" Danny, sensing the drama he'd created, tried to change the subject.

"Ready for the Tigers?" he asked.

"Ready as ready is," I replied. "How about you?"

"A little bit sore, but otherwise ready, willing and able," Danny said, sounding a bit unconvincing. The image of Danny's emotional collapse during the race against the Spartans flashed through my mind.

"I'm sure you're physically ready," I cautiously ventured. "What about mentally?" Danny gave me a curious look. "We need to win this meet more than we've ever needed to win before. If you run well, the team runs well. You don't run well and we're screwed. We can't survive another loss." Danny gave me a small smile.

"Don't worry. The woods won't be haunted in Tolono," Danny said. "I'll be okay."

"Were they haunted last week?"

"Only in my mind, but I'm okay now." Danny absentmindedly fingered Corey's ring as he spoke. The white skin that showed from under the ring contrasted with the deep tan of his hands, a product of countless hours of training under the merciless sun on the county roads.

"You're still wearing it," I said.

"What?"

"His ring. You're still wearing his ring." Danny looked at his hand as though for the first time, carefully inspecting the ring. He took it off, as if to place the ring in his pocket and then, on second thought, put it back on his finger. "You want to talk about it?" I asked.

"Nothing much to talk about."

"Are you sure? Nobody's going to judge you evil if you decide to get on with your life."

"Get on with my life?"

"Danny, he's not coming back. His name's already on a plaque in Holden Park. You have to move on."

"He's never left me," Danny said softly.

"Maybe he needs to."

"Maybe."

"Well, I'm here when you want to talk."

"Wish I could talk to her," Danny said looking at Shelly. "I can't talk to my folks, that's for damn sure, and Shelly, well, we just want such different things. She has this fairy-tale image of what life, our lives, are going to be like. She just refuses to face reality. All she sees is the pony. I can't get her to see the horseshit too."

"Is that such a bad thing?" I asked.

"I wish she could be more like…" Danny didn't finish the thought.

"Like Jill?" I asked. Danny gave me smile.

"Like I want her to be."

"And what do you want, Danny?"

"Not much."

"Not even to be rich and famous?" Danny gave me another smile.

"I want to do the right thing."

"And what is that?"

"I wish I knew. I'd ask my parents but they aren't much help, never really have been."

"How are your parents, and Hannah? I haven't seen them since the funeral." Danny let out a sigh.

"Hannah asks when Corey is coming home almost every day. My mother can't get through two sentences without crying. My father sits and stares at Corey's service picture for hours on end, and then rags on me about following in his footsteps. Family honor and all."

"He knows about the scholarships?" I asked.

"He's in denial, but hoping for the best."

"The best?"

"That I'll come to my senses and enlist, and make him as proud of me as Corey did."

"Is that the best for you or the best for him?"

"I owe something to him, don't I? He's my father."

"That's not what I asked." Danny looked at his teammates and then looked at me.

"I don't know what's best for me, but I know if I don't start winning some races, it won't be the best for them and it won't be the best for you." The waitress came by with an "anything else" look on her face. Danny politely waved her off. Shelly, looking up, gave us both her sweet smile and went back to her unenviable task of helping Candy tutor Carl.

"You know," I finally said, "it's not only your responsibility."

"I thought you just said it was my responsibility," Danny shot back.

"It's not but it is. I guess it's all our responsibility. Like Frank says, we're masters of our own fate."

"Michael, I know if I screw up we're not going to win state. I won't let that happen. I won't have my teammates coming home from friggin' Vietnam in body bags. I won't have it be my fault."

"Now you're beginning to sound like Frank," I accused him.

"I could think of worse people to sound like." The clap of closing books announced that Shelly and Candy had finished with, or given up on, Carl. Candy and Carl gave us a wave and, hand in unlikely hand, started toward the door. Shelly scooted into our booth, cuddling up next to Danny.

"That was torture," she said. "I don't think he'll ever pass algebra." Remembering our conversation, I was about to let Shelly know what the stakes were but before I could get the words out, Danny waved me off.

"He's a good kid," Danny quickly said. "We should all have his character."

"Yes, we should have his character," Shelly concluded, "but maybe we all could use a few more brain cells, too." I couldn't disagree with either Shelly or Danny. As long as Carl had Candy to look out for him, he would find his way in the world; not easily but he would find his way. Being a member of a team is important. Carl and Candy managed to team up in some inexplicable way. There had to be a reason why these two found each other. It just couldn't be a random act. I watched the unlikely pair through Mabel's large windows as they sauntered away into the darkness of the scalloped lit sidewalk. She was six inches taller, 50 IQ points smarter and unfathomably more worldly than him. I doubted God's existence more often than I should have in those days, but I had to assume He had a plan for these two. It turns out I was right.

Shelly and Danny were a different story. I was pretty sure God didn't have a plan for them other than wishing the two of them good luck in their separate lives. Just as Carl and Candy were an unlikely pair, so were Shelly and Danny. She was content to dispense with reality, plan for a life that only the virtuous deserved and the lucky received, and leave the worrying to others. On the other hand Danny was discontent with most things, not out of vindictiveness but because he knew there had to be a better way. Danny was the one who worried for the likes of Shelly. He carried the world on his shoulders. All Shelly had on her shoulders was a strap for a purse full of cosmetics. If Danny and Shelly ever walked down the aisle, it might be me who raises his hand when the preacher asks, "Is there anyone present who knows why these two should not be joined in holy matrimony?"

I wasn't sure Shelly liked me a whole lot. I can't think of more than a dozen words she ever said to me out of anything other than necessity. She had a way of creating awkward silences, and Danny filled this one by fingering Corey's ring.

Danny was living in a world of conflict. He was nearly engaged to a girl who I'm not sure he did more than tolerate. He was respectful of a father who was not deserving of his devotion. He was honor-bound to follow a family tradition that cost him his brother and would put him in harm's way. If only the war in Vietnam had been as virtuous as those his father and uncles had fought in, Corey's death would have reinforced Danny's sense of duty instead of making him question it. To me, the solution was obvious but unspoken, like the elephant sitting at the dining room table that everyone ignores as they chit-chat about the weather. Somebody had to broach the topic.

"Why don't you just tell your father you don't want to enlist?" I asked naively. Danny clearly didn't appreciate the question, particularly with Shelly there.

"I thought you already told him," Shelly quickly said. Danny stopped twisting Corey's ring.

"How do you tell your father that you reject the very fiber of his being?" Danny asked. "You have to understand my family. We're mostly just a random collection of people who happen to share relatives. There's only one thing that any male member of my family has in common with any other male member."

"And that is?"

"Service. We serve. We answer the call to duty and we serve our country. There may not be much you can say about the O'Neals. We won't win Nobel Prizes and we won't cure cancer, but you can depend on us to answer the call to duty."

"That sounds a bit dramatic."

"Does it? You've seen the shrine in my living room. If I don't enlist the way Corey enlisted, my father will die of a broken heart."

"Is that worth your dying instead?" I asked. Danny looked at me but didn't say anything. Shelly took his hand in hers.

"You promised, Danny. You're not enlisting, right?" she almost pleaded. Danny didn't answer right away.

"Danny?" Shelly was suddenly frightened, her seemingly perfect plan in the balance. Danny stopped fingering his ring and put his arm around Shelly.

"The Hawks are winning state," he finally said. "Nothing will prevent that."

CHAPTER 24

The meet against the Tolono Tigers was an away event, a 30-mile drive across the same county roads we trained on. The Hawks got out of class early and met Coach Dillon in front of the gym to load themselves into his station wagon. Everything is new at one time or another, and so I have to assume that there must have been a time when Frank's station wagon sat gleaming in a dealer's showroom. That was long ago, forgotten to most, and likely unbelievable to anyone who gazed on Frank's primitive means of transportation. Coach Dillon's 1953 Chevy wagon had once been painted white, but that sheen had long since given way to patches of primer or simply been worn away by age, leaving rusty splotches behind. The floorboards were layered with cardboard to cover the holes that would otherwise reveal the passing roadbed or, worse, admit the muddy splashings from the puddles that dot county roads. The headliner had long since disappeared and so only a thin sheet of metal separated the occupants of Frank's station wagon from the heat of summer and cold of the winter. Only two gears of the manual three-on-the-tree transmission worked. Considerable skill was required to navigate the shift from first-to-third, but most Hawk runners mastered the technique before graduation.

In spite of its lackluster looks and questionable safety, Frank's station wagon was as endeared to the Hawks as a live mascot would have been. That automobile was the continuity that bound Frank's teams together across the years and marked the seasons no less than the calendar. A new team member was only an initiate until his first road trip in Frank's station wagon. Track seasons could not officially begin until Frank dragged the track with his station wagon.

Barrel High's running track was fashioned of rocky silt dug out of the widening of the Illinois River. Every spring, an endless supply of rocks emerged on the surface of the track from hidden depths, like mushrooms sprouting on a wooded trail. And every spring, the team walked the track and filled wheelbarrow after wheelbarrow with the rocks that floated to the surface. Most were the size of marbles and some the size of baseballs. Occasionally we came upon a boulder that peeked up through the dirt like the tip of an iceberg. We would dig around it to reveal an enormity that required us to summon Amos so that his Herculean strength could dispatch the boulder into a wheelbarrow. Our preliminary tasks done, Frank would then drag the track.

I'll never forget the sight of Coach Dillon circling the track endlessly in his station wagon, leveling its surface and skimming off the remaining protruding rocks. With Coach Dillon at the helm, the Chevy trailed a section of a chain link fence tied to its bumper and weighed down by barrels of rocks. Clouds of dust billowed behind him as the fence scraped clean and leveled the track. After a few circuits around the track, the entire stadium was hidden in a dusty haze. Only the choppy rumbling of the Chevy's engine emanating from somewhere inside the clouds gave notice of Frank pursuing his ritualistic task.

The Hawks, Frank and Diane sealed themselves into the station wagon and set out for Tolono. Diane and Danny sat in the front seat with Frank at the wheel. Amos, Billy and I crammed ourselves into the small backseat while Carl and Shaun squeezed themselves into the luggage space in the rear. The dust that oncoming cars raised from the tar and gravel road allowed us to open the windows by only infinitesimal cracks, depriving us of the coolness of rushing air and enabling the sheet metal ceiling to elevate the inside temperature to oven-like proportions. We sweated no less than during an afternoon-long interval workout.

"Open a window up there," Shaun pleaded, "its hot and it stinks back here, and I think it's Carl." Billy twisted in his seat and sniffed at Carl.

"Yeah, it's Carl," he confirmed. "What do you wash with, piss?" Carl was stoic under the assault.

"This is my natural smell," Carl finally defended himself.

"Ever smell a goat?" Amos, our farming authority, asked. "That's a natural smell too, but I wouldn't want to bottle it."

"Boys, be nice," Diane refereed. Our heads grazed the ceiling as the station wagon nearly became airborne navigating the undulating road.

"What can you tell us about the Tigers, Coach?" I asked, trying to change the subject.

"The Tigers are a good team," Frank began. "They won the conference five or so years ago, but their coach retired and they've haven't been as good since. But don't let that make you too confident. They're still a darn good team."

"What about Eddie McCarthy?" Danny asked.

"He's a keeper," Coach Dillon answered. "Ran a 14:50 three mile at an all-comers' meet this summer. They've got three other runners under 15:20, but they really don't have depth beyond that."

Neither do we, I thought.

The city of Tolono was supposed to have been a temporary assembly of cheap squalid buildings and Quonset huts to house the workforce that built the nearby levees during the Depression. Instead, Tolono became a permanent assembly of cheap squalid buildings and Quonset huts that far outlived their temporary status. Given that Tolono was surrounded by thousands of acres of picturesque woods, the contrast was stark. You might have thought the townspeople would have burned the city to the ground just to eliminate the eyesore. It was the sort of place that driving through town made you want to take a shower.

When we finally arrived at Tolono High School we were greeted by a horrendously ugly edifice that gave testimony to the fact that even unimaginative architects can make good livings. The Tigers' home course was equally as unimaginative. With thousands of acres of woods surrounding the city, their three-mile cross country course was an out-and-back affair on a straight-as-an-arrow paved road starting and finishing in the faculty parking lot. "We used to have a course through the woods," their coach explained, "but our runners kept on getting lost." So much for the myth that runners are deep thinkers. The course did present one challenge: The quarter mile leading into the turn-around-point was a steep hill.

The Hawks emptied out of Frank's station wagon and began stretching. It would be a sparsely attended meet. The Tolono Tigers couldn't even attract a crowd at their own high school. We had that much in common.

"This place makes me grateful to live in Barrel," Shaun commented, looking around at the bleak surroundings.

"Appearances can be deceiving," Amos said. "For all we know, there's a Disneyland on the other side of town."

"Disneyland?" Shaun asked.

"I've always wanted to go."

"Yeah," Billy concluded, "there's got to be something good about this place. I can't imagine Barrel being better than anyplace else."

As we left to jog the course, a familiar car pulled into the parking place. The car wasn't familiar because I recognized the model or year. It was its strange appearance that made it familiar. The car was terribly lopsided, as though the tires were flat on the driver's side and over-inflated on the passenger side. The door groaned opened, and the enormous bulk of Coach Sid Benson emerged. As he extricated himself from the confines of his car, the driver side popped up like a cork released from the bottom of a swimming pool. Coach Benson, cigar firmly planted in the side of his mouth, waddled slowly across the parking lot to where Frank was in conversation with the Tolono coach.

"I happened to be in the neighborhood," Sid explained.

"Always good to see you, Sid," Frank greeted him, wondering what the real reason was Coach Benson had driven all the way to Tolono.

"If your guys don't win this meet, Frank, you can forget about state." Sid was never one to mince works.

"I'm aware of that."

"We'll talk later," and with that Sid took a seat on a nearby bench to watch the proceedings. He pulled a rolled newspaper from his back pocket and began reading.

The meet was a test for us, a test of confidence. We were capable of beating the Tigers, but did we have the heart to be champions or were we just pretenders? The Tigers were good, not great, but good. Champions should be able to beat them by the power of their will alone, if they are indeed champions.

As we finished our warm-ups, Shelly and Candy arrived, providing what I thought would be our only fans. They waved as we lined up at the start-finish line, alternating Tiger-Hawk-Tiger-Hawk. We were all unusually docile, particularly Danny. We shook each other's hands, wishing the other team well while Danny just stared back at the parking lot, fingering Corey's ring as though he were rubbing a genie's lamp.

"You ready for this?" I whispered to Danny. He didn't answer, still staring back at the parking lot. I followed his stare, and then it struck me.

"Maybe she's not coming," I said. Just then, a beat-up old Ford turned into the parking lot and screeched to a halt. Jill jumped out and began running toward the small crowd at the starting line. Danny turned to the course.

"I'm ready now," he said. The Tolono coach, starting pistol in hand, brought us to attention.

"This isn't a hard course, boys," he said, "and it's not rocket science. I pull the trigger, the gun makes a noise and you run straight ahead. When you get to the top of the hill, you turn around and run back here as fast as you can. Don't take any turns, don't think too hard." I think he was talking more to his own runners than to the Hawks. "You think too hard, and you'll screw up. Everyone got it?" We all nodded.

"Easy course," Carl said. The boy didn't say much but when he did, he was usually right.

"Anything more to add, Coach Dillon?" Frank waved him off as he walked towards his car to drive to the mile-marker. As though a second thought, he pointed at Jill, inviting her along. She bounded after him.

"Okay, boys," the Tolono coach said raising the starting pistol, "have a good race." He pulled the trigger of the starting pistol and we were off.

The Tolono Tigers were fast off the line. Eddie McCarthy and three teammates quickly took the lead. They must have covered the first quarter-mile in 65 seconds. It was a pace we knew they couldn't keep up so we held back, with Danny leading a cluster of the Hawks peppered with the rest of the Tigers.

"What the hell are they doing?" Shaun asked between breaths.

"Don't go crazy. They'll come back to us," Billy said.

Eddie McCarthy and the three Tigers opened a gap, a big gap. We began getting nervous. They weren't supposed to be that good. Deep down we knew that they would come back to us but we lacked the confidence that came with past success. We probably would have done something stupid like trying to close the gap too early had Danny not kept a reasonable pace. If Danny wasn't worried then maybe we shouldn't be worried, but I was. We held back for a while, allowing the gap to grow.

"Danny, shouldn't we go after them?" I asked. Danny thought for a brief moment, nodded his head and picked up the pace a bit. Our pack began to string out as the chase group formed. I was at Danny's heels with two Tigers. Shaun and Billy were close behind. Amos and Carl were running in a cluster with the last two Tigers. By the time we covered the first half-mile, Eddie McCarthy and his teammates were a good 50 yards ahead of our chase group.

"2:22, 2:23, 2:25," the assistant Tolono coach called out as Danny and I passed the half-mile marker. We were running a fast pace, probably too fast, so what were Eddie McCarthy and the Tigers thinking? They must have run the first half-mile in 2:15. We were already running a 14:30 pace and I didn't feel like picking it up by much, but I could tell Danny was beginning to get antsy. His cadence quickened. The two Tigers and I went with Danny. This was beginning to get serious very early, too early. I took a glance behind me. Billy and Shaun were trailing our group, but not by a lot.

The flatness of the course made the distance go quickly. There were no turns to slow the pace and no jostling on a narrow path. The first mile marker appeared far too soon. Coach Dillon and Jill were standing a few yards beyond by the station wagon with Diane at the wheel. Eddie McCarthy was lengthening his lead while his teammates strung out behind him, but they were still way in front of us.

"4:52, 4:53, 4:54..." the timer called out as we passed. That was a good pace and Eddie McCarthy and the Tigers were still way ahead head of us. Crap.

"4:39," Jill called out. "He ran 4:39!" Eddie McCarthy had run the first mile in four minutes and thirty-nine seconds and wasn't slowing down. I glanced at Danny.

"He'll come back to us," Danny said without confidence as he picked up the pace another notch. I latched myself onto Danny and went with him as we separated ourselves from the rest of the Hawks pack, and pursued Eddie McCarthy and his teammates. What was supposed to be a walk in the park was rapidly turning into a nightmare. If we lost to the Tigers, the season would be over for us. Goodbye scholarships, hello Vietnam.

In another quarter-mile, Danny and I were at the base of the hill, just catching the small pack of Tigers behind Eddie McCarthy. Danny looked behind him to gauge where his teammates were. Billy and Shaun were still entangled with a cluster of Tigers. Danny looked ahead. Eddie McCarthy was already deep into his climb to the turn-around.

"I've had enough of this shit," Danny mumbled, and with a determination that I had yet to see in Danny, he began accelerating up the hill. The suddenness of the change in his pace startled me, but only for a moment, as I mentally hooked myself onto him and tried to keep contact.

Had a film crew been present that day, Danny's display of running prowess would have become standard viewing for cross country coaches and novice runners for decades to come. His acceleration up the hill in pursuit of Eddie McCarthy can only be described as perfection in motion. The rhythm of his gait, his lean into the slope, the height of his knees. There wasn't a wasted effort on the part of a single sinew. He was driven by a purpose, by a determination that seamlessly transmitted his sheer will to succeed through his nervous system to the muscles that drove him up the hill. I subconsciously emulated his form, bringing in my flailing elbows, raising my knees in an exaggerated fashion, and the speed came to me as well.

The distance between Danny and Eddie McCarthy rapidly closed. They were dead even at the top of the hill and in a few steps after the turn-around Danny took the lead. For any other runner, the pace Danny sustained down the hill would have been called reckless. For Danny, the pace seemed natural. Eddie, already suffering from his fast opening mile, tried to keep in contact with Danny but was rapidly falling behind. When Eddie glanced behind him to see where I was, I knew he was through. Nobody looks behind if he's gunning for first place. He was running for second place. It would just be a matter of time before I caught him.

One advantage of an out-and-back course is that after you start running back from the turn-around-point, you can view the progress of the race behind you. Billy and Shaun had broken from their opponents and were confidently working their way up the hill. They looked determined, the sweat of their efforts glistening in the afternoon sun. They played off each other like Gemini twins, each using the effort of his partner as a source of power. Their Tiger opponents, already 20 yards behind, were suffering, and I wasn't surprised. The Tigers weren't good enough to sustain their opening pace and now they were paying the inevitable penalty. They flew too close to the sun and their waxed wings melted.

What did surprise me was what was happening with Carl and Amos. The trailing pack of two Tigers and Amos were methodically stepping up the hill, Amos remaining unbelievably vertical as he moved up the incline, his pace not a second different than on the flat. Carl, trailing and last up to the base of the hill, suddenly burst through the rear pack, his stubby legs turning over at a blurring rate. He built a lead of 30 yards on the pack before the effort of his enthusiasm took its toll. The pack caught Carl at the crest of the hill and passed him on the downhill.

The outcome of the race was decided by the time we were all back on the flat of the return leg. Danny only extended his lead as he powered toward the finish line, finishing a comfortable first in an outstanding 14:29. I was 10 seconds behind. Eddie McCarthy was caught by Billy just yards before the chute. Shaun barely missed doing the same. Amos split the Tiger pack in half, cementing our 19-36 victory. Even Carl beat out the last Tiger.

After the disappointment of our loss to the Spartans, beating the Tigers and Eddie McCarthy was a much needed morale booster. We congratulated each other on our cool-down run, confident that we were well on the road to the state championship. With one victory, we went from the despair of likely losing our scholarships to the undeserved optimism of becoming state champions and winning haven from the war in Vietnam.

Sid waved a smiling Frank over to join him on the bench, the prospect of raising his enormous mass apparently too great an effort to come to Frank. Coach Dillon sat by his one-time almost-mentor.

"Looks like we're on our way," Frank said, obviously proud and no doubt relieved by his team's victory.

"This race doesn't mean crap," Sid spat. "All you've shown is you can beat a second-rate team. With a performance like that, you won't raise a bead of sweat on the Spartans."

"This was a good effort, Sid," Frank countered. "You can't take that away from the boys." Sid removed the cigar from his mouth and pointed at the Hawks.

"It's depth that will win state and you don't have depth. You don't have a fifth and sixth man that can do the job," Sid began analyzing, "and without them, you'll never win state." Coach Dillon began to object but Sid waved him off. "Danny and that Michael character, they'll probably come through. Shaun and Billy, I wouldn't call them superstars, but they can be depended on. The farmer and the retard; well, they're going to kill you."

"Their names are Amos and Carl." Coach Dillon was annoyed.

"Whatever. One of them has got to come through. You've got to have a fifth man to displace the Spartans' fifth man, otherwise they've got you." Sid pulled a small notepad out of his rear pocket and began flipping through the pages until he found his scratchings. "I've done all the scenarios, Frank. The Spartans' third and fourth men are simply too strong. You're not going to win unless your fifth man finishes in front of the Spartans' fifth man." Frank took the notepad and scrutinized Sid's analysis. He wanted to find fault with it but couldn't. The Hawks' performance against the Tolono Tigers was testimony to its accuracy. Yes, the Hawks beat the Tigers in the dual meet, but they might have lost to them in a race with a dozen other teams. You can win a dual meet with only three or four good runners. To win the big meets, to win state, you needed depth and the Hawks didn't have depth.

"Shaun and Billy are getting better. The state meet is still weeks away. They'll be five places better than you think," Frank rationalized.

"Get real, Frank. You think the Spartans aren't training too? They're as motivated as you are." Frank gave Sid back his notepad.

"Why do you say that?"

"Say what?"

"That the Spartans are as motivated as we are."

Sid put the notepad back in his pocket and the cigar back in his mouth. With no small effort, he lifted his girth off the bench.

"Because, Frank, I offered them the same deal. Four scholarships if they win the state championship."

"You did what?"

"Don't get crazy on me, Frank. This is business. I can't hold those scholarships out to your guys without covering my bets. The Spartans are the better team, they'll win and I'll get them with those scholarships."

"You said four scholarships for Spartans. The Hawks are running for five."

"The last one's for Danny. Either way, I'm going to have him." Frank stood up and put his hand on Coach Benson's shoulder.

"We need six scholarships, Sid."

"I don't have six to give you. I've only got five." It hurt Sid to lie but he was in too deep to change his position.

"What if I pay for one of the scholarships myself? Will you take all the Hawks on the team and get them accepted to Illinois State?" Sid guffawed at the suggestion.

"Do you think I make up the rules myself? Or that I'm screwing the dean's wife? Quit trying to save the world."

"You know how to make these things happen. I know that, Sid." Coach Benson chewed on his cigar.

"I'll think about it, Frank, but don't get your hopes up."

Frank nodded and began walking away. "One more thing, Frank," Sid called after him. "Remember, the state finals will be at Pioneer Park. Good luck!"

Frank sat down on the bench as the memories came flooding back. Pioneer Park. It was 1942 again. The Illinois State Cross Country Championships. Frank was a senior in high school and standing at the starting line in Pioneer Park waiting for the race to begin. Standing at his side was his best friend, Pete Lorenzo. They joked about the half-mile-long hill at the end of the course, the hill that might spell the difference between their becoming champions or going home as commoners. That hill would be their last running steps as Hawks for they had already promised each other to enlist, to answer the call of duty, in the days after the race. The championship race hadn't been held in Pioneer Park for 25 years. Now it would be again. The Hawks were returning to Pioneer Park and to the finish hill to battle for the state championship. But this time the stakes were greater than ever. It would be a race for survival. Win the state championship and receive haven, lose and find yourself in a foxhole in Vietnam.

Frank shook his head into the present, leaned on his cane and began walking toward Diane. He failed to notice Carl, who had stood silently within earshot of his conversation with Sid Benson.

"Only five scholarships," Carl said to no one but himself.

CHAPTER 25

Danny and I nursed milkshakes at Mabel's, replaying and analyzing the afternoon's race against the Tigers. Shelly was otherwise occupied, giving Danny a rare and appreciated Friday night out with the boys. We gazed out the picture window that framed our booth as we talked. Mabel's was situated on Barrel's main throughway. It was difficult to go anywhere in Barrel without passing by the picture windows that lined Mabel's façade. Friends, acquaintances and strangers passed by in the evening's darkness as Danny and I talked.

"He's good," Danny said of Eddie McCarthy. "It was only his running a stupid race that let us beat him."

"Do you think he's a threat to win state?" I asked.

"No more than Denton Bentley," Danny surmised, not forgetting his Spartan nemesis. A convertible filled with drunken high school boys drove by. A bare ass mooned pedestrians as it passed. Danny smiled as he returned a wave from one of its inebriated occupants. I knew Danny was deep in thought. He was fingering Corey's ring, a signal no less obvious than a flare.

"Nice night," I ventured.

"Yeah, it is."

"It'll start turning cold soon."

"Probably."

I wasn't getting very far. A small cluster of junior high school girls noisily passed by. A hand-holding pair of grandparents crossed in the other direction. Danny seemed intent on their progress.

"We got Corey's duffle-bag a couple of days ago," Danny finally offered. "I guess it's standard procedure, sending the family the personal effects." Danny turned to me. "It was mostly uniforms, a couple of paperback books, a camera, his shaving kit..." Danny turned back to the window and continued gazing. "I wonder why the United States Marine Corps thought we'd want Corey's shaving kit, used razor blades and all? And now that we've got it, we can't throw it out, but, Jesus Christ, a shaving kit? What do we do...?" Danny didn't finish the sentence.

"What did your folks do?"

"Mom cried. Hannah still thinks Corey's coming home. Dad sent his uniforms to the cleaners. If you're going to make a shrine out of them, I guess they ought to be pressed." Danny reached into a pocket of his letterman sweater and pulled out a Kodak envelope. He tossed it across the table to me. "There was film in the camera."

I never personally knew or met Corey. To me, he was a beloved memory of Danny, his family and friends. He was no closer to me than a portrait hanging in the O'Neals' living room wall or one of the countless etchings on the plaques in Holden Park. He was as inanimate as a wooden soldier. But as I flipped through the small stack of black-and-white photos, Corey O'Neal suddenly came to life.

The dozen images seemingly chronicled Corey's tour in Vietnam. Corporal O'Neal arriving at his first billet with his company mates. A curious Corey tasting the temptations of the raw nightlife of Saigon. Corey O'Neal, battle-weary and mud-streaked, leading his squad as the point of a seek-and-destroy patrol. A smiling Corey holding a Vietnamese baby, a pack of cigarettes twisted into the sleeve of his t-shirt. Corporal O'Neal, holding the hand of a wounded soldier as a medic tended to his needs. The undeniable leadership that he provided for his men was evident from the determination that leapt out of the photographs.

It all suddenly dawned on me. Danny was Corey and Corey was Danny. Both were committed more to those they had been given, or assumed, responsibility for than they were committed to themselves. It cost Corey his life. I wondered what it would cost Danny.

I gave the photos back to Danny.

"Can you picture Billy or Shaun there?" Danny asked. "Or worse, Carl?"

"No. No I can't. I can't picture anyone there."

"Neither can I. That's why we've got to win." As we talked and gazed out the window, Danny's eyes brightened. It was Jill, ever so fresh, ever so intense, approaching Mabel's. She walked arm-in-arm with a tall, bearded and shaggy-looking young man, wearing moccasin boots and a camouflage green Army jacket, plastered with peace symbols and embroidered with beads, a situation that more than piqued Danny's curiosity. They climbed the stairs to Mabel's and walked toward our table. As they neared, the closeness between Jill and her escort could not be hidden.

"Danny, there's someone I want you to meet," Jill said, more sweetly than Danny could have hoped for. Danny stood, unsure of what his response should be but knowing that he should meet Jill's escort face to face.

"I'm Danny O'Neal," he offered, extending his hand.

"Nice to meet you," the young man responded grasping Danny's hand. "I'm Craig, Craig Burke."

"My brother," Jill explained. Danny looked at Jill and then Craig, somehow knowing there was more that needed to be told. "Craig was in Vietnam," Jill went on. Danny's heart began racing. Still clasping Craig's hand, Danny peered into his eyes, looking for the answer he hoped was there. A familiarity leaked from deep within Craig's soul.

"You knew my brother," Danny said. "You were with Corey in Vietnam."

"It was my honor serving with him," Craig proudly said.

In that instant, they began an unlikely friendship, at first bound by only a love and respect for a man that they separately knew in ever so different circumstances, and eventually bound by a respect for each other. On one side was Danny, a still innocent and idealistic high school boy unsure of his duty and full of questions. On the other side, a man only a few years older, but decades more experienced, a man who had served his country, tasted combat and returned a changed individual. Craig was anxious to provide the answers that Danny craved.

Jill, Craig, Danny and I spent hours deep into the night in that booth at Mabel's, learning from Craig and so learning about ourselves.

"I remember the day I arrived in Vietnam," Craig recounted. "I was as naïve a grunt as there ever was. I believed all the bullshit propaganda they fed us in basic training. I thought we were there for a grand purpose and I, with guns a-blazing, would fulfill that grand purpose, rid the world of the Communist menace and restore freedom to the peoples of Vietnam." Craig lit a cigarette and took a long drag. "It was, of course, all a load of crap. There was no plan. There was no higher purpose. There was only the body count, theirs and ours.

"The first company I was assigned to fought for and captured the same Goddamned hill four times." Craig paused as if forming the memory. "There was this hill a couple of hundred yards from our firebase. Charlie would sit on top of that hill and lob mortars over the perimeter. We'd take about a week of casualties until some genius gave the command, 'Take that hill, clear out Charlie and return with a body count.' So we slugged our way up the hill, killing as many of Charlie as we could and Charlie killed as many of us as he could, until there wasn't anything left of Charlie to kill and the hill was ours. We counted their dead bodies, doubled the number and went back to base, carrying our own wounded and dead with us. By the next night, Charlie was back on top of the hill, lobbing mortars at us. A week later, we'd do it all over again."

"Why didn't you just occupy the hill?" I asked. Craig shook his head, put out the stub he was puffing on and lit another cigarette.

"Capture and hold territory? Seems like a good plan, but that was a different war," he answered. "This war is about body counts." The waitress stopped by the table, wanting to clear the dishes, but thought better of it and walked on. "We lost 50 men taking that hill time and again. The only thing that seemed to matter was that we killed more of Charlie than they killed of us."

"Is that where you met Corey?" Danny asked.

"It was few months later. I got reassigned to a different company and ended up in Corey's squad," Craig continued. "At first, I thought he was just another one of those lifer assholes who walked around in clean fatigues and polished boots, and mindlessly followed any bullshit order given to him." Danny leaned forward and with his eyes firmly on Craig, almost absentmindedly took Jill's hand, as though he needed her support to survive the truth he was about to hear about his brother. Jill's eyes were only on Danny.

"In some ways, I was right. Corey was a soldier's soldier," Craig recounted, "a solitary professional in the midst of a sea of incompetence that spanned the chain of command. He wouldn't tolerate one ounce of crap from anyone in his squad. He forced us to clean our weapons when we thought they didn't need cleaning. He inspected our packs and if we didn't have the right ammo or clean socks, he'd ream us a new asshole and make us get the right stuff. If one of us lit up a smoke on night patrol, he'd be on our case faster than shit out of a monkey." Danny squeezed Jill's hand tighter as Craig took another long drag.

"But it didn't take long for us to understand that Corey wasn't doing all those things because they were the regs. He didn't give a crap about the regs. He was doing whatever he could do to save our lives. If we were ordered to go out on a useless patrol whose only purpose seemed to be to make targets of ourselves in front of an unseen enemy, Corey was going to do everything in his power to make certain we all came back alive. And if that meant chewing one of us out because we didn't have a clean weapon or dry socks, that's what he did."

Craig paused and looked a Danny. "Don't worry, kid, your brother was a righteous man. He was making us be better soldiers because the better soldiers we were, the more likely we were to come home alive. Corey didn't give a shit about politics or what some general had for breakfast, unlike all those other brown-nosing bastards. Corey got up in the morning and went to sleep at night thinking about how he could carry out his orders and keep his men alive. He saved more lives than I can count, including mine."

"How long did you serve with Corey?" I asked.

"Couple of months before I got wounded and came back stateside," Craig answered. Danny's grip on Jill's hand loosened but he still held her. Craig put out his cigarette and leaned forward. "I was on point. There was no moon. It was dark beyond reason. Then out of nowhere, we started taking fire from both sides. All we could see was muzzle flashes. I got hit in the leg and started bleeding like a stuck pig. Got hit in the femoral artery. I knew I was screwed beyond imagination. I just knew I was going to die in that jungle. I was on the ground with my hands around my leg trying to make the bleeding stop, getting woozy real fast from losing all that blood. I began to panic. Then in the middle of the firefight, there's Corey kneeling next to me, calmly getting a bandage around my leg, talking soothing to calm me down too. I passed out but the guys told me he somehow managed the battle and carried me to safety. I woke up in Saigon two days later, alive and I still had my leg. I never saw Corey again, but I think about him a lot. I didn't know he'd been killed until Jill told me."

"Thanks for telling me that," Danny said, his eyes filled with tears. "I wanted to believe Corey was..." Danny paused. "Thanks, now I know."

"Jill asked me to come here," Craig explained. "As you may have gathered from my getup, I'm no longer in the employ of the United States Marine Corps. In fact, I'm one of the founders of a group called Vietnam Vets Against the War. Ever heard of us?" Danny was beginning to get uncomfortable.

"Not really, but I guess its name is self-explanatory," Danny said, a bit more critically than he might have wanted to.

"You disapprove?" Craig asked with a smile.

"I don't know enough to approve or disapprove."

"Do you approve or disapprove?" Craig asked again. Danny looked at me as if asking for permission to answer. I shrugged, not wanting to get in the middle of this.

"My grandfather served. My father served. My brother served and he died for his country," Danny said a bit defiantly. "There are thousands of boys in Vietnam this very minute risking their lives for their country. It seems disloyal not to support them."

"So to support the troops you've got to support the war. Is that it?"

"Isn't it the same?"

"And, Danny my boy, you think that if you don't serve like your brother then you're being as disloyal as I am. Do I have it right?" Craig asked with a bit of a smile. Danny didn't answer. The silence needed to be broken.

"It's not as simple as that," I interjected, finally getting involved.

"No shit," Craig responded. The waitress came by again with a coffee pot and Craig pointed at an empty cup. Nobody spoke as she filled it.

"Jill explained your predicament," Craig said. Danny looked a bit puzzled. "Your father, the scholarships." Danny nodded.

"It's not so much a predicament," Danny tried to explained. "It's a decision I've got to make."

"And what's that decision?" Jill squeezed Danny's hand. "Whether to serve?" Craig lit up another cigarette and looked at me.

"What do you think?"

"About what?"

"About Danny's predicament. Should he enlist or let himself get drafted?"

"I guess that's his decision."

"What about you?"

"I'm not planning on enlisting, if that's what you're asking."

"Not afraid of being disloyal?"

"No, I just don't want to die for no good reason."

"What's a good reason to die?" Craig looked at his watch and began to get out of the booth. "I can think of a few good reasons, but can you two?"

Danny and I looked at each other but said nothing.

"Seems to me like the two of you need some more data," Craig went on. "You can't make a good decision without data. Vietnam Vets Against the War is putting on a demonstration in Chicago on Sunday. If you want to get another side of this story, let me take you up there. Jill will tell you where to meet me." And with that, he and Jill left Mabel's.

CHAPTER 26

The Hawks had a rare Saturday morning workout. Next week's meet against the Danville Titans was going to be a tough one and Coach Dillon didn't want to miss a day of preparation. The Titans were a team on the move. They were almost all half-milers and milers who ran cross country mostly to stay in shape for track. They were always fast off the line and so it was always a game of catch-up for their opponents. The lucky ones would catch the Titans before the finish and eke out a win. The unlucky ones lost. Seeing as though the Hawks didn't have much in the way of legs full of fast twitch fibers, this race would be a challenge.

It was an incredibly foggy morning and just getting light when I jogged up to the entrance to the gym. I was the first Hawk to arrive but Coach Dillon's station wagon was already in the parking lot. I wandered into the gym in search of the Coach, and found him in the process of posting the article from the morning's *Barrel Gazette* about our meet against the Tolono Tigers. "Tigers are Barely Kittens as Hawk Harriers Sweep Meet" read the headline. There was a photo of Danny finishing the race in first place and me visible behind him as I hurried in for second place. If I hadn't known better, the photo could have been of Frank and Pete Lorenzo. I stood by Coach Dillon as we both read the article and, without thinking, I pointed to myself in the photo.

"First time in the paper?" Coach Dillon asked.

"Yeah, I guess it is," I answered sheepishly.

"It won't be the last. You'll be taking the first place stick one day."

"It is better to win," I softly said, more to myself than the Coach. He smiled and put his arm around my shoulder.

"That's for darn certain. Let's get this workout on the road." Coach Dillon and I walked out to the parking lot. The rest of the Hawks had arrived and were clustered around Frank's station wagon.

"Morning, Coach," Amos said.

"What's it going to be today?" Shaun asked.

Without saying anything, Frank got into the wagon and started the engine. Smoke rings puffed out the tailpipe like a grizzled cigar smoker. This was not a good sign. The workout wasn't going to be a few easy laps around the track. We gathered around the driver's window; Frank deliberately and slowly rolled down the window. He turned to us and said the single, dreaded word, "Fartlek," put the car in gear and drove off. We all looked at each other with expressions of fear and began trailing after the wagon.

Fartlek is a training technique that is rumored to have originated in Sweden. It's basically a group long run. You jog for a while. Then somebody calls out, "Build for half a mile," and everyone picks up the pace, progressively running faster for a half-mile. The group reassembles, jogs for a while until another runner calls out "Sprint for a 220," and everyone lights out into a sprint for 220 yards. After another short jog, someone might call out, "A mile at three-quarter pace." This goes on for about 10 miles, mixing up jogging with bursts of builds, sprints and sustained paces. It can be, and usually is, utterly exhausting. Frank's variation on the fartlek theme is that he would call out the pace from the window of his station wagon, then drive ahead measuring the distance on the odometer.

We jogged for about a mile when the station wagon suddenly appeared out of the foggy gloom. "Build for a mile," Frank commanded through the open driver's window, and then gunned the engine as he drove ahead and disappeared into the fog.

"You heard the man," Danny said. "Build for a mile." We began slowly picking up the pace, holding plenty in reserve for what we knew would soon come. Danny and I went to the front, matching each other's stride step for step, not quite a competition but not far off. Shaun, Billy and Amos formed a nucleus behind us. Carl trailed from the start. After you run enough miles, you get a pretty good sense of distance, and with every quarter mile that passed by, the pace markedly quickened until in the final 220 yards, we were nearly sprinting. Our arms were pumping, our knees were rising high. We leaned forward like sprinters, digging into the pavement with the balls of our feet. The coldness of the air made our throats burn. We nearly ran into the station wagon that suddenly appeared out of the fog signaling the end of the mile.

We regrouped and jogged for about a half mile while Frank slowly drove in front of us.

"What about Sunday?" I asked Danny, a bit breathlessly, as we jogged. Danny didn't answer.

"Sunday, what's happening Sunday?" Billy popped in.

"There's a demonstration in Chicago," I said.

"What sort of demonstration?" Shaun asked.

"Antiwar," was my one word answer.

"You mean a real antiwar demonstration?" We'd only seen such things on television.

"Shit, you thinking about going?" Billy asked incredulously.

"I don't know."

"My father would freak if he knew I was at a demonstration," Amos admitted.

"Not as much as mine," Danny finally said. "It wouldn't be pretty." Frank slowed the wagon and we caught up.

"Full pace for a 220, jog for a 220. Keep that up for a mile," Frank ordered and he drove off into the fog. We ran the first 220 far too quickly. We tried to catch our breath in the next 220 worth of jogging but failed miserably. By the end of the next sprint, the burn had already begun in our calves and thighs, and the tightness that appeared across our chests made it difficult to breath. We were nowhere near recovered by the start of the third 220 sprint. I can't describe the agony of the fourth. As we jogged before the next installment of pain, we regrouped again. I looked around counting noses.

"Where's Carl?" I asked.

"Haven't seen him since the second 220," Amos answered and then, as if on cue, Carl appeared out of the fog.

"Got lost," he said. I was about to ask how you can get lost on a straight-as-an-arrow county road but thought better of it. Shades of Tolono. The next segment was a half-mile at half-pace, followed by a half-mile at full-pace, followed by a third half-mile at half-pace. By the end of the third half-mile, we were strung-out for a quarter-mile. Danny and I jogged in little circles while the rest of the Hawks finished.

"Well?" I asked

"Well, what?"

"Are you going to Chicago?"

"You already asked that."

"And you didn't answer."

"I don't know, are you?"

"It's not important that I go," I answered. "It's important that you go."

"Why is that?"

"Because I know I won't do something stupid but I'm not sure you won't."

"And what might that be?" Danny asked me, truly puzzled.

"Follow in Corey's footsteps just because your old man wants you to. The problem is that you believe all that bullshit your father feeds you."

"It's not bullshit. My brother didn't die for bullshit."

"How do you know? Like Craig said, you need data."

"I've got all the data I need." Billy and Shaun finished and stood with their hands on their hips, trying to recover.

"Data for what?" Billy asked.

"Never mind. There's Frank," Danny said. And for another 45 minutes, we suffered incredibly through one fartlek segment to another. We finished with a sprint back to the high school, ending with a lap around the track. We all fell in a heap in the infield, almost too tired to move. The fog had finally burned off and the warmth of the sun's weak morning rays felt surprisingly good. I rolled over to where Danny was lying in the grass.

"I'm going to the demonstration," I told him. "I'll ask Jill and Craig to stop by your house on the way to Chicago. I expect we'll be getting an early start."

Danny was waiting for us on the corner when we arrived.

CHAPTER 27

You can't spend three hours in a VW microbus with three other people without learning something about them. The ride to Chicago with Jill, Craig and Danny that Sunday morning gave me insights that explained much. Jill and her brother were closer than I expected. Before they were teenagers, their father had gone out for a loaf of bread one evening and never returned, leaving an unprepared mother to raise an introverted daughter and rebellious son. With her mother working and having few friends, Jill just hung around her middle school in the afternoons waiting for the end of the day. If not for the concern of one of the boys' coaches, it would have just been just one wasted afternoon after another. Seeing Jill alone day after day, he put her to work cleaning up his office and organizing his files to occupy her empty moments.

After a while, he had Jill follow him around with a clipboard, recording times as he orchestrated after-school practice for the boys' cross country and track teams. After watching the grace of Jill's form as she ran around the track just for the joy of it, he came to understand the magnitude of her talent. He took away her clipboard and had Jill join the team during practice, even if only unofficially. There weren't girls' sports teams in those days but she didn't seem to mind. She found in the company of runners the kinship that had eluded her in the hallways.

Craig was another story. To describe him as a juvenile delinquent may have been extreme. Describing him as rambunctious was not quite extreme enough. Schoolwork didn't interest Craig and he wasn't very good at sports. But Craig was good at hanging out, breaking windows and smoking cigarettes; and so that's what he did, much to the disappointment of his mother. Needless to say, he was far from being the valedictorian of his high school graduating class. He received his diploma and his draft notice on the same day. Faced with the reality of having to serve, Craig chose to enlist in the Marines instead. He was in Vietnam before the summer was over.

We arrived in Chicago a bit before noon. Craig parked his WV microbus in a vacant lot already nearly filled with heaps like his, emblazoned with painted flowers and peace symbols. "We'll have to walk from here," Craig told us. We got out and began navigating through the crowds toward Grant Park. The streets were clogged with a mix of humanity that was beyond imagination, an unlikely collection of the conservative and liberal, the curious and devoted, the reporters and the reportees, all with their own agendas if not motivation.

The protest had been planned for weeks, with no less purpose than to be the lead story on the evening news, a conveniently orchestrated segment to complement reports on the weekly totals of casualties in Vietnam and the Senate's impotence to stem those casualties. The Democrats had recently announced that they would hold their convention in Chicago the following spring, and the Democratic National Committee was touring the city, casing out the joint, so to speak. The protesters saw an opportunity to embarrass the DNC on national television and expertly leveraged that opportunity with planning that generals would envy. The DNC and the antiwar movement should have been allies but were never able to see beyond their differences. This gathering would prove to be merely a harbinger for the events at the next spring's convention. To some, it was a dress rehearsal for a march on Washington DC in only a few weeks time.

For a boy raised in the innocence of Barrel, the sights at Grant Park that morning were surrealistic at best, resembling figures from a Napoleonic playbook. Riot gear-outfitted police stood in rows two deep and 50 wide on one side of Buckingham Fountain, which dominates the small park. They stood at attention, wary of even the rustle of leaves. They were opposed by the war protesters on the other side of the fountain, ragtag in appearance but intense in their purpose. The protesters milled about without discipline, as though they were corralled by invisible barriers. They were an unlikely mix of flower children and bearded Vietnam vets, grandmothers and idealistic high schoolers, all in their own minds altruistically pursuing a mission of the highest priority, saving a generation of youth from the prospect of war.

The flower children began as the offspring of the privileged. They were unfettered with responsibility, and unhindered by the challenge of providing for a family and loved ones. They came from the cities and from the suburbs that begat the baby-boomers. They came from the seemingly endless middle class, a generation born after World War II and too young to remember Korea. They were facing their first war. They rejected the conformity of the 1950s and rejected the values of their parents to create their own order, one based on rebellion laced with idealism. They matured to be astute enough to understand and take advantage of a system that provided them and their parents with their means of survival, while not acknowledging the gifts that same system had granted them.

Now, years into the movement, the flower children found purpose beyond their own narcissistic needs. An unlikely coalition of hippies and Yippies, Vietnam vets and draft dodgers, and Black Panthers and Weathermen joined forces to protest against the war. It was an undertaking that, with the exception of those who had served, was more likely motivated by fear of serving than altruism.

Craig led us into the midst of the soon-to-be protesting crowd. Danny and I were no less awed than if we had been probed by aliens. We knew these sorts of people existed, we'd even seen them on television, but to actually walk among them was something neither of us had ever expected to do, at least not in Barrel. Jill, surprisingly, seemed to be as much at home as Craig. As we snaked our way through the crowd it was clear that Craig was recognized and admired. Even the hippies and Yippies were practical enough to know that protesting a war they had no intention of being part of, and were deathly afraid of, frayed their credibility beyond belief. It was the company of Vietnam vets like Craig that gave substance to their words.

Craig scanned the crowd ahead, obviously looking for someone. Jill stood on an overturned trash can to get a better view.

"There he is!" Jill said, pointing toward the fountain. "Phil, Phil!" she screamed, not being heard above the noise of the crowd. Jill took Craig's hand and ran through the crowd as best they could. Danny and I, not knowing what to do, followed as best we could, and nearly lost them in the humanity.

When we finally caught up, we found Craig down on one knee, embracing a young man in a wheelchair. Jill, her arms around the man's neck, had tears of joy running down her cheeks. "Danny, Michael, this is Phil, our best friend in the world. Phil, these are my new friends from Barrel."

Phil was a good-looking guy, about 22 or 23 years old. Unlike most of his friends clustered around him, Phil was clean-shaven, with a boy-next-door haircut. His carefully ironed army-fatigue shirt was bereft of the beads and embroidery that adorned Craig's and most of the other vets' jackets. He could have been featured on a recruiting poster. Phil looked up at us and, smiling, put out his hand to shake ours.

"Any friends of Jill's are friends of mine," he said. As I reached over Craig to grab Phil's hand, Craig stood up and it was then that we saw that Phil had no legs. His crisply ironed jeans ended about six inches above where his knees should have been. Danny couldn't help but stare at the emptiness as I took Phil's hand.

"Nice to meet you," I managed to say. Danny opened his mouth as though to say something but the words wouldn't come out. It wasn't as though Danny had never seen a legless man before, it's just that those men were of a different generation. They were World War II and Korean War vets whose wheelchairs were pushed by their fellow vets in the 4th of July parade. They were wheezing World War I vets, barely able to speak from their nursing room beds. They were not, like Phil, only a few years older than Danny. The cheerfulness and vitality that Phil seeded around him was, in Danny's mind, incongruous with having no legs. It was nearly acceptable to Danny to be young, to go to war and to die. But to be young and have no legs; that was something Danny could not accept. Danny may have in some way seen his future sitting in that chair. What he saw was Phil, a good-looking kid from some small town, who climbed aboard an airplane to a place that only a few months before he did not know existed, and returned without his legs. Phil sensed our discomfort.

"Land mine," Phil said, still smiling. "I lost my legs stepping on a land mine." Danny was little comforted. "Craig and I served together in Vietnam."

Phil was interrupted by the echoing of a bullhorn. A uniformed police officer was blaring at us from a hastily constructed platform surrounded by riot geared subordinates.

"I am Superintendent of Police Conlisk. This is an unlawful…" he began, but one of the superintendent's lackeys stroked a hand across his throat giving Conlisk the universal "cut" sign. Apparently, the WGN camera crew wasn't quite in position. After a few minutes of plugging in cables and jostling for position, the camera crew gave the go-ahead and the Superintendent began again.

"I am Superintendent of Police Conlisk. This is an unlawful gathering. You must disperse now. This is an unlawful gathering. You must disperse now. If you do not disperse, you will be forcibly removed." The crowd of protesters became suddenly silent. They all turned to look in the direction of the superintendent, flanked by the rows of riot-geared police. It reminded me of the battle scene in *Spartacus*, the peasant army on one side, the Roman legions on the other, neither all that excited about the upcoming confrontation but both realizing that the ball game was already scheduled.

"Looks like we're getting ready for action," Phil commented as he cinched the belt that secured him to his wheelchair. The protesters, having nothing in common other than their conviction that the war in Vietnam was immoral, or at least inconvenient, began self-organizing in response to the police superintendent's challenge. A dark haired man we later learned was Abbie Hoffman moved to the front of the crowd with his bullhorn and readied himself to exchange amplified accusations with the superintendent. The hippies and Yippies, vets and dodgers, Weathermen and Panthers, donned their backpacks and checked their signs, as Abbie keenly looked on. This was a dress rehearsal for protests to be held in Washington, D.C. in only a few weeks and he wanted to soak up as much learning as he could. Abbie, seemingly satisfied with the siting of the camera crews and positioning of his own ragtag troops, brought his bullhorn to his lips.

"Hey, hey, LBJ, how many kids did ya kill today?" Abbie Hoffman screeched through his bullhorn. A slight echo reflected from the Congress Hotel across the street.

"Hey, hey LBJ, how many kids did ya kill today?" the hippies and Yippies began chanting.

"Hey, hey LBJ, how many kids did ya kill today?" the draft dodgers and vets joined in.

"This is an unlawful gathering. Clear the area immediately," the superintendent retorted through his bullhorn as the television cameras refined their focus and the photographers snapped their first images on their new rolls of film. "If you do not disperse, we will forcibly remove you."

"Hey, hey, LBJ. How many kids did ya kill today?"

"This is an unlawful gathering."

"Hey, hey, LBJ..." Danny was mesmerized, like a child's first visit to Disneyland, not quite sure how much that he was experiencing was real and how much was not. This is the sort of thing you saw on television, something that somebody else experiences, not Danny O'Neal from Barrel High, where the height of protest was wearing a skirt an inch shorter than the dress code allowed. It wouldn't hurt to stick around, Danny thought, because this isn't real.

Abbie took a few bold steps forward toward the line of police. The crowd surged forward with him. The riot-gear-adorned police raised their shields and gripped their nightsticks, and responded by moving a few feet forward themselves, narrowing the distance between the legions and peasants. A photographer ran into the gap between them, quickly snapping a picture in both directions before retreating. This was beginning to look not very good.

"Maybe we ought to get out of here," I shouted towards Danny. He looked at me as though ready to agree.

"Push me to the front," Phil commanded to no one in particular, and almost instinctively, Danny grabbed the handles of Phil's wheelchair and pushed him through the mass of humanity in the direction of Abbie Hoffman.

"Danny!" I called out, but my voice was lost in the "Hey, heys" of the crowd. I pushed my way through the crowd, put my hand on Danny's shoulder and let him pull me forward.

"Clear the area."

"Hey, hey LBJ..."

"This is..."

"How many kids..."

"...an unlawful...."

"did ya kill..."

"...gathering."

"...today?"

Phil directed Danny to position him at Hoffman's side. Danny still held the handles of his wheelchair. It seemed almost a stalemate between the police and protesters. Abbie Hoffman, the showman that he was, sensed that the reporters and cameramen were beginning to lose interest. Following a seemingly prearranged plan, Abbie nodded to Phil, who glanced up at Danny, motioning him forward. Abbie handed Phil the bullhorn and Danny pushed his wheelchair into the no-man's land in front of Buckingham Fountain. As if on cue, the Superintendent of Police stopped his tirade, and the hippies and Yippies, draft dodgers and vets became equally as silent. The impact of a legless 22-year-old veteran, wounded in combat in the service of his country, is compelling, for there is no questioning his qualifications to speak his mind. Phil raised the bullhorn to his lips.

"The war in Vietnam is not a war for freedom or a war of liberation," Phil began, "it is a war against the people of Vietnam, a people that neither welcome us nor support us. We accomplish nothing in Vietnam other than perpetuating corruption. We do so by sending our young men to die in place of those who will not fight their own battles. I am an example of the cannon fodder that we send into this unwise battle. I returned from that battle without my legs but I consider myself one of the lucky ones because I lived to see my family again. The body count of those who were not so lucky increases every day."

The sincerity of a preacher's sermon could not have been greater. The message Phil delivered could not have been clearer. Reporters held out their microphones. The police superintendent put down his bullhorn. Only the snapping of shutters spoiled the moment. "What price will we continue to pay to fight a war nobody wants and cannot be won?" Phil put down the bullhorn and nodded to Danny, who wheeled his chair back into the crowd of would-be protesters.

It was as though the planets had miraculously aligned, creating a zodiacal event that might never be replicated. The police stood in thoughtful contemplation of Phil's words. The protesters held out the offer of reconciliation. A policeman took off his helmet, as if to signal his acceptance. From this one event, a groundswell of reason and understanding might have erupted across the country. Peace might have blossomed in a way that was unthinkable until that moment. Time nearly stood still. But the alignment of the planets was fragile and unraveled as quickly as it was knit.

"You fucking pigs!" a voice cried out as a beer bottle arced over Buckingham Fountain and crashed into the head of the unhelmeted police officer. Blood spattered on the concrete. The riot-geared police, jolted back from their short journey of contemplation, had been given their cue. With batons and shields raised, they began advancing towards the hippies and Yippies, draft dodgers and vets.

"Hey, hey, LBJ. How many kids did ya kill today?" the crowd began chanting again, moving forward toward the police with their signs raised. What only seconds before had been a peaceful protest erupted into the chaos of unreason. The police moved into the crowd with their batons swinging. The protesters, greatly outnumbering the police, swarmed over them. The officers were pulled to the ground and were beaten with their own batons. There was no logic to these events. There was no good that could result. But each side was committed beyond logic to see it to the end. I tried to find Danny in the mêlée but he had been consumed by the chaos. Being at the front of the swarm of protesters, he fell under one of the first swings of the policemen's batons. Jill grabbed my hand, pulling me in the opposite direction that the protesters were surging toward the police, extricating us before we too were consumed. We passed Craig as he fought his way through the crowd toward the front lines.

The swelling from the cut over Danny's right eye took a few days to subside. It was sore for a lot longer. The stitches didn't come out for yet another week. It's surprising how much damage one swing of a nightstick can do. Danny would sport a dashing scar.

CHAPTER 28

The meet against the Danville Titans the following Friday was on our home course. The meet wasn't supposed to be a challenge. It almost turned into a catastrophe. For a few days, it looked as though Danny and I wouldn't be at the starting line. That would mean a sure loss and the end of our quest for scholarships and relief from Vietnam. In fact, if not for Principal Milo's lack of imagination and Ben O'Neal's crushed spirit, we might have lost Danny for the season.

The scene in Principal Milo's office on Monday morning was far from pretty. Danny and his parents, me and my parents and Coach Dillon crowded into the small room. Principal Milo used words like "expelled" and "suspended for the season" more than once. Coach Dillon was passionate in his defense of Danny and me, displaying an eloquence he rarely needed to display. He rose to the occasion like the champion he was. "Victims of circumstance" is what I think Frank argued, as though instead of participating willingly, we had been kidnapped and spirited off to Chicago against our wills.

"I have never been so ashamed of my son," Ben O'Neal said. "An insult to the memory of your brother," is something else he said.

Danny and I were largely silent. We had spoken by our actions and any additional explanation would have likely only deepened the hole we were already standing in. If you're standing in a hole, it's best to stop digging. In the end, Principal Milo couldn't do too much about suspending us for what we may or may not have done over the weekend on our own time in a city a three-hour drive away. So the rhetoric soon died, and our punishment was left to our parents to devise and deliver.

The much anticipated punishment was, however, neither devised nor delivered. Dinner at my house that evening was filled with the usual good-natured chatter of my mother and the telling of unbelievable schemes by my father. Unlike the O'Neals, my family had no legacy of service to perpetuate or moral standards to defend. It was difficult to imagine that a con man who made his living defrauding the public would have too much to say about social responsibility, and so my father neglected his fatherly duties once again. My mother dared not ask for an explanation for fear she would get one and my father was more interested in avoiding a conflict than creating one. With our silence we all agreed to delegate the episode to a boyish indiscretion, no more or less important than being caught with your hand down your girlfriend's blouse.

The surprise of this episode occurred at the O'Neals' house. Dinner that evening was as tense and silent as most any other evening. The surprise was that there were no accusations, rationalizations, sermons nor forgiveness. There were neither ultimatums nor explanations. There was only the unspoken, heartbroken and bitter disappointment that follows a father's realization that his son may have rejected that which sustained the moral fiber of his being. Ben O'Neal was raised in this shadow of his father's service to his country. Ben O'Neal became a man while fighting a war in distant lands in the service of his country, an experience that molded his worldview in an irrevocable and uncompromising way. Ben O'Neal's brother and eldest son gave their lives in the service of their country. Ben O'Neal raised his youngest son with the unfaltering expectation that he too would serve his country. He now understood that that expectation was likely built on a foundation of sand.

Those few hours in Chicago also changed Danny irrevocably. Never before had he spoken with seemingly intelligent adults whose worldviews were so divergent from those of his parents and teachers. Never before had the lines of ideology been so clearly drawn in such a stark manner. Never before had he experienced the rage and illogic of unbridled emotion. Young men died in wars. Danny knew that. Young men returned from war changed in body and mind. Danny now knew that as well. What Danny understood only after Chicago was how war changed those who never carried a weapon nor wore a uniform. They were changed, Danny learned, by the conviction of their beliefs, by the sympathies they harbored and by the pride they expounded. They were also changed by the guilt they felt and by the envy they hid because there were those among them who had the courage to serve and they themselves lacked that same courage. Danny was changed no differently than they were.

But Danny changed more than just philosophically. Danny was, by any measure, a good-looking, clean-cut kid. His hair usually just touched his ears and was always combed. His shoes were always laced and shined. His pants were always cleaned and creased. His face was always shaved and scrubbed. He probably said "sir," "ma'am," "thank you" and "you're welcome" more often than any teenager I knew.

In spite of those qualities, Danny began a not-so-subtle transformation the day we returned from Chicago. I first noticed it when the Hawks assembled for our morning run. In place of the Hawks jersey Danny always wore on these morning jaunts, he wore a tie-dyed t-shirt and a leather string bracelet. His hair, parted on the left from the day he was born, was now parted down the middle. On Tuesday, Danny showed up at school wearing Corey's army jacket with a beaded peace symbol sewn on its back. By Wednesday, he had given up wearing socks and shaving. As the Hawks and I waited by his locker before classes on Thursday, it was anyone's guess what surprise Danny would spring on us. Shelly was beyond herself with shame. She was, in fact, suddenly embarrassed to be seen with Danny.

"I don't understand what's gotten into him," she complained as we waited.

"Maybe it was that knock on the head," I ventured.

"Whatever it was, I hope he gets over it soon."

"It's hard to believe his father lets him out of the house looking like he does."

"That would mean they were talking to each other," Shelly said.

"Not talking?" I asked. That didn't come as much of a surprise to me but I asked nonetheless.

"Not a word since Monday. Danny's mom called me," Shelly admitted. "There he is." Shelly pointed down the hallway, where Danny was weaving his way through the before-class throng of his fellow students. Two things looked different. Danny was wearing a beaded necklace and Jill was by his side.

"Shit, this can't be good," I mumbled to myself. I glanced at Shelly. She looked calm and composed, though I knew her well enough to notice the small quiver of her lips that telegraphed that she was pissed and afraid at the same time, a bad combination in a woman of any age.

"Hey, Danny, Jill," I called as the pair arrived.

"Where did you get that?" Shelly spat, pointing at Danny's necklace.

"Jill made it for me," Danny said. "She sewed the beads on my jacket too. Pretty cool, huh?"

"She did, did she?" Shelly said with a coldness that fogged the hallway. Jill's look of pride crystallized into one of fear of Shelly.

"Danny wanted something more, ah…," Jill tried to explain.

"Contemporary?"

"No, more hip, so I sewed on some beads. It wasn't hard."

"A skill no doubt learned from your brother.'

"As a matter of fact…"

"Well, I guess we should thank you for your fashion sense and originality," Shelly snarled. "Lord knows you can't buy this stuff in a respectable store." It was beginning to get good when Danny stepped between the girls.

"Let's get to class," Danny said as he took Shelly's arm. "See you later, Jill." Danny and Shelly disappeared into the crowd. I stayed behind with Jill.

"Are you going out of your way to piss off Shelly or does it just come naturally?" I asked with a smile. "Not that I object." Jill relaxed and leaned against the lockers.

"Danny's confused," she ventured.

"Yeah, about a lot of things: the war, duty, you."

"Me?"

"Yeah, you." Jill smiled uncontrollably.

"He shouldn't be. Shelly's a class act, a bit of a tight-ass, but a class act," Jill admitted. "She wants Danny bad. All he's got to do is say the word and he could have her for life. Why give up a sure thing like that for a flake like me?" I hesitated for a minute. Jill wasn't your run-of-the-mill girl, but she wasn't a flake. She was Shelly's anti-particle. Shelly craved security; Jill sought adventure. Shelly was needy; Jill gave comfort. Shelly had her life planned decades into the future. Jill didn't know what she was doing after school. Shelly owned three evening gowns. Jill's version of formal attire was wearing Pumas instead of Adidas. You might think that with Danny's confusion about his future, Shelly's stability would be an anchor he should hold onto like a boa constrictor. That seemed not to be the case.

"She's not right for him." I hitched my backpack onto my shoulder before continuing. "But you are." I started walking to class, leaving Jill behind. She gave it a few seconds thought before catching up to me.

"He's not talking to his father. I think it's my fault," she admitted.

"No shit," I chided her.

"Well, mine and Craig's. If we hadn't taken him to Chicago…"

"Then it would have been something else," I interrupted. I stopped walking and pulled Jill to the side of the hallway out of the stream of students.

"Neither of us have known Danny very long," I started. "But something tells me we know him better than even his family does and at least better than Shelly." Jill nodded. "I know he loved his brother. Hell, he still wears his ring. I think he must love his parents. What I don't know is if he loves himself enough to do the right thing."

"And what's that?" Jill asked.

"I know it isn't enlisting."

"I can't imagine Danny doing that now."

"I don't know," I thought out loud. "He's had almost 18 years of honor, duty, country and *semper fi* crammed down his throat. He lives in a shrine to brothers, uncles and grandfathers who served and died doing it. It's as though it's in his genes."

"Well, all you've got to do is win the state championship and he won't have to worry about that," Jill challenged.

"Neither will the rest of us," I said, certain there would be six scholarships. The bell rang, signaling the start of the school day. I suddenly realized Jill and I were nearly alone in the hallway. "We better get to class."

"Thanks," Jill offered.

"For what?" I asked.

"For being Danny's friend." I couldn't help but smile

"Don't give up on him," I advised my new confidant. "I think you two need each other."

CHAPTER 29

We were expecting an easy workout the day before the meet, but Frank had different ideas. There was a note in the locker room, "Meet me at my car. Coach Dillon." We all knew what that meant. We climbed into the 1953 Chevy station wagon and with Frank at the wheel began a drive to points unknown. "Where're we off to?" Billy asked. Frank didn't answer. Sitting behind Frank, I glanced at the odometer. "13,010." I had to assume that it had flipped over 100,000 miles more than a few times.

We drove in silence as the wagon jiggled along the county roads in the direction of the hill. We expected we'd stop there but Frank drove up the backside of the hill, down its face and kept going. After a while I glanced at the odometer. "13,015." We drove a bit longer without anybody saying much. I gave a quick look at Danny's tie-dyed t-shirt, the beginnings of a scrawny beard and his beaded necklace. A lot had changed in a short period of time. A few weeks ago, Danny was a poster child for the establishment, clean-cut and patriotic. Now, he would not have been out of place in Haight-Ashbury. But looks can be deceiving. So can actions. Was Danny changed as much inside as he was on the outside? Most metamorphoses change worms into butterflies. This might be the first metamorphosis to reverse the process. I looked at the odometer again. "13,019."

As I watched the fields flick by, the farmers go about their chores and the children ride their bicycles in their front yards, I could not have imagined a more Rockwellian indictment of the foolishness of what we had witnessed and become a part of in Chicago. This is the heartland. This is where fields are sown, crops are nurtured and the bounty that feeds the country, if not the world, is harvested. Babies are born, children grow through the seasons not unlike the corn in the fields and emerge from their adolescence as the backbone of a country that has created, by the will of their labors and ingenuity, the best that the planet has to offer. These are the fields that produced the greatest generations, the generations that pulled us out of the death-spirals of two world wars. Why should we have doubts that the government they elected would act in anything other than their best interests? Wouldn't it only make sense that the wisest of the wise, the best of the best, the most ingenious of the politicos who sit in Washington, would make decisions that protect the children of the greatest generation, now and in the future, and not thrust them into danger? And if in that wisdom, our leaders ask that their lives be put at risk to protect that future, in Vietnam or elsewhere, shouldn't we have faith in those same leaders and answer the call to duty?

Frank came to a stop at an intersection while a tractor sputtered across our path. I glanced at the odometer. "13,023." Coach Dillon punched the accelerator and we were off again in a cloud of dust.

If the answer was so obvious, if answering the call to duty was so clear an obligation, some would say a privilege, then why are there thousands, maybe millions, taking to the streets in protest? Do the actions of the many trump the wisdom of the few? Was it only Vietnam and its specter that so terrified us, or was it something deeper inside that made us question our duty to country and place duty to self first?

I feared that it was our character, or lack thereof. I suddenly feared that even in good wars, my generation might not have the fortitude to serve. Life has become too easy. If we were displaced in time 25 years into the past, and the threat to our freedom was Nazis goose-stepping into Paris instead of black pajama-clad Viet Cong who dig punji-stake pits and disappear back into the jungle, would we have answered the call to duty or found reason to protest? Would we have joined Coach Dillon and his teammates? Would I have gone back into the water?

The odometer clicked over to "13,027."

I took a closer look at Danny. If there was a center of the heartland, around which the Midwest values that made us great revolved, it was Danny O'Neal, or at least what Danny used to be a few weeks ago. If you couldn't make your case to Danny, what hope did you have to make your case to the privileged aristocracy of the Chicago suburbs? I think Lyndon Johnson was wrong. It isn't all lost when you lose Walter Cronkite. You've lost it when you lose Danny O'Neal, and we've probably lost Danny O'Neal.

The sliding tires of the station wagon coming to a halt on the gravel road interrupted my contemplation.

"Everyone out!" Frank ordered. I looked over his shoulder as I climbed out of the car. "13,032." Great. We've got a race tomorrow and Frank's got us taking a 22-mile run. I hoped he knew what he was doing.

The Hawks congregated around Frank, who teetered on his cane as he tried to keep his balance. Sitting in one position for a long time stiffened his bad leg and I could tell he was in pain. The sun was warm on our skin but not too terribly warm. The unusually dry breeze coming out of the west was strong enough to ripple our t-shirts.

"Okay, gentlemen, this is the plan," Coach Dillon began. "I know you're a bit leg-tired and we've got a race tomorrow. I know you'd rather be jogging a few slow miles before the meet. That would be the easy thing to do, but doing the easy thing doesn't make you champions. A champion can turn on the speed and kick in that last half-mile no matter how tired he is. He's not afraid to burn his reserves because he knows he's put in the miles and he's confident in his ability to rise to the challenge. Making that extra effort when you're dog-tired just has to become second nature. It's what champions do. There will be a time in the state finals when your legs are burning and you're going to have to punch through the wall. A champion will the make the effort. Any questions?"

We all looked at each other with the confidence of champions. We had put in countless miles on the roads and run countless intervals on the tracks. We were invincible. The state finals would be merely a formality. There wasn't much we couldn't do. As we silently congratulated each other, the wind seemed to pick up a bit. Dust blew off the road.

"You know the way home, gentlemen," Frank said smiling as he pointed with his cane to the west. Just follow the yellow-brick-road."

"Sure thing, Coach," Billy said as Coach Dillon climbed back into the station wagon. "We'll see you in a couple of hours." As the engine roared to life, Frank popped his head out the window.

"By the way, gentlemen, I'll be seeing you along the way," and Frank sped off in a cloud of blue exhaust that quickly blew away in the breeze.

"I wonder what he meant by that?" Shaun asked a bit innocently.

"We'll find out soon enough," Amos answered. Danny stooped to tie his shoes. His hair was already tied back into an embryonic ponytail. A brilliantly white peace symbol was sewn on the rear of his running trunks, something new from yesterday. Amos seemed a bit annoyed.

"Do you have to wear that?"

"Wear what?"

"That." Amos pointed at his rear end.

"It's a peace symbol. You got a problem with peace?"

"And free love?" Billy chided.

"My dad calls it the footprint of the American chicken," Amos explained. "This is redneck country. Why take a stick to a sleeping dog?"

"Would you rather I run without any pants on?" I could see this wasn't going anywhere.

"Let's get started," I more than suggested and started running. Everyone but Carl started trailing behind me. He just stood there. "Carl, what's the matter?" Carl opened his mouth a few times before answering.

"Long way."

Once again, Carl's few words pretty much summed up the situation; and with that, we began our run back to Barrel.

There are two things runners dread encountering on flat county roads, farm dogs and headwinds. We can deal with most anything else. Farm dogs diligently sit at the end of a driveway that spills out on a county road, guarding the portal with a sense of mission and dedication to duty that even the Swiss Guard at the Vatican would admire. It's their job to protect their master's homestead against intrusion, real or imagined, and it's a job they take more than seriously. When eyeing one of these canine sentinels, a wise runner will move to the opposite side of the road, pick up the pace a bit and avoid eye contact with the hope of not drawing attention to himself. The old grey backs will raise their heads, twitch their ears, assess your presence as non-threatening, and return to their afternoon naps. The youngsters will light out after you as much out of sport as concern, yapping and snapping at your heals. Once you've been chased an acceptable distance, they will stop their pursuit and, with tails wagging, return to their posts.

Wind can be your friend or your enemy. Given the choice you would prefer a tailwind to a headwind. Even a light breeze at your back can make the miles click by seconds faster, a 10-miler seems like nine, a steep hill seems like a shallow grade. A dry but light headwind on a searing day can be as much of a blessing as a tailwind. The coolness that comes from the wind evaporating the sweat off your chest is refreshing enough to compensate for the extra effort of overcoming that headwind. But when that headwind broaches an unspoken speed, the one-time ally becomes an enemy. The wind can bleed energy out of your body no less than a festering virus. The effort of running headlong into a wind makes your body react no differently than assaulting a steep hill. Your arms begin swinging, your body begins leaning forward, your gait rotates to the balls of your feet. But unlike running a hill where relief comes at the crest, redemption during a 22-mile run into the wind comes only with its completion.

As we began our trek back to Barrel, the wind began picking up dust by the handful. It was a very bad sign. Our normal banter quickly petered out, as the effort of fighting the wind and the dust began to take its toll. The unusual dryness sucked moisture out of us. We all soon had cottonmouth.

The miles clicked by slowly. Our pace was pedestrian. The fields, nearly harvested, gave us little to gaze at to take our minds off the strain of our effort. The unforgiving grid of the county roads gave us little opportunity to think that by some divine intervention, or Scotty transporting us, we had gone further than we had. Each intersection marked another mile. There could be no arguments, no compromises, no fantasies. Mile one gave way to mile two, followed by mile three; the pattern repeated itself mile after mile. The occasional truck rattled by us, raising a cloud of dust that quickly dissipated in the wind, but otherwise it was a lonely run. Simply to distract myself I counted the swings of Danny's arms for a few miles, using the glint of the sun off Corey's ring to measure the cadence.

With the exception of Carl, who fell behind and was nearly out of sight, we ran in a closely-knit single file. Like bicycle racers, we took our turns at the front of the line, breaking the wind for our teammates. One of us would stay in the lead until the effort was too much to continue, maybe half a mile at a time, when he would slip to the back of the line and it would be the next Hawk's turn to be at the point. When Amos was in the lead, we were like a Volkswagen in the slipstream of an 18-wheeler. He was a godsend.

Carl, dear Carl, suffered for his falling behind. Running alone, he had nobody to break the wind. His effort was many times that of the rest of the Hawks. There were times when the wind gusts literally blew Carl backwards. But in his silent devotion, he harbored no thought of quitting, no thought of walking. There was only one possibility, one option; keep moving forward, no matter how slowly. Every step was one less step that needed to be taken.

We had covered nearly 18 miles of unrelenting headwinds when we approached the base of the hill. Our legs were heavy, our mouths were dry. Salt from dried sweat outlined our eyes giving us the appearance of tired owls. Danny spoke the first words since the start of our trek.

"There's Frank."

Coach Dillon was poised at the bottom of the hill, leaning against the station wagon, as we arrived. We slowed to a walk over the last few yards. The wind swooped down the hill hitting us in the face.

"What's up?" Billy asked cautiously.

"Where's Carl?" Frank asked.

"Back there, somewhere," Amos answered, jerking a thumb over his shoulder. Coach Dillon walked a few yards back the way we came.

"There he is," Frank said, eyeing Carl as he slowly approached our position. Frank walked out to meet him. He put his arm around Carl's shoulder and spoke a few words into his ear. Carl smiled and nodded his reply. We were curious what that was all about but were too tired to ask. When Carl and Frank rejoined the group, Frank took off his sunglasses, inspected them, brushed off some of the road's dust and put them back on. He also gave each of us an inspecting look, as if gauging our resolution.

"Run the hill," he finally said.

"We were planning on that," Shaun said lightly, "that's the way home."

"Ten times," Frank added, "building to full pace." We were stunned. We could hardly stand in place as the wind careening down the hill tried to topple us over.

"Coach, we've come almost 20 miles already," Danny pleaded, "into the wind."

"Run the hill," Frank repeated, "10 times, building to full pace. Learn how to accelerate when you're tired."

"But Coach," Amos began to protest, but Coach Dillon cut off the debate with a look of sternness I had rarely seen.

"Who here has given up on winning the state championship?" Nobody said a word. "Who here has given up on earning those scholarships?" We looked at our shoes, ashamed to look Frank in the eye. "Who here wants to enlist or get drafted?" I began to answer but Danny waved me off. "Okay. Run the hill, 10 times, building to full pace."

With little more to say, we lined up at the bottom of the hill and waited for Coach Dillon's command. Sand blowing off the road and into our eyes made us squint like looking into a searchlight.

"Go."

With legs weighed down with the effort of 18 miles into the wind, we started our first assault of the hill. We barely moved. It was like running up a flagpole in a hurricane. The forces pushing us down the hill were far more than we could muster going up. It must have taken a minute to go the first 200 yards. Carl was blown backwards onto his ass twice. With each futile step, our legs got heavier and our arms got stiffer. The wind sucked every bit of moisture out of us. I looked at my teammates, who were doggedly fighting the hill. Even Danny was flailing. Only Amos, his massive build seemingly impervious to the force of the wind like a stone statue in the park, moved methodically up the hill. He reached the top long before any of the rest of us.

We were so exhausted, that our jog back to the start would have been impossible if it hadn't been downhill. Just by putting our feet forward, gravity pulled us downhill, and if not for gravity, the wind would have blown us down the hill. Coach Dillon watched us with the scrutiny of a jeweler inspecting a gem. I knew this was test, but I didn't quite know what we were being tested for. We had a meet the next day against the Danville Titans. It seemed like a bad time to be testing our mettle and making our legs stiff, sore and tired, but that is exactly what he was doing. Frank was taking us to the cliff edge, pushing us beyond what we thought we could do. It wasn't clear to me whether we were going to hang on by our fingernails or plunge off that cliff.

When finally assembled at the bottom of the hill, it was all we could do to shuffle our feet. Lifting them would have wasted precious reserves. Frank never took his eyes off of us.

"That's the first one. Nine more to go. You've got to get it into your minds that you can push yourself when you think you've got nothing left. Learn to run on empty. Get used to running a hill when you're exhausted." Frank was pointing up the hill with his cane. "This is just a dirt hill. You're the Hawks! Hawks don't let a pile of dirt get the best of them! Hawks have been mastering this hill for 25 years! Don't let it master you! Look at the way Pete attacks the..."

Frank stopped in mid-sentence. He tried to restart but couldn't.

Pete. Peter Lorenzo. Frank's teammate and best friend from the Hawks of 1942. Peter Lorenzo. The soldier Frank couldn't save on the beaches of Normandy on D-Day of 1944. They must have run this hill a thousand times together. What was it about that day that took Frank back 25 years? We all looked at each other, too embarrassed to look at Coach Dillon.

"Nine more to go," Frank finally said. "Build to full pace. Go!"

It was dark for an hour before we made it back to the gym.

CHAPTER 30

The Danville Titans arrived at our home course aboard a beat-up school bus that belched black exhaust and was so tilted to one side that I thought it was missing tires. The bus pulled into the parking lot and rolled to a halt with the finality of an old nag finishing her rounds of pulling a milk wagon. It was reassuring that there was at least one other school in the league that was as destitute as Barrel High. In spite of their less than auspicious entrance, as the Titans walked off the bus we knew there would be a race that afternoon. There is just something about the appearance of a runner that tells you that he will be a force to contend with. It is neither a swagger nor a display of bulging muscles. It is neither bravado nor intimidation. It is an unspoken, almost telepathic transmission of confidence. I have come to run a race today. Run with me if you can.

Our confidence drained like water through a sieve. Our legs were heavy, tight and sore from yesterday's efforts. There wasn't one Hawk who was anywhere near the top of his form.

"Shit," Billy said, "look at those guys. I thought this would be a cakewalk."

"It might've been if we had some rest yesterday," Shaun complained. "I can't believe Coach did that to us."

"He wants us to learn how to race when we're tired," Danny defended Coach Dillon. "He knows what it's going to be like in the state finals. He's been there."

"Yeah, well we're not going to make it to the state finals if we lose this meet."

"We'll win," Danny said.

Danny was right, but only barely. The mind is very good about protecting itself from unpleasant experiences but is far from perfect in doing so. Moments of anxiety, and sometimes terror, are neatly balled up and stored away in the recesses of your mind so as to not interfere with your daily goings on. It is only during nights of fitful sleep that those balls leak their contents into your conscience, creating sweaty sheet-soaking nightmares whose only benefit is waking you from the sleep that brought those same memories to the surface.

The race began in ways we could not have predicted. Within a half-mile of the start, the entire Titan team was ahead of us save for Danny, who struggled to stay in their pack. The gap between the Titans and Hawks widened to more than 15 seconds before the first mile was completed. Our legs were just too heavy, our sinews just too sore, our throats just too raw from Thursday's tortuous workout to be part of this race. We looked ahead and saw the backs of our opponents, and saw our state championship running away from us, our scholarships dissolving into nothingness with another loss. The specter of Vietnam came menacingly closer as the Titans pulled away. The nightmare of a squandered opportunity was born as we approached the mile-and-half marker, and it was a pajama-soaker. We had nearly given up. We were tired but should not have been that tired. Races are won or lost between the ears. We had to learn that, and Frank was our tutor.

Coach Dillon positioned himself on the road as the course emptied out of the woods. As each of us passed, he made eye contact and in some telepathic way transmitted the confidence we needed to build in ourselves, the confidence that separates want-to-be champions from those who make good on their ambitions.

Push yourself when you're tired. Dig down into the depths of your soul and draw upon the investments you have made through the intensity of your workouts. Become singular in your purpose. Will your body to do your bidding. Feed and feed on your teammates.

Frank had said those words many times and when he said them, they were just words, the sort of coach's drivel that athletes take for granted. It took the challenge he had placed before us that day in the race against the Titans to make those words part of our psyche. My legs did not lose their heaviness and my sinews did not become less sore, but Coach Dillon's telepathy did something to me that made that discomfort less important. I put my faith in Coach Dillon no less than my faith in God, and pulled from the depths of my conditioning the reserves to lift my legs higher, to turn them over faster and begin closing the gap between me and the Titans.

That act would have been worthless had the others not also put their faith in Coach Dillon's words. As I surged forward, I felt the same commitment from Shaun and Billy and Amos as they flanked me. It took more than just one of us to be converted to win the championship. It took all of us. Teams win the state championship, not individuals. As I glanced to each side and behind me, I saw the conviction of the converted in my teammates' eyes, no less than in the eyes of those who witness miracles under the tents of roadside evangelists. I trusted that Carl had also seen the light but he was still far behind.

We caught the Titans well into the third mile, merging our two packs into a single massive group of runners. Danny, who had been mired in the Titan pack unable to break free, was reenergized by our arrival knowing that he was no longer alone in his battle to secure this victory. As I took my place by Danny's side, synching my stride with his, the Hawks' network was completed, its intensity as blinding as a searchlight in front of movie premier. The Hawks' nucleus began moving forward, an unstoppable force, splitting apart the Titans pack and leaving them behind. They were the unwashed and we were the converted. Hallelujah, brother!

We won the meet against the Titans 17-38. But more importantly we came away from that victory with the confidence that we could be champions.

CHAPTER 31

Career Day of 1967 at Barrel High was, with one exception, no different than career days at the countless other high schools that dotted the prairies of downstate Illinois. That one exception was that Career Day of 1967 marked the completion of Danny O'Neal's transformation. It was my first Career Day at Barrel High but I knew what to expect. The auditorium was filled with a student body that was rapidly becoming bored, policed by an already bored squad of teachers who weren't clever enough not to get roped into assembly duty. On stage sat a Village People collection of the trades and professions who were tasked with inspiring an uninspirable student body to become contributing and hard-working members of our society. There was a doctor, a plumber, a nurse, a carpenter, an accountant and a marine sergeant major.

Given the choice of being bored in class or being bored at the Career Day assembly, the choice was obvious. At least homework wouldn't be assigned at the assembly. I sat next to Danny and as the lights were dimmed we both slouched in our seats with our feet on the back of the seats in front of us, readying ourselves for the ordeal ahead. The doctor stepped to the podium, pulled out sheets of his carefully prepared prose, signaled for the first slide and began his spiel.

"The medical profession is demanding but rewarding. First slide please."

Click.

And then the plumber clumsily followed the doctor, speaking from his handwritten 3 x 5 cards.

"Plumbing can be a demanding but rewarding profession. First slide please."

Click. Click.

And then the nurse, the carpenter and the accountant.

"Accounting is an always demanding but always rewarding profession. First slide please."

Click. Click. Click.

Through this monotony, it was difficult to tell if Danny was engaged or bored out of his mind. He sat motionless, save for twirling Corey's ring on his finger. I did my best to pay attention to the sincere but hopelessly inept speeches of our would-be mentors, but there are some things that are almost too much to ask of 17-year-old boys and this was one of them. I amused myself by looking around me, trying to imagine the jobs and professions in which my classmates would find themselves in 10 years time. Jerry, a linebacker on the football team, would make a good policeman. Emily, who volunteered for anything that had to do with kids, would probably become a teacher. Vince, who was as close to a savant as Barrel High was likely to produce, might end up an industrial mogul. Kelly, whose skirts were short enough that we knew when she wasn't wearing panties, might pursue the oldest profession.

At long last, the accountant finished his droning and returned to his seat with polite but scattered applause at his back. As if on cue, the Marine sergeant major strode to the podium with turns so close to right angles it would have taken a protractor to prove otherwise. His appearance was stunning. His dress blue pants, trimmed by a red strip, had creases so sharp they could have sliced bread. His chevrons were bold upon his sleeve and ironed flat to an atom's precision. The rack of ribbons on his chest gave testimony to three wars' worth of bravery. His crew cut was so sharply trimmed he could have just stepped out of a barber's chair. His sandy hair was only beginning to become peppered with gray. He stood at the podium with mechanical precision, his eyes brighter and sharper than the shining brass belt buckle that reflected the spotlight. His commanding presence silenced the murmurs and whispered conversations that provided a background hum during the previous presentations. The sergeant major stood silently for what seemed like an eternity. Every eye in the auditorium was upon him. Danny leaned forward in his chair, his attention equally rapt.

"To be a soldier, to be a Marine," the sergeant major began, "is to serve your country. It is an honor and it is a privilege of being a citizen of this great nation. When you become a soldier, you accept the responsibility of defending your country against attack, of securing its borders against our enemies and defending our freedom wherever you are called upon to do so. There is no nobler profession. You will command men and you will command respect."

The sergeant major was in friendly territory. It was like preaching to the choir. Looking around at my fellow students, I saw heads nodding, smiles erupting and chests expanding with pride. They elbowed each other with the friendship and familiarity of a shared fate. These boys had been preprogrammed to fulfill the destiny of the young men of Barrel by serving their country with unquestioned loyalty. Answering the call to duty was as natural a response to them as shielding you eyes from the noontime sun. All the sergeant major needed to do was to press the button to execute their programming.

"Should you be fortunate enough to serve in combat," the sergeant major continued, "you will find bravery in yourself you never thought you had. You will perform gallant acts you thought only occurred in the movies. You will wear your medals with a pride you thought you never deserved. You may begin the battle as a boy, but you will finish the battle as a hardened Marine."

The sergeant major scanned the crowd in such a way that every boy later swore that he had looked directly into his eyes. "Are you worthy of this challenge?" The auditorium was cast into a silence so deep that the creaking of an unoiled folding chair seemed deafening. Then a single pair of hands began clapping, and then a second and then a third, and then the entire auditorium. The applause, cheers and whistles that erupted were truly deafening. The sergeant major smiled broadly. His mission was nearly complete. So mesmerizing was the spell he cast, he could have given lessons to snake oil salesmen and rainmakers, maybe even my father.

It was only then that I noticed Danny was no longer sitting by my side. I looked around in the darkness of the auditorium and there he was walking down the aisle toward the stage. By the time the applause died away, Danny was standing in the front of the auditorium, staring up at the sergeant major on stage behind the podium. The contrast could not have been greater. The sergeant major was broad and muscular, crisp and chiseled, standing tall, as if having just stepped out of a recruiting poster. Danny, on the other hand, wore the uniform of the opposition. His tie-dyed shirt and faded jeans hung on his runner's thinness like a poorly dressed mannequin. His rubber-banded ponytail and old-tire sandals spoke volumes of his newly found disrespect for the high school dress code. His only concession to the establishment was Corey's ring that he still wore. The sergeant major gave Danny only slight notice as he continued his oration.

"The war in Vietnam gets a lot of bad press these days. Those long-haired hippies you see on TV protest against a war they know nothing about while burning the flag of our great nation." A chorus of boos and catcalls peppered from the audience. "Let me tell you the truth about the war in Vietnam. It is a war to stop Communism. It is a war to secure the freedom of the Vietnamese people. It is a war no less glorious than the wars your fathers and grandfathers fought. It is our war to win. It is your war to win. It is the war you will tell your grandchildren about." Applause erupted into a crescendo that hurt my ears. Through the din of the applause, I could barely hear the words Danny was shouting up at the podium.

"Tha…load…bul…."

The sergeant major motioned for silence and the applause quickly dissipated.

"Our pony-tailed friend here has something to say," the sergeant major said, pointing down at Danny. "Let's give him a chance." All eyes turned to Danny while Danny's eyes never left the sergeant major.

"That's a load of bullshit," Danny yelled up to the podium. The ensuing silence echoed through the auditorium.

"Say again," the sergeant major commanded, not quite sure he could believe what had been said.

"I said that's a load of bullshit." One of the men teachers leapt out of his seat in the direction of Danny as if to haul him away but the sergeant major waved the teacher off.

"And why is that?" the sergeant major asked.

"Because you make the war sound like a glamorous vacation," Danny accused, "when it's really about killing and trying not to get killed. Why don't you tell these boys how many of them are going to come back from Vietnam in body bags? How many will come back without legs? How many will be killed by an innocent-looking South Vietnamese mama-san or a Saigon whore who's really a Viet Cong agent?" Danny turned to face the audience. "Don't you know when you're being lied to?" The sergeant major seemed unfazed.

"Heroes die in wars," he said.

"Heroes die in just wars," Danny countered. "Fools die in trumped-up wars." It was then that two huge boys, they must have been football players, launched themselves from the second row toward Danny.

"Get the Commie!" one yelled. Danny was cornered between the vectors of the oncoming hulks and the stage behind him. With no place to go, he stood his ground as the boys grabbed his arms.

"Get the hell off me," Danny commanded. The brighter-looking of the two football players put his face inches from Danny's.

"Shut the fuck up, Commie." Danny eyed his opponent and then began yelling.

"Hey, hey LBJ! How many kids did ya kill today? Hey, hey, LBJ! How many kids did ya kill today?"

It was then that things began happening quickly. Amos rose out of his seat, not unlike a bear rearing back on his haunches, and in only a few of his impressively large steps stood in front of the football players who still held Danny's arms. As huge as the players were, Amos hovered over them.

"Let go of my friend," Amos said as calmly as though he was ordering a milkshake at Mabel's.

"Go fuck yourself," the not so bright football player retorted. Amos, with almost uncanny deliberateness, grabbed the football player's collar, lifted him off his feet and tossed him into the first row of seats like a rag-doll. It was then that the other football player landed a punch on Amos's jaw. Amos, looking more startled than hurt, just picked him up and threw him into the first row of seats to join his friend. Before either Danny or Amos could beat a retreat, they were both assaulted by boys who began streaming down out of the seats yelling "Get the Commies!" and "God-damned hippies!" Before I knew it, the rest of the Hawks and I were in the midst of the pushing and shoving as well. I'm not certain who threw the next punch that ignited the melee, but I'm proud to say I landed a few myself.

That evening I answered a knock at the front door to find Danny waiting in the darkness of our porch wearing his backpack full of books and carrying Corey's duffle bag stuffed full of clothes. His performance at the Career Day assembly pounded the wedge a few more inches deeper into the crack that separated Danny from his father. A philosophical separation was now a physical one. I opened the screen door and let in my new roommate. That was also the first night I heard Danny call his brother's name from the deep recesses of a sweaty nightmare. That was also the night I learned that not all casualties of war occur on the battlefield.

CHAPTER 32

The cross country meet against the Selby Sharks should've been a cakewalk. They were good but not that good, while the Hawks were simply getting better and better every week. But within the span of the few minutes of the Career Day slugfest, a sure victory turned into a likely defeat. Only two days before the meet, Danny and Amos were suspended for a week for their part in the melee. That left us with only four runners. Even if we swept the first three places, we'd lose the meet for lack of a fifth man.

It was a sullen and sorry Hawks who gathered in the locker room, ashamed at what they had done and deathly fearful that their quest for scholarships and their tickets out of Vietnam had disappeared in the flailing of fists. It would have been easy to blame Danny for having started the snowball rolling downhill that sucked Amos into its path, resulting in both of them getting suspended. It also would have been easy to forget that it was only by luck that the rest of us weren't suspended as well.

It also would have been difficult to blame Danny. Like his brother before him, Danny put himself in harm's way to protect others from danger. Danny knew the fate that awaited his classmates, those who enlisted and those who were drafted, because he knew all too well the outcome of Corey's answering the call to duty. In Danny's mind, duty to self trumped duty to country when the cause was as unjust as he judged the war in Vietnam to be.

Frank sat on the bench on one side of our row of lockers and the Hawks sat on the bench on the other side. The disappointment that was written on Frank's face needed no translation and overshadowed the pride he felt for Danny for his Quixote-like performance at the Career Day assembly. Coach Dillon tried to teach us to choose our battles wisely and we had ignored his tutelage. Think of the big picture, he had implored us. Don't lose sight of the prize, he had advised us. Let the small thinkers have their say, he had counseled us. We had collectively chosen not to heed his wisdom, and it might have cost us dearly.

"I'm not going to spend a lot of time restating the obvious and making you feel worse than you do," Frank said, amazingly calm in spite of the disappointment he must have felt, "but you let your emotions get the best of you." Frank was looking straight at Danny but then shifted his gaze to the rest of us. "Be passionate about what you do but be smarter than the next guy. We're lucky it was only Danny and Amos who were suspended. It could have been all of you." Frank got up and balanced himself on his cane, almost walking a full circle around the pivot. "This is the situation," Frank began explaining. "We've only got four eligible runners. Without a fifth man, we forfeit the race. That means no state finals, no state championship, and no scholarships. We can't let that happen."

"This is not a problem," Shaun tried to say with some confidence. "The Sharks just aren't that good. We'll go 1-2-3 on Friday. So all we need is somebody who can finish the race and we'll win."

"And if we don't go 1-2-3?" Frank asked. Shaun started to answer but thought better of it. Frank pointed in turn at Shaun, Billy and me. "The three of you are going to have run the race of your lives or it's all over. You understand that, don't you? This could be the biggest race you'll ever run, even bigger than the state championships." We nodded in unison, as though our heads were all tied together. "But we still need a fifth man, and who's that going to be?"

"What about Dennis Fisher?" Amos asked, trying to redeem some credibility with Frank. Dennis was a quarter-miler who played football in the fall. Frank thought for a moment.

"Maybe. I've never been able to get Dennis to run more than a half-mile, but maybe."

What about Jill?" Danny asked.

"What are you talking about?" Billy seemed to object. "A girl can't run on the team."

"Yes, she can," Frank corrected, conjuring up the state high athletic regulations in his mind. "Since we don't have a girls cross country team, Jill could run for us."

"You can't be serious," Billy came back with. "We'd be a laughingstock."

"Do you want to win or not?" Shaun said, now joining ranks with the opposition. "Besides, she's a lot faster than Carl or anyone else we could find." Carl winced as though he had been slapped across the face. It was bad enough he was the worst runner on the team. Now some girl off the street was going to be called on to save the season. Carl seemed to be thinking up a response, and slowly stated his case.

"I'm not slow." Carl's defense was ignored as being worse than unimportant. If Jill could run, then all Carl needed to do was bring up the rear.

"Then Jill it is," Coach Dillon said, half as a statement and half as a question. Nobody objected so the deal seemed to be done. There was one missing piece to this puzzle.

"Will she do it?" I asked. Without the need for a cue, all of our eyes turned to Danny. It didn't take but a second for him to respond.

"I'll ask her."

Danny didn't join us for the morning workout. Instead, he sat on the curb outside Jill's house in the early morning chill, waiting for her to emerge for her morning run. Jill was more than a little surprised to see Danny outside her door, his twirling of Corey's ring giving notice that he was deep in thought.

"What do I owe for this privilege?" Jill asked as she took her steps two at a time, startling Danny.

"Oh, nothing much. I didn't feel like running with the Hawks this morning, and didn't feel like running alone..."

"So I'm your third choice?" she asked playfully.

"No, I didn't mean..."

"Fourth choice? This isn't impressing me."

"No, really…"

"That's getting to be one good-looking scar," Jill said, gently moving Danny's locks off his forehead to expose his souvenir from the Chicago mêlée. "I hope it was worth it."

"I guess it will be if girls think it's dashing. Do you?"

"Let's get moving," Jill said with a smile and lit off down the street. Danny picked up after her and was soon by her side.

As they ran miles together on the county roads, they talked about school, about Chicago, about wanting to be part of something bigger than Barrel, about Jill's dreams to see the world, about Danny's confusion about where his duty lies. As they ran, they discovered that they had more in common than they ever imagined, their visions of their future lives intertwining like jumbled string. At the turn-around point, Danny slowed to a halt and stood clearly at a loss for words.

"Tired already?" Jill asked.

"There's something I need to ask you," Danny said.

"Sounds serious."

"It is."

"Well, you can't be dumping me because we're not dating."

"It's not that type of serious. It's more like…I need you to do me a favor. I need you to do the Hawks a favor."

"What type of favor?"

Danny told her about the suspensions, the cross country meet on Friday and the plan that Jill run in the race to secure the Hawks' victory over the Sharks. Tears welled in Danny's eyes when he confessed the risk that he and Amos inflicted on their teammates. Everything, but everything depended on the Hawks winning a race they expected Danny to lead but would be standing on the sidelines instead.

Jill raised her hand and with a finger across Danny's lips, silenced him. She took both of Danny's hands in hers, stood on her toes and kissed Danny, a long, tender but passionate kiss. Standing in the intersection of nameless county roads in the after-dawn during the middle of a morning run, Danny felt an emotion, an elation that Shelly never sparked in him. They held each other for all too short a time, their embarrassingly brief running outfits allowing them to touch in a most sensual way. They finally let go of each other, both smiling, both a bit embarrassed, both happy.

"Does that mean yes?" Danny asked.

"You bet it does, but only if you can catch me!" and Jill took off running back towards Barrel. Danny happily gave chase.

CHAPTER 33

The cross country meet against the Selby Sharks was mostly unremarkable; but in one respect, it was a watershed for the Hawks. The roster for the Hawks listed only five names, a little bit unusual but not outrageously so. The fact that one of the names was "J. Burke" was not at all a point of concern for the Selby coach. There was nothing deceitful in that. No lies were told but no truths were revealed. Jill arrived at the meet wearing baggy sweats and her hair hidden under a baseball cap. She showered three times to remove the fragrance of her favorite perfume. She kept to herself as she warmed up so not to draw attention to herself. The fact that her running style was more boy-like than girl-like aided her anonymity. Danny stood with Coach Dillon and Diane, carefully watching to see if Jill would become a point of contention or even be noticed at all. When Jill took off her sweats for the start of the race, her oversized t-shirt and running trunks made her look as unisex as most any adolescent boy. She stood at the far end of the starting line, avoiding conversation and eye contact with any of the opposing runners.

The race was an easy victory for the Hawks. Billy, Shaun and I effortlessly outdistanced the Sharks' first runner. We ran smoothly and confidently like the champions we aspired to be, and crossed the finish line together in an indistinguishable pack. Jill held back, running easily at the rear side-by-side with Carl. She wisely allowed at least a few of the Sharks to remain ahead of her. But as the race moved into its final mile, Danny could sense Jill's agitation, her wanting to run to the front. She moved the pace up, pulling Carl with her, encouraging him, building his confidence. When they passed the Shark ahead of them, a change came over Carl. His legs began turning over faster, his form began to resemble that of a runner. He was finally in a position to make himself valuable to the Hawks. Jill could have run to the front, leaving Carl far behind, but instead slowed to allow Carl to grab his finish stick ahead of her.

It was a good day for Carl.

"Did you see that?" Billy asked Frank after the race. "Did you see how easily Jill ran? She could be our fifth or sixth man. Let's just keep her on the team."

"That's not a bad idea," Coach Dillon answered, "except for one thing."

"What's that?"

"Jill's not going to get drafted and doesn't need a deferment. Carl does."

CHAPTER 34

I was leaving school, walking by Frank's office, just as he was tacking up the newspaper clipping of our latest victory of the season on the hallway bulletin board. The headline read "Hawk Harriers Win Another—On to State Prelims." There was a nice photo of Danny grabbing the number one stick at the end of the finish chute. Frank stood back and scrutinized his work. He pulled out one of the tacks, straightened the clipping and replaced the tack. He then carefully read all the articles, telling the tales of the season's cross country meets, as though he was reading them for the first time. It was an impressive display. Even if I had not been a member of the team, I think I would have been awed by the story they told. Runners from a backwoods high school running their way to victory after victory, only the reader couldn't know the reasons why. We were running to be champions, running to seal the deal with Sid Benson and procure the scholarships that would grant us the safety and haven of college. We were running for the luxury of turning deaf ears to our country's call to duty. Had our readership known, would they have been so awed?

But that deafness was justified. It was a wasteful war conducted by a callous and unknowing leadership who lost no sleep at committing young men to fight and die in battles whose only measures of goodness were fabricated body counts. This was the truth we accepted. This is the truth we believed. This was the truth because we wanted it to be the truth. We were uninterested in other versions of the truth.

I stood back in the shadows watching Frank examine the clippings. There was an indescribable pride in his slow scrutiny of the articles. Occasionally Frank would stop and reread a paragraph or two, his finger tracing the lines of text. It finally struck me that he was analyzing his own coaching. The articles were a record of his success no less than they were a record of the Hawks' victories. They were Frank's report card. A slamming door down the hallway swung Frank's attention toward me. Having been seen, I sheepishly stepped out of the shadows. Frank silently motioned me toward him and I walked to his side.

"What do you see here?" Coach Dillon asked, pointing to the articles. Knowing Frank rarely asked questions without a purpose, I looked for some hidden meaning. All I saw were headlines, words and photos, the makings of a scrapbook but nothing profound.

"Not much," I admitted.

"Look again." I glanced over the clippings one more time.

"They're just a bunch of clippings." Frank looked disappointed.

"Come with me," he commanded and began limping up the stairs toward his office, the click of his cane against the linoleum echoing in the hallways. When we arrived at his office, Frank motioned me to a chair. With inexplicable reverence, he opened a file drawer and took out a well-worn manila folder. He opened the folder as though he was opening the frail pages of a Gutenberg Bible. The folder contained stacks of yellowing *Barrel Gazette* newspaper clippings, each stack held together with a paper clip and a label: "1949," "1950," "1951"…The folder was a time capsule of Coach Dillon's legacy, preserving the record of the victories and losses his teams had enjoyed and suffered, as reported in the *Barrel Gazette*. Each stack froze in time the teams that Frank had mentored. Every year, Frank took on the task of transforming a collection of undisciplined high school boys into a team of athletes, of elite runners who gave much but received more. They carried away lessons from the experience that would enrich their lives forever. But even as they matured into adults with lives far beyond the confines of Barrel High School, they would also live forever in Frank's memory just as they appeared on those yellowing scraps of paper. And for some that is the only life they would enjoy.

Coach Dillon took the paper clip off of the stack of clippings from 1949 and gently handed me an article with a photo of the Hawks from his first year of coaching. He pointed at a grinning boy whose gap between his front teeth was large enough to spit seeds through.

"That's Gary Tuttle," Frank said. "He was a consistent third man on the team for a couple of years and one of the best half-milers I ever coached. He just loved running the 880. I think he ran cross country just to please me." Frank smiled a smile of remembrance. I took the article and looked carefully at Gary's photo. It was as though I was discovering a long lost relative. We were members of an extended family that wasn't related through anything other than shared experiences and the devotion of our coach, but sometimes that can be thicker than blood.

"Gary's family ran a dairy herd just north of town," Frank continued. "All Gary wanted to do was graduate, marry the girl next door and spend the rest of his life on the family farm. That was his world and the only world he wanted but there was a bigger world that beckoned. We were at war, his country called for his service and he answered he call. He put duty to country above duty to self and enlisted."

I handed back the article and Frank solemnly returned the clipping to its stack. "Gary was killed in action in Korea in the battle at the Chosin Reservoir. They'd run out of ammunition and his company was surrounded by Mao's Chinese. They had no place to go, so they stood their ground and fought hand to hand with bayonets until there were none of them left."

We spent the next hour reliving Frank's memories of his past cross country teams. They were teams but they were also individuals, all as dear to Frank as his own flesh and blood. We laughed and admired their accomplishments, and held back tears at the retelling of tragedies that befell them. I came away knowing Coach Dillon in a way I would have never otherwise known. I was a member of Frank's long gray line, accepted without question or prejudice. Frank made an unspoken commitment to me as he had to the runners before me and as he would to the runners that would follow me. I will train you and I will mentor you but I will also protect you, a vow that intensified with the years. Pete, Gary, Corey. Frank would not tolerate this legacy continuing.

CHAPTER 35

Practice would be a tough one. We had only a few weeks left before the state finals. I didn't know that much about coaching but I did know that these next few weeks were absolutely critical to how we would perform in the championship race. Whether we won or whether we lost, whether a year from now we were in college or in some shithole in Vietnam, depended on what we did in these few weeks.

The stakes were high, very high. They could not be any higher for either Frank or the Hawks. If we won, we would be rescued from a fate that we could only vicariously imagine yet feared with a reality that was no less hard than the rockiness of our track. If we lost, Frank would have failed yet again to rescue his runners from that same fate. In his mind, Frank had failed Pete Lorenzo on the beaches of Normandy so many years ago and he had to atone for that sin. Frank would not, could not, now fail his Hawks.

I arrived at practice a little early, not having bothered with my last class of the day, not so much out of callousness but out of boredom. I changed into my running trunks and singlet, and jogged around the deserted track, just enjoying the coolness of the afternoon as I waited for my teammates. I enjoyed the solitude, a time to be alone with my thoughts. As much as I wanted those thoughts to be pleasant, light and bright, they quickly turned seriously gray.

Much had changed for me in the few months since I arrived in Barrel. On my first day in Barrel, I only had a glimmer of the magnitude of the impending call to duty that awaited me. My first walk through Holden Park should have been enough to make that call something more than just an annoying thought. The voices of the young men, most no older than me, who had paid the ultimate price called down to me from their vantage points on the memorial spires in Holden Park. Had I been more aware of the decision that lay ahead of me, I might have listened more carefully as the breeze wafted their muses towards me. Were those voices warnings or encouragement? Having bested their fears on distant battlefields, would they portray their ordeal as patriotic and heroic, and so entice me to follow them? Or would they do their best to protect me from suffering their own fate? It was impossible to retrieve the words the winds had carried away and so I could only speculate on their message.

The war in Vietnam, once only a distant thought that was easier to ignore than acknowledge, was rapidly becoming as real as the voices of those who did not return. Corey O'Neal's death focused the prospect of my obligation and intensified my fear of fulfilling that obligation. The chaos of the Chicago demonstration made real the raw emotion and conflict between those who saw Corey as a patriot and those that saw him a patsy. The intensity of Danny O'Neal and Frank Dillon's efforts to save me from the prospect of sharing Corey's fate created an opportunity I could not have imagined only a summer ago.

With every lap around the track, I glimpsed the memorial spires in Holden Park as they momentarily showed themselves through the branches of trees that were rapidly shedding their leaves. On the opposite side of the track, I could see across the fields to the elementary school yard where children innocently played their afternoon's games. The distance between the playground and Holden Park could be measured in yards, in years or in sacrifice. From giggling on the jungle gyms and swings of the playground to becoming an etching on the spires of Holden park had been only a scant six or seven years for some. How much life could they have lived in those few years? Had they hit a home run, owned a car or kissed a girl? Had they been worldly enough to even know they had a choice?

In spite of Danny and Frank's scheming, in spite of the deal with Sid Benson, in spite of the countless hours the Hawks had trained to win the championship that would excuse them from their duty, the distance to Holden Park seemed terribly short. The state championships were nearly upon us. The victory we needed to put great distance between us and Holden Park was at our fingertips but was only achievable with a stretch that might extend us beyond our abilities. We started the season with a loss to the Spartans that cast a dark shadow on our prospects of becoming champions. But Danny, whose failure may have cost us that first victory, harnessed his seemingly limitless running talent to lead what was on the surface an unremarkable team to a string of unbroken victories that were as surprising as they were deserved. But we would still have to beat the Spartans to win the state championship. Much had changed from that first meet but much had not.

Sid Benson had it right. We were a team that was at the threshold of winning the state championship, earning scholarships and receiving a reprieve from Vietnam only because of a fluke of a hundred-year-old scoring system. You could win dual meets with three or four good runners by scoring an unbeatably low point total no matter how weak your fifth runner was, and that was good enough to get you to the state finals. But to win the championship, you needed seven finely tuned athletes. Five would score your small tally of points and two would finish ahead of your opponents and so increase their totals. The Hawks didn't have the depth to win. Sid knew it. Frank denied it. We didn't think about it.

Danny was in his own right an individual champion. If he did not win the state finals, it would be a travesty. Shaun, Billy and I would score well. We were good runners, maybe even good enough. On a good day, Amos might also score well. Amos, his tree-trunk-like legs pounding the ground like pile-drivers, would power his way from the back of the pack, picking off opponents in the last mile and finishing the race with a pace imperceptibly different from that at the start. But our depth ended with Amos. Carl had the heart of a champion but having heart was only part of the equation.

As I jogged around the track, I noticed Coach Dillon, Candy and Carl standing by Frank's station wagon behind the gym. It was an odd time for Candy and Carl to be out of class, just as it was odd for me. I was out of class because I didn't care but Candy would only miss class for national emergencies. Something was up. Frank was doing most of the talking, swooping and pointing with his hands as though directing a construction project. Candy listened intently as Coach Dillon spoke, jotting down notes on a small pad of paper. Carl stood by, characteristically silent, nodding with the cadence of Frank's hands. I completed more than a few circuits of the track while they talked, trying not to be too obvious as I observed from afar, my curiosity building with each lap. Frank eventually handed Candy his car keys and a stop watch, and walked back into the gym, his cane lifting up puffs of dust from the surface of the gravel parking lot. Candy and Carl got into Frank's station wagon and drove off in a cloud of exhaust to points unknown.

I ran a few more laps before the rest of the Hawks began appearing. They fell into a group with me jogging around the track.

"I may be flunking sociology," Billy confessed. "My parents are going to kill me."

"You wouldn't be flunking if you opened a book and read an assignment once in a while," Shaun countered.

"I do, once in a while."

"That's a bunch of crap. You haven't read anything since the letters in the last issue of *Penthouse*."

"Do you think they're real?" Amos asked.

"Do I think what's real?" I said.

"The letters in *Penthouse*. Do you think they're real?"

"What if they are?"

"Then there's a lot of perverts in the world."

"Does it matter? Just enjoy the entertainment value and while you're at it, look at the pictures," Shaun taunted. "It may be as close as the two of you will ever get to seeing a naked woman." Amos smiled. Adonis that he was, I wanted to believe he'd done more than just see a naked woman. "As for me," Shaun continued, "let me tell you guys about the view of the underside of Kelly Martin." We completed another lap or two as Shaun entertained us with the story of his exploits with Kelly. I guess Shaun's stories were a bit like the letters in *Penthouse*. It wasn't so important that they were real as long as they were entertaining.

Danny was not so oddly silent. Since Corey's funeral, we were getting used to Danny being physically with us but mentally being someplace else. He ran ahead of us, his now pony-tailed hair tied with a rubber band bouncing on his back, his scrawny beard hiding his boyish good looks. The only thing familiar about Danny's appearance was Corey's ring, off which the afternoon sun glinted. We caught up with Danny and ran in silence for half a lap.

"Pioneer Park," Danny finally said. "The state finals are at Pioneer Park. We've got our work cut out for us."

"Shit," Billy said.

"Is that bad?" I asked.

"Not if you're a damned mountain goat," Shaun explained.

"The course ends on a hill," Amos said.

"Not just a hill," Shaun went on, "it's an are-you-fucking-with-me-hill, the mother of all hills. It's a damned mountain. Two feet higher and you can talk to God."

"And we've got to beat the Spartans on that hill. We're screwed." Billy complained.

"They'll kick our asses," Shaun concluded. Danny suddenly stopped, a look of anger on his face I had never before seen.

"What the fuck is wrong with you guys?" he blurted out. "Don't you understand what's at stake here? We're just a few races away from getting scholarships, from getting deferments. No Vietnam, no coming home in body bags or without legs. And you assholes don't care enough about staying eligible to read an assignment. Yeah, the Spartans will kick our asses if you let them. Give a shit. Isn't your life worth it?"

"Give them a break, Danny," I said. "They were just talking."

"Well, I don't want to end up with my ass in a foxhole in Vietnam because they were just talking." Amos moved in front of Danny, put his hands on Danny's shoulder and stared in straight in the eyes.

"We're in this together. You can count on us as much as we're counting on you," Amos said. Nobody said much more after that until Coach Dillon, limping across the infield, his cane occasionally getting stuck in the grass, arrived with his stopwatch and notebook. He knew something was not right and began as though to ask what the problem was but must have thought better of it.

"We've run a lot of miles this season," he began, "and our base of endurance is solid. Whatever pace we choose to run we'll be able to sustain it for as long as we need to. Now what we've got to do is increase that pace. Over the next few weeks, we're going to emphasize speed. We've got to get our legs used to moving faster." His good leg began twitching like a dreaming dog. "We've got to get used to turning up the pace when you think you've got nothing left. When it comes down to that final half-mile, the winner will be the team that accelerates into the finish. We're going to be that team."

"How does that translate into accelerating up a hill? The state finals end on a hill." Coach Dillon whirred around and looked at Amos, surprised as we all were at his asking that question.

"Your legs will move plenty fast up that hill," Frank answered.

"What about the Spartans?" Shaun asked.

"Forget about the Spartans. Just worry about yourself." Frank's look told us that would be the end of that conversation. Frank stared at his clipboard for a moment before continuing. "The first set this afternoon will be 30 quarter-miles in 65 seconds. Let's get started."

"Shouldn't we wait for Carl?" Danny asked.

"Carl will be running on his own for a few workouts. Like I said, let's get this started, gentlemen. We have a lot of work to do." We quickly toed the start-finish line on the track. Frank eyed us as if assessing our fortitude. "Sixty-five seconds, gentlemen, each one like the last. Go!" We leapt off the line and began around the first turn.

***

The hill towered over Carl no less than Everest towered over Sir Edmund Hillary. Like Hillary had with Everest, Carl had been tasked to conquer the summit, and conquer it he would. But unlike Hillary, whose fame was based on a single courageous and confident climb of the summit, Carl's courage and confidence would build over a hundred quests of his summit. The hill was no stranger to Carl, as it was no stranger to the Hawks. Carl and the Hawks had battled the hill countless times, sinew against rock, determination against an unemotional and unchanging foe. The hill is 1050 yards long and 350 feet from the base to the crest. Grueling climbs up the face of that hill consumed the efforts of generations of Hawks. For some, the battle built the confidence, muscle and endurance that propelled them to the brink of greatness. Others were beaten by the challenge, never to excel beyond their own ambitions. Frank Dillon, Pete Lorenzo and the Hawks of 1942 used the hill to their advantage and became champions in the process. The jury was still out on the Hawks of 1967.

Carl stood at the bottom of the hill, looking upwards toward Candy, barely visible near the summit. She waved a pink scarf above her head like the starter of a thoroughbred horse race. She clicked the stopwatch as the scarf came down, signaling the start of Carl's climb, and he began his battle against the hill. Carl brought up his knees, planting the balls of feet on the gravelly surface and did his best to synchronize his gait with the swinging of his arms. Remembering Coach Dillon's instructions, Carl leaned into the hill, letting gravity work to his advantage. All he had to do was move his legs under his falling body and he would climb the hill. Carl's short legs and stubby stature were a liability in virtually any running scenario you could imagine except running up a hill. Coach Dillon knew this. Carl needed to learn it.

In spite of the coolness of the fall afternoon, Carl's shirt was soaked through with the perspiration of his efforts before he reached the first marker. The pounding in his chest nearly drowned out Candy's encouraging voice from the summit. Carl struggled to achieve the rhythm of Coach Dillon's words.

Plant right foot, lift left knee, swing arms, lean forward, plant left foot, lift right knee, swing arms, lean forward.

The process was simple but nearly impossible to master on such a steep slope. Carl's throat became raw as his chest pumped air in-and-out at a monstrous rate. Sweat stung his eyes.

"Only a few more yards, sweetie," Candy yelled, her inexperienced hands gingerly holding the stopwatch as though it was a fragile heirloom, her index finger on the plunger as Frank had instructed. Carl slipped on the gravelly surface, momentarily falling to one knee. His burning thigh muscles tempted him to stay down, but Candy's encouragement told him otherwise. Carl lifted himself back into his gait.

Plant right foot, lift left knee, swing arms, lean forward, plant left foot, lift right knee, swing arms, lean forward.

Coach Dillon's words rang in Carl's ears like a gigantic bell. At last at the summit, sweat burning his eyes, he crossed the finish line only to fall in exhaustion at Candy's feet. "4 minutes, 3 seconds," Candy said, her hand softly at the nape of Carl's neck. "Now, get to the bottom and do it again."

***

The long shadows that crossed the track disappeared into the dusk of the evening. The gym and the parking lot had long since emptied out. Dinners were starting all over Barrel. Televisions were being turned on to watch to Walter Cronkite's evening news. These common events of the evening were foreign to us. We were alone in the world, deep into a workout whose end was somewhere in the undefined future, as mysterious and undecipherable to us as the Dead Sea Scrolls. Thirty quarters were followed by a half-dozen half miles and a set of three miles at race pace. Exhaustion was far too inadequate a word to describe our state. Desperate might have been a more accurate term. There comes a time when your legs grow too heavy to lift and your storage of calories has long since been depleted. You are certain you cannot go on.

We were jogging a rest lap. It was so dark we could barely see across the track. We hoped the darkness would spell an end to this workout. That hope was dashed when we heard the clack of the master switch and were momentarily blinded by the stadium lights flashing on. After a few blinks, we saw Frank walking back to the start-finish line from the equipment shed, flipping through his small notebook. We walked into the starting line, hands on our hips, breathing almost as hard as at the end of the last mile. We were too tired to lift our heads.

"We're just about done, gentlemen," Frank said. "Eight 220s, building to 110 percent pace. On your toes from the start. Go!" We hesitated an instant, not out of defiance but because our legs just didn't seem to want to obey the command to move. Suddenly, Danny started screaming as though a hot poker had been jammed up his ass, and bolted off the line.

"Aaaaahhhhhh." Danny accelerated into the turn, his ponytail bouncing off his back.

"Aaaaahhhhhh." His legs began turning over, his arms pumping.

"Aaaaahhhhhh." Danny's hair shed drops of sweat like chunks of dandruff. The Hawks stood mesmerized as they watched Danny.

"Aaaaahhhhhh." Danny rounded the turn, flailing like a madman. All sense of control was lost in his exhaustion. He was operating on the adrenalin he willed into his bloodstream.

"Well?" Coach Dillon asked the rest of us. We all looked at each other. Amos was the first to move.

"Aaaaahhhhhh," Amos screamed, his tree-trunk legs, digging into the track, left visible footprints as he accelerated into the turn.

"Aaaaahhhhhh," Billy hollered, following Amos.

"Aaaaahhhhhh," Shaun bellowed at Billy's heels.

"Aaaaahhhhhh," I screamed as I tucked in behind Billy.

No pain, no gain. No guts, no glory.

***

Carl sat in the middle of the road at the bottom of the hill, engulfed in the darkness of early evening. He looked at his legs as though urging them to move but without success. His natural dullness deepened with his exhaustion. His body was so depleted by his treks up the hill he was nearly incapable of processing speech. With unexpected suddenness, he was illuminated by what he thought was a spotlight. A horn blared. He looked up to see Frank's station wagon pointing down the hill with its headlights on. Candy was reaching in through the driver's window with her hand on the horn. "Let's go, sweetie," she yelled, still the voice of encouragement after a dozen assaults up the hill. Carl pushed himself up onto his short legs, wobbling at first before getting his balance. He looked up the hill to see Candy smiling and waving her pink scarf. She was a saint in a knee-high skirt. Candy and Carl were as different as different can be. It must be love. There could be no other explanation. Candy brought the scarf down and clicked the stopwatch.

Carl started up the hill, his feet barely clearing the small stones in the gravel, his already minuscule stride now immeasurably short. Carl was breathing hard before he passed the first tree.

Plant right foot, lift left knee, swing arms, lean forward, plant left foot, lift right knee, swing arms lean forward.

Conquer the hill, reach for the crest.

"You can do it, sweetie. Just one more time. Go, sweetie, go!"

Plant right foot, lift left knee, swing arms, lean forward, plant left foot, lift right knee, swing arms, lean forward.

Each step brought Carl closer to becoming the master of his own fate and those of his teammates. A year in the future, would Carl be a soldier fighting a war nobody seemed to want or attending a seminar in European history? It might be as simple as Carl conquering the hill.

"It'll all be worth it, sweetie!"

Plant right foot, lift left knee, swing arms, lean forward, plant left foot, lift right knee, swing arms, lean forward.

There will be a reward for all the work, for all the effort, for all the hours on the roads and tracks and hills.

"You're almost done, sweetie. Don't let up!"

No pain, no gain. No guts no glory.

CHAPTER 36

The State Cross Country Championship hadn't been held at Pioneer Park for 25 years, not since 1942 when Frank Dillon led the Hawks to Barrel High's first and only state championship. Decade-long complaints by coaches and runners finally wore down the State Athletic Association and the 1943 State Cross Country Championship moved to a prettier and flatter site, and for the next 25 years, that's where the state meet was held. It was only an unexpected construction project, something called a shopping mall, that forced the SAA to find a substitute venue. The lack of any financial gain for hosting the meet led the SAA back to its roots, Pioneer Park, a freebie even if it was as undesirable and depressing a place as it was in 1942.

Our three-car caravan arrived at Pioneer Park with a dignity that defied our appearance. Spewing exhaust and dripping oil, the 1953 Chevy station wagon ferrying the Hawks and Frank rolled into a stall in the rapidly filling parking lot. Diane, Jill, Candy and Craig followed in the peace symbol-emblazoned Volkswagen microbus trailing catcalls and raised middle fingers from the patriotic and uninformed. Sid Benson pulled up the rear in his shock absorber-challenged Pontiac. Climbing out of the station wagon, the Hawks gazed upon Pioneer Park with the reverence that Red Sox fans display entering Fenway Park. Though both places are dumps that even the homeless shun, they command a hallowed respect for what has transpired there in years past.

Pioneer Park was a largely abandoned and scrawny prairie with dried-out grass spotted with discarded tires, rusting shopping carts and the crumbling skeleton of a 1930s Chicago streetcar whose only explanation for being there was that it fell out of the sky. The small prairie was lined with dense woods and punctuated with a hill at its center, rising out of the flatness like a volcanic island in the middle of the ocean. The white chalk starting line, with neat lanes like the teeth of a comb, was framed by a banner blaring "ILLINOIS STATE CROSS COUNTRY CHAMPIONSHIP." The chalk line that defined the course disappeared into the woods and undulated unseen through the trees before reappearing on the opposite side. It snaked to the bottom of the hill before it turned upwards, like the contrail of a jet at takeoff, toward the summit where the race would finish. The finish chute, lined with flags flapping in the breeze, loomed over the field. The winner's tape, already strung across the finish line, taunted the runners no less than a streetlamp-hugging hooker. There were only a handful of runners that day who had the talent to be first up the hill and grab the number one stick, but we all lusted for it, hoping against hope that today would be the day we ran the race of our lives. For some of us, it would be a race for our lives.

We slowly walked toward the fields, where other teams were already clustered with their coaches. It was an unusually hot morning for being so late in the year. Others were jogging along the chalk line, inspecting the course for unseen flaws and strategizing their race plans. Were there hidden holes that might grab your ankle? Where was the best place to jump the log? Should you take the turn sharply on the inside where there would be a crush of runners or pay the penalty of running further on the outside where the traffic would be less?

"I guess this is it," Diane said, taking Frank's hand. "It doesn't seem like 25 years since we were last here." Frank gazed across the prairie. The memory of his victory was still fresh in his mind but so was the sacrifice of his teammates.

"It was only yesterday," he said, and to Frank, it was only yesterday. The last time Frank had set foot on the fields of Pioneer Park, his country was at war. The young men who so innocently vied for glory in the race of their lives knew that they would soon be fighting in a conflict that might cost them their lives. They looked forward to that service with the same enthusiasm they looked forward to the crack of the starting pistol. Seemingly nothing had changed in the intervening 25 years except for the enthusiasm for the service that lay ahead. Today was yesterday and yesterday was today. Frank had done everything in his power to ensure that the pattern would not repeat in the tomorrows of his Hawks.

As we walked toward the field, Danny put his arm around my shoulders. We didn't need to say anything. We had both come a long way in the months since we met on the top of our hill on my first day in Barrel. The words had already been said during that journey. Although Danny's appearance was nearly unrecognizable from that first day and his rebellious verbiage was as foreign to Barrel as Incan dialects, what emanated from his soul was a familiar aura that both comforted me and gave me confidence. But something was oddly different.

Without a word, he gave me a short hug and jogged off toward Jill. The sun was bright and Corey's ring should have glinted like a beacon, but Danny's finger was bare. Even as Danny distanced himself from me, I could clearly see the band of white skin that had for two years been hidden beneath Corey's ring contrasting against his deeply tanned hands.

When Danny caught up with Jill he ever so easily fell in by her side. It was a comfort, a kinship, an unspoken love I had never seen with Shelly. Danny put his arm around Jill with a gentleness that I was almost envious of.

"I don't see Shelly," Jill said playfully as she took Danny's hand. "She might not like this." Danny smiled in a way that I hadn't seen in a long time.

"Shelly's not here."

"She's not? This is a big day for you. You'd think she'd be here."

"Shelly's a great girl," Danny admitted, "but she'll never be you."

"Do you want her to be? Would you like her to be more like me?" Danny stopped as though hit by lightning.

"No. No, I don't. I don't want her to be anything she doesn't want to be. I just want you to be with me."

Danny reached into the pocket of his sweat pants and pulled out a necklace chain. Corey's ring dangled from the silver strand. Danny placed the shimmering loop around Jill's neck as though she was an Olympic gold medal winner. Jill not only shared Danny's psyche with him, now she shared Corey. She took the ring in her fist and squeezed, hoping to make the connection stronger. They put their arms around each other and kissed.

"This will be a good day," Jill said softly.

"It already is," Danny replied.

The Hawks were stretching in a group when Frank slowly walked over. With a wave of this hand, he motioned for us to gather around him. In spite of months of preparation for this moment, I could tell that Coach Dillon was still carefully choosing his words. He knew there was nothing more he could do to physically prepare us for the morning's race. Our muscles were as toned as they were going to be. Our hearts were as ready to pump blood as one could humanly expect. Without bursting, it would be difficult for our lungs to process any more oxygen than they were ready to do at that moment. Coach Dillon's years of experience had trained us, challenged us and taught us to perform as champions. The countless miles, the endless laps, the gut busting hill climbs were all part of his strategy to mold six young men into running machines that would perform beyond their abilities. So it wasn't the physical Frank was forming his words to address. It was the mental. Frank knew that most races were won or lost between the ears.

Twenty-five years ago, Frank, Pete Lorenzo and the Hawks of 1942 stood on that very spot. They were committed to each other but they were also committed to becoming members of what would one day be called the Greatest Generation. Their selflessness, their willingness to put duty to country over duty to self, made me ashamed to compare ourselves to them. The Hawks of 1942 came together that day prepared to run the race of their lives and fulfill their ambitions of bringing glory to their friends, to their families and to their undistinguished town, a fitting tribute to their youth before enlisting in the defense of their country. The Hawks of 1967 also came together ready to run the race of their lives. However, we would not run for the greater good but rather for individual good, placing duty to self over duty to country. Should we have been ashamed?

It would be an all or nothing proposition. There would be no shades of gray. It was red or black, odd or even, fold or call. A victory would be as much of a reprieve for Frank as for the Hawks. The Hawks would succeed in cheating the system out of that which we owed it. Frank would succeed in atoning for his failure to save Pete on the beaches of Normandy. Second place would gain us a trophy but would spell failure as boldly as a last place finish.

We sat clustered on a picnic table. Our few supporters stood by our sides. Jill held Danny's hand as tightly as fear would allow. Frank stood balancing on his cane when, inexplicably, he let the cane fall to the ground, as though willing his body back to the vitality it enjoyed when last he stood on that spot. Coach Dillon looked at each of the Hawks with an inspecting but caring eye. Had he done his job well enough? Did these boys, these young men, have the heart and sinew required to be champions and relieve Frank of the fear that the Hawks of 1967 might relive the fate of his own teammates? Coach Dillon was finally ready.

"You've come a long way and you're close to finishing this journey. But before you do, there's one more race to win. Every mile you have run, every hill you have climbed, has prepared you for this moment. You have become the masters of your own fate. You are the Hawks. There has never been a better team. Believe in each other as much as you believe in yourself. There will be a point some time during the race when you will need strength from a teammate. Take what you need from him because he will be willing to give, and you to him. No single runner is greater than this team. But at the same time the Hawks are no better than any single runner. You are a team. You are champions. Run a race you will be proud of 25 years from now." The Hawks and Frank put their hands together in a circle. "This is what you've trained for. This is what the season is all about."

Billy began chanting, "Hawks! Hawks! Hawks!"

The crescendo of the chant grew as the other Hawks joined in. Then there was silence leaving only the touching of hands between teammates and coach, between friends.

We walked to the starting line and took our places in our lane. I stepped in front of the line and looked upon the competition. There were 30 teams, more than 200 runners nervously toeing the line. It was an impressive array. The Spartans were only a few lanes from us.

Frank and Sid stood side-by-side watching the teams line up. Both vicariously placed their toes at the starting line. Coaches can't help themselves. They want to be their runners. Frank tried to take advantage of the shared moment.

"What about the sixth scholarship, Sid? What's it going to be?"

"Give it a rest, Frank. We'll talk about it after the race."

"You won't know anything more then than you do now, Sid."

"Sure I will. I'll know whether your guys won."

The president of the SAA and Miss Illinois, a shapely lass if there ever was one, climbed the handful of steps to the top of the starter's platform.

"Welcome to the 1967 Illinois State Athletic Association Cross Country Championships," he said through a static ridden PA system. "Congratulations to all the teams who have made it this far. It is an accomplishment in its own right. So with no further ado, let me introduce Miss Illinois, who will start the race." The president ceremoniously handed Miss Illinois the official starting pistol. In Coach Dillon's eyes, it was the same pistol that started his race 25 years in the past.

"On you marks, get set...." Miss Illinois closed her eyes, pointed the gun skyward and squeezed the trigger of the starting pistol as though the ground would swallow her up if the hammer came down. We stood motionless at the starting line, the tips of our shoes embedded into the chalk line, adrenalin pumping into our bloodstream, waiting for the retort of the pistol that would launch us forward.

The crack of the starting pistol pierced the tension and the race that would decide our future erupted into our lives.

As though connected by a steel rod, the front line of runners surged forward. I was squeezed between Danny and the human wall of runners in the next lane. As the mass of runners thundered up the prairie toward the woods, those teams with the ambition to win the race quickly moved to the front to claim a position before the course narrowed. The Spartans went to the front of the pack in a well-executed plan of dominance. The Hawks weren't so quick to respond and we were just as quickly trapped in the middle of the pack, confined no less than a pig in the coils of a boa. It was early, very early, but we couldn't let a gap open between us and the Spartans.

Danny took the initiative and began weaving his way through the pack of runners, spending far too much energy with the race less than a minute old. I instinctively followed him. Without needing to look, I could sense Billy and Shaun were close behind. Amos methodically pounded step after step while nearly creating holes in the prairie. He used his Herculean dimensions to open a path through the pack. Carl was consumed by the pack. He was jostled back and forth like a steel ball in a Pachinko machine and was barely making headway.

Danny quickly caught up with the lead cluster of Spartans and positioned himself behind Denton. The Spartans, perhaps smarter than we gave them credit for being, boxed Danny in with Kyle and Brian taking positions on each side. I bullied my way into the lead pack, catching and giving an occasional elbow. The prairie surface was rough, with patches of grass alternating with cracked dirt and punctuated by gopher holes. We were weaving back and forth to keep our footing. I took a quick glance behind. Less than half-a-mile into the race and the pack was strung out for more than a hundred yards, more than 200 runners raising a cloud of dust like chariots in the Hippodrome. Billy was only seven or eight places behind me. I didn't see Shaun. Amos, towering a head above any runner around him, was barely visible through the dust. Carl was lost to the world.

I was surrounded by Spartans and half-a-dozen would-be champions from no-name schools in no-name towns hoping that a miracle might occur and they would grab the number one stick. How many miles had been run preparing for this one morning? How many lives would crescendo on the finish hill?

The Spartans already had four runners in the top 10, five in the top 15. We barely had three in the top 20. This was not a good start.

The heat of the day was already taking a toll. Sweat rivered into my eyes, stinging and making me lose concentration as I tried to wipe my forehead. Stains of effort already showed through the backs of the jerseys on the runners around me. For those whose ambition outweighed their abilities, their legs were already getting heavy, their muscles tightening, their throats getting raspy. For them, a miracle would not occur. They were slowing and falling behind, making the lead pack more exclusive.

The course took a 90-degree turn to the left at the half-mile mark, looping around a massive oak tree. A course official stood by the tree, ready to flag any runner who cut it short. A 50-yard-wide course funneled into a path only five feet wide. The traffic jam would be horrendous. As we approached the turn, the lead pack instinctively strung out. The lead group was small enough that we could take the turn only a few across. The mass of humanity behind us had no choice but to duke it out with elbows flying.

Denton went into the lead with Danny shadowing him. Kyle and Brian were at Danny's heels. As Denton leaned into the turn, he looked behind, smiled and nodded his head. It was a vicious, calculating and rehearsed smile. I remember thinking that odd. Why at the beginning of the race of his life, would Denton do that? But when Kyle nodded in return, raised his arm and began reaching toward Danny's back, I suddenly understood the plan.

"Danny, look out" I yelled, but was unheard over the thunderous footsteps and heavy breathing of 200 runners. As Kyle's hand approached Danny's back, I picked up my pace. As the inches closed between Kyle and Danny, the gap closed between Kyle and me. I had no idea what I would do if I caught him. Just as Danny leaned to his left to take the turn, Kyle's palm hit between his shoulder blades, and at the same instant, I grabbed Kyle's shirt. Danny, already barely balanced as he negotiated the turn, was sent crashing into the base of the tree. I thought Danny would spring back up, as though he had bounced off a trampoline, but instead he lay crumpled on the ground. The official saw nothing. The act was hidden from his view by the broad trunk of the oak.

I wanted to stop, to see what I could do to help Danny but instinct told me to keep going. I rounded the tree with my hand still firmly attached to Kyle's shirt. I looked back. Danny still wasn't moving. Kyle began wildly flailing his arm behind him, like he was swatting away bees.

"Get off me, motherfucker," he yelled, and with no plan of my own, I let go.

"You'll be disqualified," I managed to say between breaths. Kyle only smiled.

I looked behind me again. Billy and Shaun were already around the turn. I could tell by the surge of runners leaping over an unseen object on the ground that Danny still hadn't gotten up yet. A fear beyond fear struck me. Suddenly it was up to me. The championship and the scholarships lay at the bottom of the tree unless I had the race of my life.

I looked ahead. There were barely 50 yards before we entered the woods onto a narrow path. If I had thoughts of winning, I had to position myself better. I increased my pace, passed Kyle, giving him an elbow as I went by, and weaved my way through the runners in third and fourth place, finally ducking behind Denton as we entered the shadows of the woods. Shit, I thought, what I am doing here?

I was outclassed and outgunned but I had no choice. I let Denton's momentum suck me along the trail.

***

Frank, Diane, Jill and Sid perched on a picnic table. Candy and Craig stood nearby. Frank, binoculars to his eyes, called the race like an announcer at the Kentucky Derby. Diane took notes. Jill stood on her toes, trying to catch a glimpse of the young man whose brother's ring hung around her neck. A much less animated Sid Benson chomped on a cigar, his massive weight almost tipping the table like a seesaw.

"Where are they?" Jill screamed as the lead pack looped around the oak tree and headed for the woods.

"Looks like Denton's in the lead," Coach Dillon reported.

"Okay, here we go." Diane stood ready to record. "Spartans, first, fourth, sixth, eleventh and looks like fifteenth." Sid shifted his weight, nearly launching the rest off the table. "Mike's in second, Billy twelfth, Shaun sixteenth..." Frank's voice trailed off.

"Danny! Where's Danny?" Jill pleaded. Frank lowered the binoculars.

"I don't see him, Jill."

"Amos?" Diane ventured.

"Carl?" Candy pleaded.

"They must be lost in the pack."

"Where could he be?" Jill asked. Sid sat down, the effort of holding up his own weight apparently too much for him.

"Your guys are screwed already."

***

Danny was just getting to his feet as Amos rounded the tree. Blood gushed from a deep cut on his knee. The sea of runners enveloped Danny and Amos, locking them into their slow pace. Danny fell in behind Amos. He tried to go around but was boxed in by the heavy breathing and sweaty efforts of the midland runners around them. Danny was a fly in molasses. Struggling only wasted energy. Panic was building inside him. With every second, the distance between Danny and Denton widened. It may have already been too late.

"Help me, Amos, help me!" Danny yelled, "Make a hole! Get me through!" Danny gingerly put his hand on Amos' back, urging him forward. Danny could feel his teammate's fear through his jersey. Danny was perhaps asking the impossible.

Amos, our Adonis, was a one-gait runner. His internal metronome ticked at only one frequency, his legs turned with only one cadence. His stomping pace never faltered from start to finish. Stopwatches could be calibrated with his consistency. Amos simply outlasted his less disciplined opponents, who unwisely ran to the front in the early goings, tired and fell back to be consumed by the more patient Amos.

"Let's go, Amos," Danny whispered in his ear, as though a jockey coaching his reluctant thoroughbred forward. Amos hesitated. Precious seconds were slipping by. His body just wasn't built to survive bursts of speed. Amos knew it, his body knew it. He would be sacrificing himself for the better good.

"You've got to get me through," Danny coaxed, pushing more firmly on Amos' back. Amos finally turned his head.

"Follow me."

Amos accelerated forward with a force that surprised even Danny. His legs began moving at a blurring pace. His knees were high and his arms began swinging. With every step, the pace increased until, with Danny in tow, they were sprinting. Amos plowed through the middle-of-the-pack runners like a locomotive through a flock of sheep, opening a lane for Danny behind him. Amos' daunting size and towering physique, until that day a liability for a cross country runner, became a human battering ram that rescued Danny from his imprisonment.

***

"My God, there's Amos," Coach Dillon yelled, not needing the binoculars to see the towering Amos plowing through the pack with sprinter's speed.

"Gimme those," Sid said, grabbing the binoculars. "Holy crap, look at him go. Never thought Amos could move that fast. And Danny's right behind him."

"Danny?"

"Let's get to mile marker," Diane said. Jill and Diane jumped off the table and ran in the direction of the first mile marker. Frank hobbled after them.

***

Amos' sprint led Danny straight into the woods, where Amos continued plowing ahead on the narrow path. Amos flicked a runner or two aside before he began slowing, the magnitude of his effort finally taking its toll. Danny stepped around Amos, barely missing a beat, giving his shoulder a pat as he passed, and accelerated along the path. Danny was in thirtieth place.

Amos was spent. He tried to resume his stolid and unrelenting pace but the reserves he would have normally called on to move his muscular bulk were depleted. They were expended in his gallant sprint that liberated Danny from the confines of the pack, and in doing so had sacrificed his own race. Like a jet fighter burning through its fuel with its afterburner to valiantly complete its mission, Amos was spiraling to earth on empty tanks. As Danny sped to the front, Amos slowed, his bulk nearly blocking the narrow path, forcing runners to navigate around him.

The Hawks' fifth man was being passed and falling further behind, and the race was barely started.

The path leapt over a creek and over trail-crossing logs. The small lead pack negotiated them expertly. As the pack behind them thickened, there was jostling and an occasional fall as the logs grabbed at their hurdling feet. Danny worked his way through the lead pack, picking off runner after runner.

The path exited the woods out onto a narrow, spectator-lined road just at the one-mile maker. I foolishly watched Denton speed ahead of me. He ran with the confidence of someone who knew he would be winning a race that day. A gap opened between us. I was beginning to feel the pace. Denton seemed unfazed.

"4:39," the timer called out as Denton passed.

"4:43," the timer called out as I passed.

We were running a blazing pace, but it was the state championship. Everything was on the line for both the Spartans and the Hawks. Would the winner be the one who didn't spiral to earth?

Billy and Shaun, now running like the Gemini twins they were, began moving through the pack.

"4:51, 4:52, 4:53," the timer called out as they passed.

**

"Can you see them?" Diane called out.

"Yes, yes! Spartans are 1, 4, 5 and 11," Jill said as Diane jotted down the numbers. "Mike is still in second. It looks like Shaun and Billy are fourteenth and fifteenth."

"Danny?"

"Don't see him. Yes, there he is!"

**

Danny's pace should have had him in the lead instead of watching the backs of those in front of him. He burst out of the woods thankful for the openness that allowed him to maneuver. He passed a Spartan at the mile marker.

"4:58, 4:59, 5:00."

Any other day, Danny might have cried for having run that split in the championship race. Today, it challenged him and he was grateful it wasn't slower. All was not lost. It couldn't be. There was too much at stake, and Danny had made promises he had no intention of not fulfilling. As Danny regrouped his thoughts, he finally glanced at the gash on his knee. The riverlet of blood from the gash began soaking his sock.

Danny caught Shaun and Billy a hundred yards past the mile marker.

"Where've you been?" Shaun managed to ask as Danny passed him.

"Denton, where's Denton?"

"In the lead"

"Mike?"

"Not far behind." Danny accelerated ahead.

All was not lost. It couldn't be. Danny had made promises.

Deep inside the pack, Carl's short legs chewed at the path that serpentined through the woods. Nearly unnoticed by the runners around him, Carl weaved deftly around one competitor after another. One-by-one, he moved slowly through the pack, scurrying through openings and under the swinging arms of his larger competitors. When Carl came to the logs, the runner by his side leapt them like an Olympic hurdler. Carl climbed over them like they were cyclone fences. Carl was hidden from his coach's view when he cleared the woods, a coach that would have been proud beyond words of his perseverance, a coach who knew nothing of Amos' valiant dash to free Danny from the pack while depleting his reserves, a coach who could not have known that the success of his 25-year quest to protect his precious Hawks from the prospect of war now lay at Carl's feet.

The course snaked around the perimeter of the park before coming back into the woods. The road was wide enough that Danny could maneuver though the pack of runners without expending too much extra effort. His knee throbbed but Danny put the pain out of his mind as he regained his rhythm. His uncharacteristically awkward gait quickly recovered to a smooth, fluid motion that propelled Danny forward. His arms swayed just enough to balance his lengthening strides. This was make-or-break time. The championship might be won or lost in the next half mile.

All was not lost. It couldn't be. Danny had made promises.

CHAPTER 37

The pace was relentless on the flat of the road. My legs grew heavy as the gap opened in front of me and Denton widened his lead. Brian came to my shoulder. I tried to go with him but he powered by me just as we passed the two-mile marker. I was paying for my foolish dash to Denton's side.

***

"What's happening?" Sid demanded. "What's the split?" Frank peered through the binoculars.

"Denton's still in the lead. He's at the two-mile mark now!"

"9:28. That was a 4:49 second mile." Diane called out.

"Michael and Brian, now!"

"9:40."

"He's slowing!" Sid yelled.

"Danny, now!"

"9:42"

"That was 4:42 mile for Danny," Jill called out. Frank let the binoculars down.

"I can't see the rest of them."

"You don't have to," Sid concluded. "The Spartans are winning this race."

***

Kyle passed me just as we went back into the woods. I tried to go with him, but I just couldn't make my legs move. They were heavy beyond description. I felt as though I was at 20 miles in a marathon. A moment after Kyle went by Danny hesitated just an instant as he too passed me. I felt electricity when he brushed against my arm. Something passed between us that I would never be able to explain.

"Let's go, Mike. Don't let them get away!"

I obeyed. I had no choice. My life would change in a big way in the next five minutes. I couldn't let that happen without me. I used Danny's strength to will myself forward. There was one aura and we both shared it. I latched onto Danny and went with him. Whatever happened to us, it would happen together. It was 1942. We were Pete Lorenzo and Frank Dillon.

Running through the woods on that narrow trail was like hurtling through an amusement park arcade. There was no time to analyze, just react. Pray to God that your foot lands on solid dirt and not a root or a stone. The trees passed by so quickly they looked like picket fences out a car window. In spite of the trail jostling our legs and challenging our balance, and the low-lying branches slapping at our faces, the pace was blistering. There was no time for anything other than running faster and catching the Spartans. The Spartans were smarter than us. They knew that running from the front on a course like this was the best strategy and they pursued that strategy like experts.

The course spilled out of the woods at the base of the long and dreaded finish hill. The Spartans' strategy had worked. Denton, Brian and Kyle were first, second, and third as they burst out of the woods. They were tired but not spent. Only a thousand yards lay between them and the finish. Their confidence soared. The race, the championship, the scholarships were nearly theirs. It was only seconds, but seemed like eons, before Danny and I exited the woods in fourth and fifth place. The gap between Danny and the Spartans was large, too large. I followed Danny like a shadow, attached to him by an invisible rope that pulled me along. Our fates were linked together. My own stores were exhausted. It was only Danny's aura that supplied me with the energy to move forward. But Danny's arms were too high, his gait was too short. He was tired.

Just as I affixed myself to Danny, his eyes were fixated on the backs of the Spartans in front of him. Danny had to pass them if the

Hawks were going to win this race. As the lead group of Spartans started up the hill, their pace slowed on the incredible slope. Maybe there was a chance.

All was not lost. It couldn't be. Danny had made promises.

Hundreds of spectators lined the course. Their cheers were loud but unintelligible to the runners. The runners' focus was too tight to let other senses interfere with the intensity of their efforts.

***

"They've started up the hill," Frank said, lowering his binoculars. "Let's get going." He jumped off the table, nearly collapsing on his bad leg. Diane pulled Frank up and they ran to the waiting station wagon. The engine was running. Jill was behind the wheel. Candy and Craig filled the rest of the front seat. Sid, who had squeezed himself into the back seat, stuck his large head through the window.

"Get your asses in gear," he yelled at Frank and Diane.

As Frank and Diane tumbled into the station wagon, Jill gunned the engine and navigated the service road up the backside of the hill.

***

Danny began his assault up the finish hill but unlike the Spartans, his legs felt familiar ground. The slope was less foreign to him, feeling almost like an old friend. Danny's body, without being asked to, morphed itself into a hill-climbing mode. After so many charges up the Hawks' hill in practice, the metamorphosis was an instinctive response, no different than a pupae bursting out of its cocoon. Danny's concentration was pointed beyond description. The roar of the crowds did not penetrate into his mind. The only sound was his pounding heartbeat. With each step, he closed the gap to the Spartans. Danny moved up on Kyle in third place. Denton, sensing his being pursued, stole a glance behind him. Denton was running all out. There wasn't a thing Denton could do to run any faster and he knew that. Panic began to boil inside him.

My legs no longer heeded my wishes. I could not will them faster and could not allow them to slow. They moved on their own. I let them pull me up the hill, following Danny, our fates, our futures fused together. With each step that moved Danny further up the hill, he pulled closer to the leading trio of Spartans, and he pulled me with him. Kyle's form said volumes about how foreign the terrain he was climbing felt. With each step, the hill became steeper for Kyle, while with each step it seemed to get flatter for Danny. Kyle was a runner built for the flats. His long stride was perfect for chewing up the yards on the track but served him poorly in the climb. He was exhausted and as Danny commandingly passed him, Kyle looked behind to see whether he could keep his place. It was a sign to me that Kyle would not pursue Danny. Only seconds later I passed Kyle, still feeding off of Danny's strength.

With half the hill behind us, there were still 40 yards separating us from Brian and Denton. The hill had consumed their bravado. Their strides were choppy, their paths no longer straight. The countless treks up our hill, Frank's unrelenting training, his shaping of our confidence, were paying off. Danny powered up the hill, leaning forward, launching himself up the slope, stride after stride, closing the gap between him and the Spartans duo. But the gap was large. Too many yards lay between Danny and the Spartans. The hope of catching Brian and Denton was barely a glimmer.

Danny's concentration was as sharp as a blade yet he was only human and so he was fallible. The mind stores memories you cannot recall, experiences you once thought lost, only to conjure them up for reasons that defy explanation. In the midst of Danny's pursuit of the Spartans, he turned his head and gazed at the spectators lining the course. He slowed, while looking back at the crowd again and again, and then nodded before gathering his concentration and turning back to the pursuit with renewed vigor. What had he seen? What could have stolen his attention in the midst of his pursuit? Who would have such influence?

It must have been Corey. His apparition, his spirit, concealing itself in the crowd, visible to Danny and to those who believed, speaking through the ether hoping that Danny would hear. Dressed as a proud Marine, crisp in his dress blues, intent on this mission as he had been on his last, Corey appeared not to cheer his brother to victory but to deliver a long-awaited message, to lay to rest the indecision that haunted Danny since his death. The conflict that festered in Danny was resolved in the short instant that Corey appeared to him. It was no less miraculous than an answered prayer. With that burden lifted from his shoulders, Danny surged forward, consuming the steepness of the hill with nearly inhuman intensity. I had no choice but to let that intensity pull me up the hill too. Danny and I pursued the Spartans and pursued our destinies.

Barely 50 yards behind us, Shaun and Billy, the Gemini twins, shadowed each other as they dug into the deepest recesses of their reserves. There were a dozen runners between them and the leaders, and two of those runners were Spartans. Shaun and Billy had to catch them. They simply had to. Their lives depended on it. One by one, the slowing runners ahead of them fell behind Shaun and Billy as they assaulted the hill. The countless forays up the Hawks' hill, the climbs Frank had forced them to make in the throes of their exhaustion, had hardened their sinews and expanded their lungs. Now with each runner Shaun and Billy passed, Frank smiled with the results of his craftsmanship.

Amos exited the woods a man in distress. The pain of his efforts showed on his face. Amos had been drained by the dash to deliver Danny out of the confinement of the pack two miles before. But Amos could count. There were four Hawks ahead of him but there were five Spartans. All would be lost, the championship, the scholarships, if the race ended that way. Amos was no novice to pain and not one to cave in to a challenge. He pursued that fifth Spartan through the woods, boldly powering himself through the pack that thinned as his place fell from 50 to 40 to 30. Drawing on reserves he no longer had, he began his climb up the hill, pursuing the Spartan that still lay ahead.

***

Frank, Diane and Jill pushed their way through the crowd to positions at the rope that formed the chute. They were only a few yards from the finish line with a clear view down the hill. Candy and Craig squeezed onto the rope a few yards away.

"Two Spartans are in the lead," Frank yelled back to Sid, who trailed behind him.

"There are Danny and Mike," Jill called out, "and Shaun and Billy!"

"What are their places?" Diane asked, clipboard in hand.

"Spartans first and second. Danny and Mike, third and fourth. A Spartan's in fifth. Looks like another Spartan in twelfth. Billy and Shaun are about fifteenth and sixteenth." Diane jotted down the places and quickly summed up the points. Sid, breathing as heavily as the runners, looked over Diane's shoulder.

"Doesn't look good, Frank."

***

Carl, virtually unnoticed among the towering runners around him, popped out of the woods only 20 yards behind Amos. He scurried between his opponents with the deftness that comes with being small. As he began his climb up the hill, Frank's voice played in his mind with a volume that obliterated all other thought.

Plant right foot, lift left knee, swing arms, lean forward, plant left foot, lift right knee, swing arms, lean forward.

There were few lessons that Carl had learned well, but that one he had mastered.

Amos knew what was at stake. In spite of his exhaustion, he attacked the mountain. His muscles rippled, his arms swung forward, his feet tore divots into the soil as his towering figure climbed up the hillside. At first, he gained a few yards on the Spartan ahead of him, passing four or five runners in the process, but in spite of his Herculean efforts, the gap between him and the Spartan began to widen. Amos dug down deep into his soul, lifted his knees higher and tried to increase his speed, but there was nothing left. His race had already been run.

The chute began to narrow for the lead pack further up the hill. Denton and Brian, staring at the sloping ground in front of them, raised their heads and could see the cheerleaders at the finish line waving their finish sticks. Their legs and chests were tightening. They began to pull their arms up to their chests. Their reserves were gone. There was nothing on their mind other than getting to those sticks before we caught them.

***

Candy and Jill leaned over the ropes of the chute, nearly falling onto the course.

"Go, Danny! Dig down! Get them! Get them!" Jill screamed over the noise of the crowd, knowing that Danny would hear her voice over the rest. Frank knew there was nothing more he could do. His job was over when the starting pistol fired.

"You can do it, Danny. The race is yours to win," he said, the words barely audible even to him. Sid Benson, the rope pressed against his belly, squeezed between Diane and Frank to get a better look.

"Your boys are in trouble, Frank."

***

Denton and Brian were slowing as they approached the finish line. They were only yards from the finish when I saw a gap opening between them. Brian's legs were tighter than violin strings and just wouldn't bend to the contours of the hill. Denton was pulling away from him. Danny saw the gap at the same time as I did. We might not catch Denton, but we would get Brian.

"Aaaahhhh!" Danny let out a scream that must have scared even him. Danny surged again. His heart pounded so hard I thought the ground shook with each beat. I let Danny pull me ahead with him. I riveted my eyes on his back as I synced my fate with his. "Get him, Danny," I prayed. "Get him and take me with you," I commanded. This was it. This was the end of the journey. The few dozen yards between the finish line and us would make differences in our lives we couldn't imagine. Vietnam or Illinois State. It was as simple as that. With each step, we closed the gap with Brian. Sweat burned in my eyes no less than muscle burned in my calves, but I didn't dare break my rhythm to rub them.

***

"Danny's making his move," Jill shouted.

"He's doing something," Sid concurred, crunching his cigar.

Frank was silent, his mouth moving but no words coming out. He took Diane's hand, squeezing it almost to the point of pain. His leg began shaking like a dreaming dog. Frank was on the hill too, and Pete was with him.

***

Danny caught Brian, passing him without a break in stride. Brain slowed and as he turned his head to see where I was, I powered by him just as Danny had. Brian was done with. For just an instant, Danny raised his head, and took a bead on Denton in front of him. There were 50 yards to the finish and 10 yards between Denton and us.

***

"They caught that Spartan," Diane shouted. "Go, Danny! Go, Mike." Jill jumped to get a better view.

"Danny's going to do it."

"Holy shit, he might do it," Sid admitted.

***

With each step, the gap between Denton and us shrank, the finish chute narrowed, and the crowds got closer and louder. The noise should have been unbearable but we didn't hear it. The only sounds were of our own breathing and of the voices from our inner being that drove us forward. A voice also spoke to Denton as he powered up the hill toward the finish line, a voice with the same conviction as spoke to us. Whose spirits would be stronger?

Cheerleaders waved the finish sticks at the end of the chute as we approached. There were only 30 yards to go. Denton was so close that Danny could have reached out and grabbed his jersey. Denton knew Danny was there. You could sense his awareness but he didn't change his pace. There was nothing more in him, his reserves were exhausted. Denton was running the pace that would take him across the finish line and it was our chance to defeat him. We needed one more surge, one more burst from our depleted sinews to beat out Denton. There were only yards to do it.

Finding strength from the depths of his soul, Danny lengthened his stride, climbing faster, pulling me up the hill with him. The gap to Denton evaporated. We were now a seemingly inseparable knot of three runners. Denton and Danny surged against the hill, trying to break from the other, their bodies pressing against each other as the chute narrowed. Their swinging arms nearly entangled with each other. I was inches behind them. The dirt coming off the hill from the thrusts of their feet splattered on my chest. Hands grabbed at us from spectators' enthusiasm as they leaned over the ropes. The cheerleader at the throat of the chute, the precious winner's stick in her hand, was only yards, now feet, in front of us. The sun danced behind her head, burning our eyes dare we look, as though she held forbidden fruit.

Danny inexplicably turned his head. I couldn't help myself and I looked too. I saw them as Danny saw them, flesh and apparition. It was Jill, it was Coach Dillon, it was Corey. They spoke to Danny through the ether, transmitting their strength to him. Do this for love, do this for honor, do this for the lives of your teammates. Do this to atone for Frank's leaving Pete Lorenzo on the beaches of Normandy. Do this to honor Corey's duty in Vietnam. Do this for the life we might have together.

"Aaaahhhh!" Danny screamed like a savage and, with a final planting of his bloodstained shoe into the earth, launched himself in front of Denton. Nearly airborne, Danny leaned into the finish like a sprinter in a 100-meter dash. Without thinking, I took that last step too and launched myself forward with Danny. There was shock on

Denton's face, as we propelled ourselves by him. As we came down, I saw the finish line pass beneath us. We landed in a heap, Danny sprawled on the ground unable to keep his balance. I fell on top of him and felt Denton's foot on my back as he passed over us. We lay there without the strength to get up as hands grabbed our arms, pulling us to our feet and pushing us along the finish chute. The cheerleader called to us.

"Don't forget these," she said smiling as she placed the first and second place sticks in our hands.

***

"He won! He won!" Jill screamed, hugging Candy and Craig as they jumped up and down.

Frank leaned against the rope, nearly losing his balance as he called places to Diane.

"Danny first, Mike second. Denton and Brian third and fourth!" Diane jotted down the places on her clipboard, a column for the Hawks and a column for the Spartans. Sid just shook his head as he looked at his stopwatch.

"14:27! Those son of a bitches ran the last mile in 4:45 up a Goddamned mountain!"

***

Shaun and Billy charged up the hill in pursuit of Kyle and David, the Spartans ahead of them. Kyle led David as they mingled among the other runners strung along the slope, moving into the narrowing chute. They were Shaun and Billy's targets. Pass them and the Hawks had a chance of winning. Lose to them and the scholarships would be lost. The countless runs up the Hawks' hill were paying off. The runners ahead of Shaun and Billy were soon behind them, as the conditioning of those climbs gave them speed up the incline their opponents couldn't muster. It might have been easy until Shaun stumbled on the rough and steep slope and fell to one knee, pain shooting through his leg. Shaun, stunned by the pain, courageously got up, but his pace suffered. Billy ran on alone, passing a knot of five runners, pursuing and catching David as the Spartan struggled to keep his pace. Billy, the confident and bawdy Billy, would not let his teammates down today. He fed on the strength that Danny trailed behind him, consuming it in the air he breathed. Billy caught another runner and pulled even with Kyle. Shoulder against shoulder, stride matching stride, Billy battled with Kyle for that one better place. Inch by inch Billy pulled ahead of Kyle, the chute narrowing to the one lane of the finish line. With a final lunge Billy grabbed the ninth place stick ahead of Kyle. David was only a few places back.

Shaun struggled to regain his rhythm, but that tiny instant when his knee hit the slope unbalanced his stride. He wobbled side to side, as he valiantly tried to make up lost ground. The knot of runners ahead of him was nearly at the finish line. Shaun had to break into them. He just had to. He couldn't let a random stumble be the end of his teammates' dreams. He couldn't be the cause of his teammates going to war.

Don't let it be me.

Tears streamed down his cheeks.

Don't let it be me.

Adrenalin pumped into his arteries, carrying Shaun forward. He broke into the cluster of runners as they crossed the finish line.

***

"Billy got him!" Candy yelled.

"Ninth for Billy. Spartans in tenth and twelfth," Frank called out. Diane added their places to the columns.

"Shaun? What about Shaun?" she asked. Frank counted heads as they crossed the finish line.

"Seventeen. He's seventeenth."

"The score, what's the score?" Sid commanded. Diane tallied the two columns.

"It's 29-29. They're tied."

"Shit! Next one across the finish line wins the championship."

"It's up to Amos," Jill called out, searching for him in the pack thundering up the hill.

"And Carl," Candy added, with a conviction that only love could inspire.

One of them had to beat the Spartan ahead of them.

***

Amos struggled beyond his endurance to catch the Spartan in front of him. He willed his legs to move him faster up the hill but they would not obey. They had already done their duty that day, breaking Danny out of the mire of the pack in a burst of speed that so drained Amos' reserves. Now, with each futile step, Amos willed his legs with greater emotion to carry him up the hill. But instead of that intensity translating into fluid motion, it became his enemy. His Herculean stature bent over with the effort. Amos battled against himself and was losing the battle, but he would not give up. Amos was a Hawk and his teammates were depending on him. But in spite of Amos' devotion, the Spartan ahead of him lengthened his lead.

With the Spartan getting further ahead and with Vietnam getting closer, Amos felt a small hand on his arm. He looked down. It was Carl.

"I go now," Carl said. He squeezed Amos' arm with affection and dashed ahead into the pack.

If ever there was a race designed for the likes of Carl, this was it. The narrow trails, the uncertain footing, the tortuous climb to the finish. His small feet, short legs, and diminutive arms, nothing but liabilities over any other terrain, were his weapons on this course. As though a terminal branch on the human family tree, Carl alone seemed to possess the genes needed to conquer this course so convincingly. Around him his taller, more sinewy competitors struggled to shorten their long strides to match the steep hillside. Carl was not struggling. His stride, his mentality, his singular purpose matched the steep terrain as though by godly design.

Plant right foot, lift left knee, swing arms, lean forward, plant left foot, lift right knee, swing arms, lean forward.

For countless days on the Hawks' hill, Candy had nurtured Carl beyond his abilities, following Frank's commands as though they were scriptures. Carl built muscle that was seemingly worthless on the flat, but tuned to the hill. Day after day, climb after climb, toiling after an unknown goal, Candy cheering him on, Carl burned Frank's words into his psyche; and now they guided him up the finish hill.

Plant right foot, lift left knee, swing arms, lean forward, plant left foot, lift right knee, swing arms, lean forward.

Carl passed runner after runner, his path zigzagging through the obstacle course created by his taller competitors. He deftly chose footholds no one else saw, flitting up the hillside with purpose beyond purpose. Carl did not allow the pain of his efforts to interfere with his programming, his synapses hammered into an unalterable pattern.

Plant right foot, lift left knee, swing arms, lean forward, plant left foot, lift right knee, swing arms, lean forward.

Carl looked ahead and suddenly the purpose of all those afternoons of torturous practice became clear, the unspoken goal became understood. Carl eyed the back of the Spartan running the hill ahead of him and his programming told him that was his target. He had only one sense working, that which sighted his prey.

Carl now knew why he was placed on the Earth. It was to run that hill, beat that Spartan and secure the scholarships that would rescue his teammates from the prospect of war. If Carl's life ended one yard beyond the chute, he would have fulfilled his destiny, a destiny that began on the beaches of Normandy when Coach Dillon brushed the foot of Pete Lorenzo, but failed to carry him to safety. Carl would be their savior.

***

"Oh my God, it's Carl!" Candy screamed, pointing across the ropes into the pack of runners. Jill, Diane, Frank and Sid followed her finger, and in the pack of runners, they saw one small figure scurrying up the hill faster than the rest.

"Holy crap!" Sid yelled, smiling for the first time in years. "Look at that son-of-a-bitch go!"

"Go, little buddy!" Craig yelled.

***

Carl's short legs carried him up the hillside in a single-minded mission of conquest. The places between him and the Spartan ahead of him fell away as Carl passed runner after runner. The gap between them closed.

Plant right foot, lift left knee, swing arms, lean forward, plant left foot, lift right knee, swing arms, lean forward.

The course steepened in the last yards before the finish line, and the pack of runners thickened as they slowed to overcome those last yards in the narrowing chute. A wall of runners shielded Carl from his Spartan prey. Carl couldn't let it slow him. It was his destiny that he succeed. A small crack appeared between two runners and Carl popped through it like water shot from a cannon, ducking beneath their swinging arms. There ahead was the Spartan, his prey, the finish line only yards beyond him. Carl's programming would not fail him. Carl would not fail his teammates. Carl would not let Candy's devotion be for naught. Hundreds of assaults up the Hawks' hill would not be wasted. Pete Lorenzo would be saved. With a burst of speed of divine proportions, Carl ducked under the arm of the laboring Spartan and lit by him. A step ahead of his opponent, Carl crossed the finish line and grabbed his stick, his small hand clutching that piece of wood as though it was made of platinum.

CHAPTER 38

The celebration would be remembered forever in Barrel, Illinois. There must have been 300 people crammed into Mabel's Diner the Saturday night of the state championships: friends, parents, brothers, sisters, sweethearts, cheerleaders, teachers. They were all there to share in the wonderfulness of our victory. Hamburgers, fries and milkshakes flowed like champagne at a speakeasy. To this day, I don't know who paid for it all. Frank conjured up a banner blaring "Barrel High Hawks—State Cross Country Champions 1967" that stretched across the picture windows. The Hawks and everyone else there that night signed it. I'm told the banner still hangs in the cross country locker room at Barrel High. Frank and Diane greeted people as they entered Mabel's like proud parents at a wedding. Sid Benson wedged his immense bulk into a booth, his cigar wedged equally between his teeth. He pinched waitress' bottoms and held court to the amusement to whoever stopped by.

"Goddamn, I knew they would win," Sid explained. "They'll run for me at Illinois State. I cemented the deal with scholarships. Yeah, they're good but I'll make them better. Danny and the team will win the nationals by their sophomore year. Crap, I ought to be making room in the trophy case now."

Principal Milo made a speech praising our victory. The suspensions that almost cost us this cherished moment were not mentioned. As Principal Milo introduced us, we jogged through a tunnel of cheerleaders and into the accolades of the crowd, each one of us wearing our letterman jackets with the newly sewn state championship patch recording our accomplishment. We were Barrel High's first state champions in 25 years. It was a moment to savor. Even the football players clapped at our entrance. The applause, trapped within Mabel's cramped quarters, was amplified to deafening levels.

With each retelling of the story of the championship race, our exploits morphed into even more legendary proportions. The devious Spartans who conspired to flatten Danny into a tree became more hated. Amos' selfless sprint as the human battering ram became more heroic. Danny's leap across the finish line grew a yard in length with each retelling. The seeds of tales that Hawk runners repeat today were planted that night. But the loudest applause, the most earsplitting cheers and the most animated cartwheels by the prettiest cheerleaders were reserved for Carl, whose race-saving dash up the finish hill at Pioneer Park clinched the championship, and with that monumental and unpredictable feat, secured our scholarships, and saved us from the threat of serving our country in a far away and dangerous land.

As Carl emerged from the tunnel of cheerleaders, Danny swept him up and they hugged with the love of reunited brothers. Tears ran down both of their cheeks to match the tears of most of those in Mabel's Diner that night.

"Thank you, Carl. You made this all possible."

"Only five," Carl said softly, looking down at the floor, "and six of us."

"Don't worry, Carl, everyone will get what they want."

"Even me?"

"I made a promise. To your mother, to my teammates, to my brother."

"To Corey?"

Shelly was strangely and mercifully absent from the celebration. Her expectations, her dreams, her sense of purpose, so stolidly uncompromising, were now so different from Danny's. She didn't understand Danny's transformation and didn't try to. Shelly understanding what Danny so caringly explained to her was beyond being possible. Her tears, her pounding fists on his chest, her biting words merely confirmed that Danny had made the right decision.

Had things been different, had she wanted to wait, it would have been beyond her abilities. Compromising would have been above her character, wishing good fortune beyond her humanity.

The celebration lasted until the early morning hours. Danny thanked each and every person who filled Mabel's as they left the diner and disappeared into the night. He hugged Amos and Shaun and Billy, as though it might be the last time he would ever see them. His hug-lifted Carl off his feet. Mrs. Hager and Candy received kisses that mixed with tears of joy. Sid Benson, his cigar wagging in the corner of his mouth, told Danny of future victories they would enjoy together, and waddled off into the darkness a happy man, oblivious to the decision Danny had made on the finish hill.

Save for Jill and me, Coach Dillon and Diane were the last to leave. Danny and Frank spoke softly at the bottom of the stairs while I stood with Diane at the top. She gently squeezed my hand as she watched her husband plead with Danny to change his mind. Fear, more than disappointment, showed on Coach Dillon's face. The futility, the failure of his quest of 25 years loomed in front of him. Tears welled in Diane's eyes as they did in Frank's. It was a strange reaction for such a joyous night, but I soon shared it as it became clear to me what decision had been made. Danny put his arm around Coach Dillon's shoulders and bade him goodbye as Diane took his arm and they too walked into the darkness. A night that started with such joy ended in such sadness. Frank Dillon would not need to negotiate with Sid Benson for the sixth scholarship.

Danny walked back up the stairs and sat between Jill and me on the top step. He took Jill's hand in his and we sat in silence for a few moments.

"What did he say to you, Danny?" I asked him. "What did he say to you that made you change you mind?" Danny looked at me, giving thought as to whether he should answer.

"What did who say?" Jill asked.

"He knows," I said, nodding toward Danny.

"Who is he talking about?" Jill asked again.

"Is it important that you know?" Danny finally answered me.

"Yes, it is."

Danny looked at me with the concern of a father. Danny seemed years older, years wiser from only a day before. The conflicts within him, with his family, with his destiny, were resolved. Danny was serene as he held Jill's hand in both of his and contemplated his answer.

"Some things are best not repeated," Danny finally spoke.

"I need to know because I think I saw him too," I admitted. "On the finish hill at the finals." Danny seemed not to be too surprised. The apparition was so real to him that it was not unbelievable that someone else would have seen it too. Those who believe, those who have faith, would have seen the apparition as well.

"Did he speak to you?" Danny asked.

"No, but I saw that he spoke to you and I need to know what he said."

"Who are we talking about?" Jill insisted.

"Corey," I said.

"But Corey's dead," Jill let slip out before realizing her error. "I'm sorry, but…"

"No need to apologize," Danny said. "He is dead, but that doesn't mean he doesn't visit once in a while."

"Did he tell you to enlist?" I asked. Danny gazed into the night and then turned to me.

"No."

"What did he say?" Danny locked my eyes in his.

"Serve with honor."

Danny stood up, walked down the stairs and headed out across the street. Jill and I followed him.

"We all have a duty to fulfill. Somehow we have to come to grips as to how to serve that duty, Michael," Danny thoughtfully and slowly spoke. "Will it be duty to self, or duty to country? Will the needs of your country outweigh your own personal needs? The question is simple. Sometimes the answers are easy, sometimes they're not."

We turned the corner in the direction of Holden Park.

"Twenty-five years ago, almost to this night," Danny continued, "five Hawks joined an entire generation of young men who put duty to country above duty to self. Their decision was easy because the cause was so clear and just. Nobody argued their motivation. They enlisted to save their country from tyranny. Things are not so clear today." Danny paused for a moment. "Sometimes you have to trust your leaders. Sometimes the plan or purpose is not so obvious. Sometimes you answer the call because that is what you do as citizen of this country."

We reached the gate to Holden Park and Danny swung it open. The moonlight illuminated the spires, the names engraved on their sides standing sentinel duty in the crisp air.

"Are you telling me you think the war in Vietnam is a good thing?" I asked. "Napalming children? Getting killed for a country that doesn't want us there? Those are good things?"

"No, those are not good things."

"Then why be part of it?"

"We can't choose when to serve our country and when not to based simply on whether it pleases us or it doesn't please us. The system needs our loyalty and our faith, or it unravels."

"Blind loyalty? Blind faith?"

"Perhaps blind faith is called for at times. At other times, I'm sure it's not. It's a decision that each of us must make for himself."

Danny walked to the Vietnam War memorial spire. He reached out and touched the etching of his brother's name. Jill, by his side, reached out and touched the etching as well. They now shared him.

"Is it worth adding more names to this plaque?" she said.

"Sometimes protecting freedom is costly," Danny answered, "a price that is paid by those who choose to serve for those who choose not to. I don't doubt there will be more names on this plaque and on others yet to be erected for wars that will come. We must honor those who serve."

Jill gave me a look that told me that she had accepted Danny's decision, not because she agreed with him but because she loved him.

"I can't let you do this," I told Danny. He smiled and put his arm around my shoulders.

"You can't make me not do it."

It was then that I also came to accept Danny's decision, not because I agreed with him but because I loved him too.

CHAPTER 39

It was not a usual scene, at least not for Barrel, Illinois. The Marine and Army recruiting offices opened early on Wednesday mornings and empty buses, parked at the curb, stood sentry. It was barely daylight when the first draftees and enlistees, their parents, brothers, sisters and girlfriends began arriving. It's a long ride to the induction centers and an early start was called for.

The boys who would soon become men joked with their parents, were admired by their younger siblings, and held hands with their girlfriends. The enlistees stood with pride. They hid behind their bravado the fear of what lay ahead. They were our patriots. They were the keepers of our freedom. They chose duty to country over duty to self. They made an honorable choice. Their motivations were not important. The glory of battles yet to be fought, the look of the uniform, the traditions of their families, the patriotism instilled by 4th of July parades or the embellished stories of their grandfathers' valor, it did not matter what moved them to choose to serve their country. All that truly mattered was like their brothers and cousins, and their fathers and uncles, they chose service and in doing so made it possible for us to choose not to serve.

Their youth and inexperience lifted their confidence, their invincibility, their bravado. In an earlier war Eisenhower filled the landing craft of the Normandy Invasion with soldiers who had not before seen combat. Only those who had not experienced what the weapons of war can do to human flesh would have jumped so confidently onto the surf, so certain they would be the exception and not the rule, so confident that they would wade through the surf to the beach, scale the cliffs, and so defend our nation. Thank God for their naïveté for it has secured our freedom more than once.

The draftees waiting to board the Army bus that morning were more thoughtful. They accepted a fate they had not volunteered for nor aspired to. But it was a duty they accepted, if not happily, then resolutely. They would serve because their country had beckoned. They looked forward not to adventure but to survival, not to glory but to anonymity, not to lead but to be led. In spite of their reservations, the draftees would serve valiantly and bravely, becoming brothers with the volunteers, bound by their common goals of survival. The enemy did not distinguish between the volunteers and the draftees. Neither did the medals they earned nor the headstones that marked their resting places.

With the tears of their mothers, bear hugs of their fathers and lingering kisses of their girlfriends marking the end of their adolescence, the enlistees climbed the steps of the Marine bus and took seats as their first acts as soldiers. The Marine sergeant who stood at the door of the bus, clipboard in hand, recorded their arrival with a check in a box, and firmly greeted the recruits with salutes that were clumsily but proudly returned. The bus would soon rumble away, carrying these boys on the first leg of a journey that, for most, would end in the steaming jungles of Vietnam. In some inexplicable way, their fighting and dying in that far-away place protected our freedoms in Barrel, Illinois. It was not clear then, nor now, how our freedoms were so protected, but they were. How many of these boys, our protectors, would not return as anything other than an inscription in Holden Park?

I waited with Jill across the street from the bus. We waited to send off my friend and her love, Danny O'Neal. Jill and I said little to each other as we waited. We had already said our goodbyes to Danny in words that could hardly be spoken. Still, we could not let him leave without a final glance, a final connection. Jill waited impatiently for an event that she dreaded. Corey's ring was now on her finger, hastily sized to fit with bits of masking tape. Corey gave his ring to Danny with the love of a brother and with a pledge that Danny would wear it until Corey fulfilled his promise to return from his duty. Danny gave Jill that same ring, with the love of young man for a young woman, with a pledge that Jill would wear it until he fulfilled his promise to return from his duty.

Danny arrived with his mother and father and sister, replaying a scene that had sent Corey to his destiny only a few months before. As Danny stepped out of the family car, we saw that he had undergone another transformation, from a counterculture rebel back to a Midwest innocent. His ponytailed hair was shorn to nearly the length of a Marine's crew cut. His scraggly beard had disappeared under the swipe of a razor, uncovering the brightness of the smile I remembered from our first meeting. His torn jeans and old-tire sandals were replaced by his going-to-church wool pants and wingtips with a spit-and-polish sheen. Danny wore his letterman jacket, emblazoned with the newly stitched state championship patch. His first-place medal hung around Jill's neck. Both would lose their meaning in the months ahead, but today, they were Danny's two most prized possessions.

Alice O'Neal hugged Danny with the intensity of a mother who had already lost a son to a war that she did not understand but tried to accept, and with the fear of a mother who could not let herself think that the same fate might befall another son. Ben O'Neal shook his son's hand while staring into his eyes, trying to convey the pride that he had repressed for years, that he was repressing still. Sons are supposed to somehow know the pride their fathers feel for them. I don't know if Danny ever did.

Hannah O'Neal kept her arms wrapped around her brother's waist, her head on Danny's chest, her eyes squeezed shut. The last time she bid goodbye to a brother he never returned. She blamed herself for having let go and would not make the same mistake again. Hannah was too young to understand cause and effect. It is unfortunate that our elected leaders who sent our young men to war failed to understand cause and effect as well.

As Jill and I watched these farewells, we felt hands upon our shoulders. I had no need to turn around to know who stood behind me. I knew that Frank and Diane Dillon had come to say their goodbyes. Coach Dillon had more reason than either Jill or me to bid Danny Godspeed because he had come this way himself. The parallels made me wince. Twenty-five years ago, only days after his record-setting championship race, Frank climbed onto a bus as Danny was about to, the first step in a journey that would take him to war, to manhood and to heroism. Frank left Barrel that day with the conviction of a patriot, the prayers of his family and the pride of his country. Danny had the conviction and the prayers, but instead of pride, his country felt shame for what it asked these young men to do. We owe so very much to those who chose to serve. Why did we treat them like traitors when they gallantly returned? Why did we spit on them as they stepped off their returning flights? How could we have been so heartless, so selfish?

In a way, Frank had succeeded in his quest and in a way he had failed. Coach Dillon saved five young men from a war he feared more than those who would serve, but five were not enough.

"Let's say goodbye," Coach Dillon said in a soft voice.

"We've already said our good-byes, Coach," Jill explained. Diane wiped a tear from her husband's cheek. Frank took her hand firmly in his.

"Then please help me say goodbye," he said.

I nodded and together we all slowly crossed the street.

EPILOGUE

The Hawks of 1967, members of the championship cross country team that brought fame to Barrel, Illinois, now look back at that season as the Rubicon dividing the privilege of their youth from the obligations of their adulthood. In some ways, the small enclave of Barrel shielded its young men from the rebuke of the outside world and allowed them to be what boys should be, innocent students of life. We enjoyed 4th of July parades, waving sparklers in the dusk procession and pointing with delight at the fireworks extravaganza, without feeling the sting of ridicule from our peers. We sat with fascinated respect at the barbershop while grizzled farmers told their heroic tales of beating back the elements and bringing in the harvest, without being ashamed of our unsophisticated ways. We loved each other without fearing we would be labeled as being queer.

Those times were, sadly, an end of a way of life. It was an end of an era when boys and girls learned from their parents, respected their elders and earned their entertainment by their own labors. Perhaps there are still high school football towns in the panhandle of Texas that have enviously preserved this way of life, but in large part, the innocence of the youth of Barrel has slipped into obsolescence. The shield that protected the young men of Barrel from the scrutiny and the sophistication of their more streetwise city counterparts has long since been broached by the ease with which we communicate and the passiveness with which we listen and watch. MTV makes a questioning imagination as irrelevant as tits on a bull.

Barrel was, in some sense, a time machine, preserving a lifestyle that was in many ways simple and in many ways backwards. In many ways, it was also a lifestyle that nurtured its youth. But just as the Morlocks exacted an unimaginable price of the Eloi in return for their simpler life, so did the country that so enamored Barrel exact an unimaginable price of its youth. For it was those youth who innocently and unquestionably placed duty to country above duty to self who paid the ultimate price at rates far in excess of their more sophisticated city brethren, who could afford lawyers and knew how to use them. But unlike the Time Traveler, there was no past for the young men of Barrel to escape to. There was only a future that in order to enjoy they needed to survive the consequences of their duty.

The Hawks of 1967 were a throwback to that future. With one exception, they broke with the expectations of their elders. They questioned that which had never been questioned before and placed duty to self over duty to country. Their unwillingness to serve their country was a harbinger of the selfishness of their generation that was only beginning to erupt across the nation. The Hawks grabbed at the opportunity that Frank Dillon and Danny O'Neal so cleverly engineered, and Sid Benson so reluctantly offered, not so much for the education it provided but for the enticing shelter from duty it harbored. At the time, there was no question in our minds about accepting the offer of haven. There was also no reluctance at Danny serving in our place. We sat in the black and they in the white, with no grayness in between. It is now only decades later that the guilt of our selfishness robs us of sleep no less than would the nightmares of combat. It is an indescribable buyer's remorse. Did Frank Dillon and Danny O'Neal offer us gifts, or were they apples?

We used Frank Dillon and Danny O'Neal's gifts to their fullest. We attended Illinois State University and ran for Sid Benson with no less intensity than we did for Frank Dillon, feeling gratitude if not respect for the man. We studied for exams through countless all-nighters. We debated the meaning of men landing on the moon and the likelihood that free love would outlive the decade. In lemming-like precision, we marched in anti-war protests as countless other college students of our generation did, giving little thought to the implications of what we did.

Given the questionable talent that Sid Benson procured with his acquisition of the Hawks of 1967, he aptly displayed his talents as a coach and made those same Hawks champions once again. Shaun, Billy and I rose to be the top three runners on Coach Benson's cross country teams, leading our teammates to three NCAA Division II championships. I won the individual national title in my senior year. As I stood on the dais, victoriously holding my medal above my head for the spectators to admire, I couldn't help but admit to myself that I was holding Danny's medal. Had Danny chosen the path we had taken, he would have stood on that platform in my place.

After three years of unrelenting effort, Amos finally muscled his way to claim the coveted seventh position on Sid Benson's cross country team his senior year and left college with a championship patch on his Illinois State letterman's jacket. He still wears that jacket to this day.

Carl, my dear Carl, as much our savior as Frank or Danny, sweated through every workout that Sid threw at us for four years. The intensity of his effort shamed the rest of us for if we slacked even one quarter-mile, we knew that Carl would not. Yet in spite of his unmatched devotion to training and the nearly god-like respect he afforded Sid, Carl failed to start a single race at Illinois State. Carl's momentary break from obscurity in his last high school race, that unpredictable, championship-winning charge up the hill at the state meet of so many years ago, was his crowning achievement as a runner. He never again approached that greatness, perhaps because the need was never again so acute. For four years, Carl was denied a spot in the top seven on the Illinois State cross country team not by virtue of his lack of dedication but by virtue of his lack of talent. Candy, sitting in the stands for every workout, was Carl's only fan and his undeniable source of unending support. It is as much a credit to Candy as to Carl that he graduated, if not with honors then with pride. His mother gratefully lived to see her son crest that hill as well.

The Hawks of 1967 are in many ways no different than high school classmates of other young men who are now deep into middle age. The Barrel High School class reunions go unattended, the Christmas card lists grow out of date and the events of our youth are either selectively remembered or embellished beyond recognition.

Amos took his degree in agricultural engineering from Illinois State back to Barrel and grew his family farm into a 10,000-acre agribusiness that has made him wealthy beyond expectations. Billy, now predictably on his third wife, headed to Los Angeles with a degree in journalism and virtuous plans to expose corruption. He succumbed to the illusion that is L.A., and now writes sitcoms for the networks. Shaun surprisingly found molecules more alluring than women, took his degree in chemistry to graduate school and now makes molecules for Dupont. Carl parlayed his degree in sociology into a teaching certificate and is now vice-principal of a high school in the suburbs of Chicago. Candy, his wife of more than 25 years, is still at his side.

I discovered early on that saving a system meant changing it, and that change must come from within. I took my degree in political science to law school, then to clerkships, legal aid, and to congressional staffs; and now to a Washington think-tank. We specialize in mediating conflicts. In some ways, I carry on where Frank Dillon left off.

Shelly, pretty innocent Shelly, would have never survived waiting for Danny to return from his service. His enlistment spelled the end to any relationship she could have hoped for, much to Danny's relief, I think. Shelly attended Swarthmore and married well, achieving the social status that would have eluded her as Danny's wife.

Much to our shame, it was only Jill who maintained a physical connection with Danny after high school. Their daily letters carried with them a stream of emotion that built with their every crossing of the Pacific. She wrote to him of her hopes and dreams, and Danny responded with words of optimism and love, protecting her from the reality of the war in Vietnam. They found each other much too late and so were sentenced to wait out his service to build a life together. When Danny's letters failed to arrive on schedule, Jill called me with concern and sometimes with panic. Had I heard anything? Is

Danny all right? Have you talked to his parents? You're his friend, you should know, she insisted. She was right. I was his friend, and I should have known.

The Hawks of 1967 visit with each other only once a year and that reunion is for only one purpose. Every June 11, we gather in front of panel 22W of the Vietnam Memorial in Washington, D.C. to pay our respects to Danny. The names are seemingly endless on that great expanse of marble, but those on panel 22W have been indelibly memorized by each of us. "PFC Charles D. Green, SSG Charlie Will Farmer, CPL John Body Parker, SGT Daniel Shane O'Neal." They were all patriots who chose duty to country over duty to self and on June 11, 1969, paid the ultimate price for that choice. That day was an ordinary day by almost any other measure, but was immeasurably extraordinary in our lives.

Danny was well into his second tour of duty when during a Vietcong counter-offensive in Quang Tin, South Vietnam, he heroically and singlehandedly maintained an indefensible position so that his men could retreat to safety, and in doing so, sacrificed his life for his comrades. Sacrifice had become a habit for Danny. He sacrificed for his teammates, the Hawks. He sacrificed for his fellow soldiers. He sacrificed for his country. It was a destiny he was incapable of avoiding, as if the result of an unfortunate arrangement of chromosomes that shaped his character without remorse. Danny and his brother Corey fulfilled their family's destiny and with their sacrifices enabled us to pursue ours.

Every year the Hawks of 1967 gather to remember Danny. We share memories and honor our friend, our benefactor, our brother, our conscience. We bring our wives and children who never knew Danny so they can learn about the man who served in our place. And now, grandchildren giggle at their reflection in the polished marble of the memorial, too young to appreciate the significance of the engraved stone. One day, they will be old enough and we will tell them the stories so that they too can pay homage. Jill joined us the first few years but grew distant as she found fulfillment and love elsewhere, and soon stopped her pilgrimage lest her wounds reopen. I wish her well.

I also used to return to Barrel every year, sometimes unnoticed, sometimes to visit Amos, but always to spend time with Frank Dillon. My last visit was the year Frank retired and moved away. He left no forwarding address but he did leave me that manila envelope containing the newspaper clippings that recorded the stories of his runners' triumphs and disappointments, and of the sacrifices of those who paid the ultimate price. There was no note of explanation with the clippings but a note was not necessary. I knew that it was now my duty to preserve the memories that Frank could no longer bear to carry.

In the end, Frank Dillon was not the same man who mentored the Hawks of 1967 and, with Danny O'Neal's help, kept them safe. The joy and triumph he felt for having saved his precious Hawks from war was tempered by Danny's decision to serve, and diminished to unending sadness by Danny's death. Frank grew old beyond his years after he finally came to accept the reality of Danny's sacrifice. With that acceptance, Frank finally had to admit to himself that his quest was futile. No matter what he did, there would be new wars and there would be new generations of young men to fight them. What he failed to realize is that the good of the many often comes at the expense of the few. Pete Lorenzo's sacrifice on the beaches of Normandy protected the freedoms of the many at his own expense. The same can be said of Danny's sacrifice in the jungles of Vietnam. It was just more difficult to connect the dots with Danny, but I have to believe that was the case.

With his admission, Frank's willingness to challenge what he knew to be wrong withered, and so did his ability to mentor his runners. In the end, his last teams of Hawks were just like any other high school team, lacking the soul that Frank Dillon had breathed into the Hawks of 1967. The Hawks never again achieved the greatness of that team. Danny's records still stand to this day, a memorial as fitting as his picture, which sits next to Frank and Pete Lorenzo's in the trophy case in the Barrel High gymnasium.

At our last meeting, Frank spoke to me about every one of his runners and teammates whose names are engraved on the plaques in Holden Park. We walked through the grass, pausing at the spire that held each name. He touched their letters as though a physical connection still existed, the essence of the departed somehow leaking through the etchings. The names of his teammates and runners spanned three wars, a continuum that Frank feared would stretch endlessly into the future. We paused particularly long at two engravings, Peter Lorenzo and Danny O'Neal, while Frank stared with moist eyes at the sharpness of their memory. Peter Lorenzo and Danny O'Neal were two young men, two wars apart, whom Frank Dillon, in spite of superhuman effort, was unable to save from their destinies. With the passing of time, Frank Dillon could finally speak about Pete Lorenzo, their friendship and their pledges to each other, but he could not speak to me of Danny O'Neal. The pain was still too fresh even years after the fact.

But it was not necessary for Coach Dillon to speak to me of Danny O'Neal. I knew the story better than Frank, for it was a runner's honor, Danny's honor, that opened the world for me.

The End

Made in the USA
Lexington, KY
15 January 2010